What the cri
Louisia...

"Delivers... genuinely heart-stopping suspense."

—*PUBLISHERS WEEKLY*

"Sleek, fast moving."

—*KIRKUS*

"Broussard tracks the virus with a winning combination of common sense and epidemiologic legerdemain."

—*NEW ORLEANS TIMES PICAYUNE*

"This series has carved a solid place for itself. Broussard makes a terrific counterpoint to the Dave Robicheaux ragin' Cajun school of mystery heroes."

—*BOOKLIST*

"A dazzling tour de force... sheer pulse-pounding reading excitement."

—*THE CLARION LEDGER* (JACKSON, MS)

"A novel of... "terrifying force... utterly fascinating.... His best work yet."

—*THE COMMERCIAL APPEAL* (MEMPHIS)

What the critics said about *Sleeping With The Crawfish:*

"Streamlined thrills and gripping forensic detail."

—*KIRKUS*

"Action-packed, cleverly plotted topnotch thriller. Another fine entry in a consistently outstanding series."

—*BOOKLIST*

"With each book, Donaldson peels away a few more layers of these characters and we find ourselves loving the involvement."

—*THE COMMERCIAL APPEAL* (MEMPHIS)

"The pace is pell-mell."

—*SAN ANTONIO EXPRESS-NEWS*

"Exciting and… realistic. Donaldson… starts his action early and sustains it until the final pages."

—*BENTON COURIER* (Arkansas)

"A roller-coaster ride…. Thoroughly enjoyable."

—*BRAZOSPORT FACTS*

"The latest outing of a fine series which never disappoints."

—*MERITORIOUS MYSTERIES*

What the critics said about *New Orleans Requiem*:

"Lots of Louisiana color, pinpoint plotting and two highly likable characters... smart, convincing solution."

—*PUBLISHERS WEEKLY* (starred review)

"An... accomplished forensic mystery. His New Orleans is worth the trip."

—*NEW ORLEANS TIMES PICAYUNE*

"Andy and Kit are a match made in mystery heaven."

—*THE CLARION LEDGER* (JACKSON, MS)

"Nicely drawn characters, plenty of action, and an engaging... storytelling style."

—*THE COMMERCIAL APPEAL* (Memphis)

"Donaldson has established himself as a master of the Gothic mystery."

—*BOOKLIST*

"The tension will keep even the most reluctant young adult readers turning the pages."

—*SCHOOL LIBRARY JOURNAL*

BAD KARMA IN THE BIG EASY

by

D. J. Donaldson

ASTOR
+BLUE
EDITIONS

BAD KARMA IN THE BIG EASY
Astor + Blue Editions, LLC

Copyright © 2014 by D.J. DONALDSON

Astor + Blue Editions,
New York, NY 10036
www.astorandblue.com

Publisher's Cataloging-In-Publication Data

DONALDSON, D.J. BAD KARMA IN THE BIG EASY—1st ed.

ISBN: 978-1-938231-32-2 (paperback)
ISBN: 978-1-938231-31-5 (epdf)
ISBN: 978-1-938231-30-8 (epub)

1. Detective Duo—Murder Mystery—Fiction. 2. Fiction 3. Police procedural and forensic mystery—Fiction 4. Medical thriller—Fiction 5. Post Hurricane Katrina police drama—Fiction 6. American Murder and Suspense Story—Fiction 7. New Orleans (LA) I. Title

Jacket Cover Design: Ervin Serrano

Acknowledgments

I'M GREATLY INDEBTED TO Drs. Jerry Francisco and O. C. Smith for advice on forensic aspects of this story. Thanks also to Dr. Brian Chrz for patiently responding to my far-too-detailed e-mail questions about the FEMA mortuary operation in St. Gabriel after Katrina. And I can't forget former New Orleans Homicide commander James Keen, who helped me understand the impossible circumstances members of the law enforcement community faced in the hurricane aftermath. Finally, a tip of the hat to Bruce Rolf, former navy pilot, for insights into the operation of a Kiowa helicopter. My sincere apologies to any others who provided background for the story but weren't mentioned here. I alone am responsible for any factual errors.

Prologue

JENNIFER HENDRIN HAD ALWAYS disliked being cold. Once when she was four, she asked her daddy if it would be warm in heaven. Eyes tearing, he told her she wouldn't have to worry about that for a very long time, but yes, God kept the thermostat in heaven set at a toasty snug temperature.

Thirteen months ago, a week after her twenty-first birthday, Jennifer had gone missing. Along with her father's prayers that she would be found alive and safe, he hoped she would be warm. Had he known that most of the time she'd been missing she had been colder than she'd ever been and that now her sightless eyes stared at the ceiling of a refrigerated FEMA truck in St. Gabriel, Louisiana, waiting, along with bodies 428 and 429, for justice, he might have lost his mind.

CHAPTER 1

ANDY BROUSSARD, CHIEF MEDICAL Examiner for Orleans Parish, rubbed the back of his stiff neck. *Cots must have been invented by the Marquis de Sade. There couldn't be any other explanation for the existence of such a wretched object.* Fortified with a surprisingly decent cup of coffee and two hastily-consumed sausage biscuits, he stepped out of the abandoned schoolhouse where most of the area's FEMA workers slept in former classrooms. Without pause, he set his stubby, tired legs moving, heading as fast as he could toward the makeshift mortuary next door. In most of the state, people who still had beds were in them. But here, though the sun had not yet made an appearance, the morning shift in the morgue was already well underway.

And Broussard was late.

Never mind that he'd worked most of the night shift. This was the day he could turn to the task that had been picking at his sense of order for weeks, so he was upset at having overslept.

Broussard had lived with death daily for over forty years. It was as much a part of him as his bow ties and the lanyard that tethered his glasses to his neck when he looked through a microscope. It enveloped him as completely as each of his six

1957 T-Birds cradled his massive body. He could feel its touch as surely as the steering wheels of those cars, which rubbed against the buttons on his shirt when he turned a corner. It was in his gray hair and beard and the leather of the shoes with perforated uppers he wore to keep his feet from sweating.

He did not fear death. He simply viewed it as a respected adversary that came in many guises, a cunning opponent with endless tricks to mislead those who would document and understand its handiwork, an antagonist capable of challenging his intellect at the highest level, especially when one human arranged for it to take another.

But this easy familiarity with the dark eternal did not lessen the burden he had carried for weeks as the body count from Hurricane Katrina mounted. The corpses had been flowing at a shocking rate into the row of refrigerated trucks he could already see through the chain-link fence surrounding his brightly lit destination. Over eight hundred souls lost at last count… mostly from failure of the levees. It was still incomprehensible to him that such a catastrophe could have happened. His beloved New Orleans … much of it destroyed … It was almost too much for the old pathologist to take. But he owed it to the dead to make sure every one of them was identified, and none had been murdered under cover of the storm. That, he would not tolerate.

But Lord, it was hard to keep going. Once body recovery began, he'd worked practically around the clock, quickly pushing himself beyond exhaustion, often remaining in the morgue well into the hot afternoons, when everyone but he and one or two loyal assistants fled to more temperate surroundings in the school to wait out the sun. St. Gabriel, where the mortuary had been set up, was just south of Baton Rouge, sixty miles from New Orleans. Even if I-10 hadn't been clotted daily in both directions with refugees from Orleans Parish clinging to shreds of their former lives, it was too long a commute for Broussard to go home each time he needed a few hours sleep. So he hadn't seen his own bed more than a few times since the horror started. That's why he was already breathing hard even though he hadn't covered much ground.

Suddenly, he felt light-headed.

He stopped walking to see how bad this episode was going to be. He'd had the first one a week after the mortuary started receiving bodies. An isolated event, he'd thought. But they had continued, so far, not progressing to anything worse, but occurring more frequently. He bent over and looked at the ground, muttering for this nuisance to go away. Instead, it rose in intensity until he thought he might pass out. Then, as quickly as it had appeared, it moved on, leaving him even more fully drained.

He resumed walking, heading along a well-illuminated foot path through the weeds that led to a gate in the chain-link fence five yards ahead. Three paces later, he felt something give way under his left shoe. Looking down, he saw his foot resting in the midst of a cluster of mud marbles, some of which were surely now sludgy little pancakes on the bottom of his shoe. He was an expert at wandering through fields and woods, often in much worse lighting than there was here, and had never before in his entire life stepped in a pile of armadillo scat. He should have realized that event, though small, was telling him something. But he was too tired to get it.

Reaching the fence, he held onto it and wiped his soiled shoe across some clumps of grass. He went through the gate and angled left, up the paved driveway toward the metal warehouse converted to a morgue.

Ahead, showers of sparks shot into the air as a dozen construction workers continued assembling a refrigeration facility to replace the semi trucks now being used for that purpose.

To see the living expend so much energy for the dead was both heartwarming and depressing.

He entered the warehouse through the side door. At the security desk, he was greeted by Eddie Shavers, St Gabriel's sheriff for over twenty years, now retired and volunteering his services. Shavers turned the clipboard with the sign-in sheet toward Broussard. Over the sound of the massive FEMA-installed air conditioner in the back of the building, he said, "Things are lookin' better, yeah? I heard we only got four in yesterday."

Raising his own voice to compete with the air conditioner, Broussard said, "Wish we were back in the days when the discovery of four bodies was cause for alarm, not encouragement." He scribbled his name and the time on the sheet.

Shavers's brow furrowed with concern at how Broussard had taken his comment. "I just meant…"

Broussard put a reassuring hand on the old sheriff's shoulder. "I'm just frustrated I can't make this whole problem go away. Sometimes I let it show."

Shavers nodded. "…Know exactly what you mean."

Save for the afternoon hours when it was too hot to work, there were always around seventy-five people in the building, all toiling to identify the dead. Despite what Broussard had said to Shavers, the waning number of admissions *was* a hopeful sign that someday the gruesome flow would stop. FEMA had set up the morgue and coordinated deployment of all the volunteers working there. But they had put Broussard in charge. And he had decided it was now time to cut back to one shift and let many of those volunteers return to their normal lives. This easing of the workload was also why he could finally tackle that job he'd long wanted to begin.

With plastic pipe and blue tarps, the old warehouse had been partitioned off into areas for clerical, body reception, whole-body x-ray, dental x-ray, and DNA collection. There were also a couple of autopsy rooms as well as one for changing clothes. There were no ceilings in any of these rooms, so the odor of decomposition was free to go where it would. And it went everywhere.

Thankful that his smell neurons would soon fatigue and make the odor unnoticeable, Broussard stepped into the dressing room, where he ran into Charlie Franks, Deputy Medical examiner for Orleans Parish, already suiting up. Franks was late, too, but he had an aging mother and her sister to care for back in New Orleans, and sometimes that obligation made it impossible for him to get back to St. Gabriel precisely when he wanted. Broussard understood this and no conversation about it was necessary.

Franks looked at Broussard and said something.

Hearing only half the words because of the air conditioner, Broussard leaned forward and said, "I didn't get that."

"We have to stop meeting like this," Franks repeated more forcefully as he slipped a disposable cover over his left shoe.

"Nothin' would please me more," Broussard replied. "How are you this mornin'?"

"Better than yesterday. The power came back on at my house last night."

"That had to be a thrill."

"After three weeks ... thrill doesn't cover it. Even with candles on the table, MREs ain't romantic."

"So you're sayin' now that you got electricity, you and the missus will be steamin' up the bedroom windows?"

"Oh yeah ... that's gonna happen." A look of concern crept over Franks's face. "Did you work the night shift?"

"Not all of it."

"Damn it, Andy, you've got to slow down. You can't keep going at this pace."

"Now that things are taperin' off, I won't have to."

"Meaning you'll go home tonight?"

"That's my plan."

"Hope you'll stick to it."

Franks pulled on his other shoe cover, snatched a couple of masks from a box on nearby metal shelves, and shoved them into the pocket of his disposable jump suit. He put some rubber gloves in his other pocket and grabbed a full-face shield from the shelves. "See you in the trenches."

It took Broussard about ten minutes to change. From the dressing room, he followed the makeshift corridors between blue tarps to clerical, where, sitting behind a black metal desk bearing a big screen laptop, he found Fran Durbin, their chief data-entry volunteer from Omaha, wearing out her keyboard.

Durbin had a long face and a large nose that made her a homely woman. Accustomed to noticing only a person's best features, Broussard thought once again what nice skin she had.

She looked up from her work, fatigue evident in her eyes. "And the fun goes on …"

"Is it gettin' to be more than you can handle? We're to the point now where I'm plannin' to cut some folks loose. If you like, you can be one of 'em. Your call."

She shook her head. "I'm a lousy cook. And since the Forestry Service has started preparing our meals over there at the school, I'm eating better here than I would at home. So, think I'll stick around awhile."

Broussard cupped his big stomach, which for all his travails, was still a ponderous thing. "As you can see, food is not somethin' I care much about."

Despite their grim duties, Durban smiled. "What can I do for you this morning?"

Of the countless bodies he had processed since the storm, three had remained foremost in Broussard's mind ... all collected from the same tangle of brush and trees in the lower Ninth Ward, all female, all naked. Today, his curiosity about them could finally be exercised. Hating that he had to refer to them by number, he said, "I want to take another look at 427... then the next two in sequence. Has the data we sent over to the missin' persons center turned up anything on 'em?"

For each collected body, the FEMA mortuary had provided the center with fingerprints and dental x-rays. At this stage of things, those items were of little value since family members reporting lost relatives weren't likely to have records of either. A few of those who'd become separated from family members had been able to produce pictures of the missing. But because all the bodies coming in were already disfigured by decomposition, they would no longer resemble those photos. Far more useful were descriptions of tattoos, clothing, hair color, jewelry, and any old fractures repaired with metal pins.

The three bodies in Broussard's sights this morning had been wearing no jewelry, had no tattoos, and no repaired fractures. But the peculiar fact they were all nude seemed potentially as useful in identifying them as any item of clothing they might have been wearing. Even so, Broussard's highest hopes lay with the silicone chin implant found on the whole-body x-rays of 427. That seemed like something most family members would know about and mention when filing a report.

Durbin turned to the bank of three rolling file cabinets beside the desk and pulled the middle one closer. She thumbed through the hanging files inside and selected the pertinent records, which were all still identified on the tab only by a number. "Sorry, no luck."

Durban handed the files to Broussard. "I'll have the first one there in just a few minutes."

For all the noise the air conditioner made, it didn't adequately cool the building. That's why it was so hot in there during the afternoons. Today, even though it was still early morning, the place was barely tolerable, so as Broussard walked down to autopsy area 1, he wasn't looking forward to putting on his mask and face shield.

As each body moved through the facility, it was accompanied by an escort that served as a scribe and an extra pair of hands when needed. The body bag containing corpse 427 arrived promptly on a gurney pushed by Jeff Lyons, a husky young fire department paramedic and navy reserve pilot from Jesuit Bend who Broussard had worked with many times over the past few weeks. Broussard recognized him even though Lyons was gowned and already masked.

The two men exchanged a brief greeting, then as Broussard donned his face protection, Lyons said, "You dream about any of this?"

Broussard stepped in to help position the gurney so they could move the body onto the examination table sitting under a bank of fluorescent lights. Practically shouting now to be heard through his facial gear and over the air conditioner, Broussard said, "If you mean this kind of work in general, not usually, but I've had a few since the storm." He unzipped the bag, unleashing a powerful smell that surged over the two men in an almost tangible cloud, once again kick-starting their smell receptors and making Lyons's eyes water.

Broussard moved around to the head, and they pushed the bag down so they could reach the monstrously swollen body inside. Broussard leaned over and took hold of the cadaver's shoulders, his hands sinking deeply into the macerated muscle beneath the skin. Lyons grasped the corpse's ankles.

"On the count of three," Broussard said. "One, two, three ..."

As they lifted their loathsome burden, a filthy blond ponytail, clotted with mud and leaves and twigs, unfurled from the skull.

With the transfer complete, Lyons said, "I was this one's escort when she first came in. That ponytail is one of the things I been dreaming about ... only in my dream it's soft and clean. But her face ... is still ... like that. And ... I'm in bed with her."

Broussard looked at the cadaver's ruined features: the sunken eyes, the opaque corneas, the swollen skin a disgusting palette of red, purple, and black all swirled together with green and yellow, blending like some grotesque artwork. Forgetting Lyons was even there, he moved around the table, bent down, and sighted along the plane of the cadaver's facial skin.

The feature he'd noticed when he'd initially seen the body weeks earlier was still there: a series of small elevations of the skin around the nose and mouth that were superimposed on the general facial swelling. Under these elevations, he thought there was a corresponding constancy of coloration as though she might have been injured in those areas before she died.

When he'd first observed this many days ago, it hadn't set off any mental alarm. She could have gone into the water, been hit by some floating debris as she struggled, then drowned a short while later. It was when he saw the same thing on bodies 428 and 429, both collected close to this one, both nude as this one had been when found, that his skullduggery sonar, already warming up, had begun beeping.

Back then, he couldn't do anything about it. The morgue's prime directive in those early days was body identification. There had been little time for cause-of-death analyses. Considering how fast the bodies were arriving, he was lucky to have picked up on this suspicious discoloration. It's likely that had he been able to follow up then on these cases, while he was still alert enough to avoid stepping in armadillo feces, he might have noticed one other unusual feature of the victim's destroyed face. As it was, it slipped right by him then, and did so again this time.

Realizing Broussard wasn't going to respond to his comment about his dreams, Lyons pushed the gurney out of the way and changed gloves so he wouldn't soil the records as he handled them.

Broussard's main goal now was to determine if this woman had really drowned. He had noted on his earlier examination of the body that the most reliable feature of drowning, a tenacious mushroom of foam issuing from the cadaver's nose and mouth, formed by air, mucus, and water as the victim takes a last few breaths, was not present. Nor did pressure on the chest produce any. After so long in the warm water, the absence of this foam was not by itself surprising. He did clearly remember, though, that it was also missing on 428 and 429. Pressure on the chest of those cadavers, likewise, hadn't produced any.

What he needed now was a look at the lungs.

When any body was first brought in, it was fingerprinted. In many cases, clear prints were difficult to obtain because of wrinkling and folding of the skin on the fingers. But there was a way around this. Most of the bodies, this one included, had been immersed long enough for the superficial layers of the skin of the hands to separate from the underlying tissues so the epidermis, nails included, could be peeled off like a glove. If someone with appropriate-sized hands then slipped the skin glove on, prints could easily be taken. The gloves belonging to this victim were lying on her stomach. Before proceeding any further, Broussard picked up those gloves and placed them on a nearby stainless steel table. Then he reached for a scalpel.

Blade poised above the cadaver's left shoulder, Broussard silently recited the mantra he had long ago adopted before making the first cut. *What I do now, I do for you and for others.*

CHAPTER 2

KIT FRANKLYN PULLED OFF St. Charles Avenue into Audubon Park and immediately saw where she was needed. About fifty yards ahead, Phil Gatlin's old Pontiac was parked on the shoulder behind a single NOPD cruiser. Across the leaf and branch-littered grass to the left, Gatlin and a lone uniformed cop were standing next to a convertible that had apparently crashed into a huge old live oak. Had this been a normal Thursday in the city, there would have been more official cars and at least a small crowd of gawkers present. But with most of the city's population gone and unable to return because of the flooding damage, Gatlin and the cop were the only two humans in sight.

Kit parked behind the cruiser, picked up her little digital camera from the passenger seat, and got out of her car. For the last several years, she had worked for Broussard as a suicide investigator and, occasionally, for the police as a psychological profiler. At Broussard's suggestion, she had recently completed a course in death investigation in St. Louis. Upon her return, she had become Broussard's eyes and ears in all kinds of cases when he was too busy to personally work a scene.

As she walked toward the crashed car, she thought briefly about how much she had changed since she'd met Broussard. Fresh out of graduate school when she had taken the job with him, she'd cringed at much of what she saw in the morgue and at the scene of suspected suicides ... on occasion had even become ill. When the governor's aide suggested she carry a gun on that undercover assignment, it seemed so ridiculous—Kit Franklyn, with a concealed weapon. Now, here she was, that same Ladysmith .38 strapped to her calf, its presence as much a part of her as the tortoiseshell combs she used to keep her hair out of her eyes. Who would have predicted all this?

Drawing nearer to the scene, her attention was drawn to something lying in the grass approximately thirty yards behind the crashed car. It almost looked like ...

She changed direction and headed for the object.

With a few more steps, she was able to verify that it was exactly what she'd thought. Despite her years of experience in viewing the results of self-inflicted, accidental, and intentional mayhem committed on one human by another, her stomach did a triple Axel. The object in the grass was a human head.

Kit's stomach was still performing moves she'd never felt before, as she stepped up to the head and stared down at its clouded corneas visible through half-closed eyes. There was something so surreal about a head detached from its body. It almost seemed it wasn't real at all, but merely a Hollywood creation.

But it *was* real. Not so long ago those eyes had been bright and shining with life. Now they were opaque and dead.

With great effort, she shifted her focus from the eyes to the rest of the face and let her mind shift into catalogue mode: male ... receding hairline ... prematurely silver hair ... age: early fifties, most likely. It didn't take any expertise at all to tell that the head had not been severed from the rest of the body, but had been pulled from it. The free margin of the neck was ragged and torn. And the event had not happened elsewhere, because the severed arteries and veins had leaked their contents onto the grass, fouling it with gore.

Out of the corner of her left eye, she saw a loop of rope with a trailing end. The rope was not straight, but took a sinuous course back to a large oak, where the rope had been wound around the trunk and tied off.

Good God. She didn't even have to turn around and look back at the crashed car to know what happened. The guy had …

"So, what do you think?" the voice of Phil Gatlin said, coming up on her from the direction of the crashed car. "Would you rather have dew on the grass in the morning or a human head?"

Kit turned and saw the oldest homicide detective on the force strolling her way. At six foot four, he was also the tallest. When she'd first met him, his dark hair had been shot with gray. Now, gray was its only color. His untamed eyebrows then had been black as squid ink, and oddly, still were, accenting his black eyes so he still looked as though he could see through even the most artfully conceived lie. With the city devastated, he could have been excused for not wearing the coat and tie the NOPD pre-storm regs required for detectives. But, he didn't look any different than usual, which is to say, his ill-fitting suit was shiny with wear and his tie didn't match.

"Put me down for dew," she said, answering his question about what she preferred on the grass. "I guess the rest of the body is behind the wheel of that car over there."

"Yeah."

"Anyone in there with him?"

"No."

"So one end of the rope is around his neck, the other around that tree … car takes off …"

"We end up with a guy in two pieces."

Kit's job was to determine if the case was a homicide or something else. If it *was* a homicide, she'd turn further investigation of it over to Gatlin. If not, she'd have to establish whether it was an accident or a suicide. To someone not schooled in the perversities of human behavior, it would seem there was no chance at all this could have been anything but an intentional act, either by the victim or a second party. But there were many cases of so called auto-erotic asphyxiation on record, where a male, while masturbating, would fashion some kind of ligature around his neck to decrease blood flow to his brain. The resulting denial of oxygen to the subject's nerve cells would apparently heighten the sexual experience. Occasionally, things would go wrong and the victim would die of strangulation. Was this case just an extreme variation on that theme? Too soon to say. She was sure Gatlin had already decided what he thought it was, but wouldn't express any opinion until she'd had a chance to see everything for herself.

"Let me get some pictures here."

Kit took three shots of the head from different angles, then another of the looped end of the rope. She took a distant picture of the rope leading to the tree where it was tied off, then walked over to the tree and took a final frame of the knot on the rope.

She went back to where Gatlin was waiting. "Okay, let's see the rest."

At the crashed car, the cop guarding the scene stood with his back to it, hands in his pockets. He turned as Kit and Gatlin approached, and Kit could see he was just a kid, probably newly out of the academy. His uniform, dirty and unpressed, reflected the difficult days he'd been living through since the storm. He was also apparently having trouble coping with the close proximity of the headless corpse, because his face was the color of skim milk and his lips were dry.

With a thick tongue he said, "Detective, I'd like to go back to my car and sit down, if that's all right."

"You do that," Gatlin said.

Looking at Kit, who was heading for the driver's side of the wreck, Gatlin said, "I remember when you were like that."

"Now I'm a rough, bad-ass veteran," Kit replied, not looking at him.

Gatlin nodded. "Not the way I would have put it, but yeah … the sentiment is there."

The body belonged to the medical examiner, the rest of the scene to the cops. On earlier cases, when some of the other homicide detectives arrived before Kit did, they'd move the corpse, creating a need to question them to make sure she wasn't noting a circumstance they had created. But Gatlin knew the rules and observed them, so she didn't need to ask him if he'd crossed into her territory. That was good because Gatlin was Broussard's best friend, and it would have been extremely awkward to be at odds with him. As it was, she liked and respected him almost as much she did Broussard.

The corpse was slumped over the wheel of the wrecked car in exactly the correct position for the way the vehicle had come to an abrupt stop. Because there was no head to crash through it, the windshield was intact. But on the driver's side it was covered with a thick layer of clotted blood, apparently painted by spurts from the large arteries in the stump of the neck as the heart continued beating for a few seconds after the head was torn off.

She looked back at the end of the rope thirty yards away. At first, it seemed hard to believe the heart could have continued pumping while the car covered that distance, and then kept working long enough to bloody the windshield. But then she remembered the famous chicken that had lived for several years after having its head chopped off. The cut had gone above the brainstem, preserving the primitive parts of the brain that regulated the basic body functions of heart rate and respiration. Except for having to be fed by hand directly into its esophagus through an eyedropper, the bird seemed no worse off for the experience. So stranger things than what she was seeing here had happened. It was all a function of where the brainstem was damaged.

Despite being a bad-ass veteran, the thought of a man being fed with an eyedropper made her shudder.

She took a half-dozen photographs of the corpse and a few more of the car where it was enveloping the tree. Then she looked at Gatlin, who was standing back and watching her work. "Would you mind moving the body so I can see his clothes in front? Or I'll do it and you can take the pictures."

"You know your camera. I'll move him."

Gatlin shucked off his jacket and laid it over a nearby shrub. He rolled up his sleeves and tucked his tie into his shirt, then pulled on a pair of rubber gloves from his pants pocket. He moved to the car and reached over the top of the door. He grabbed the corpse by the shoulders and pulled him back against the seat.

The victim was wearing a long-sleeved, blue button-down oxford cloth shirt that had about as much blood on the front as on the shoulders and back. Kit leaned in and looked at the front of his khaki trousers …

"Zipper's up," she said, so Gatlin could share the moment.

She took several pictures of the corpse from that angle, then said, "Okay, you can put him back where he was."

While Gatlin did that, she went around to the other side of the car and looked at the ignition, where she saw that the keys were still in it. They were in the ON position. This was another reason she liked Gatlin. He understood that for her to make the correct decision about what had happened at a scene, she often needed information that didn't come from the body. So he would make sure the integrity of the scene was maintained until she'd had a look.

She photographed the keys, then, just to be sure all the facts fit, she walked back toward the rope, looking along the route for blood spatters. They were there ... little clotted gouts of red tracking back to the point where the head lay in the grass.

Ordinarily, she would have had Glen Fry, one of the autopsy assistants, with her, but after his home was destroyed, he and his family had evacuated to Dallas. There would have also been a crime scene team to impart their views on what happened, but the crime scene vans had been flooded to the rooftops. Most of the techs were still in other cities, waiting for FEMA to bring in those trailers everyone was expecting. So she and Gatlin and the sick young cop in his cruiser were all the attention this case was going to get.

She slipped her camera into her pants pocket and walked back to the crash site. She snapped on a pair of rubber gloves and said to Gatlin, "Let's get him out of there."

Gatlin grabbed the body under the arms and hauled it off the seat. When the angle allowed, Kit grabbed the corpse's ankles. Together, they carried the victim well away from the car and carefully laid him on his back on the grass. It was obvious from the way the body moved as they carried it that rigor had not yet set in, a fact consistent with the relatively fresh appearance of all the blood at the scene.

Gatlin rolled the left side of the body up and glanced at the back pocket. "Can you get that?" he said, referring to the guy's wallet.

Kit bent down, clamped the edge of the wallet with two fingers, and pulled it free. In seconds, she found a driver's license containing a picture of the owner with his head where it ought to be. It took a second for her to reconcile the face in the photo with the head in the grass. She looked at Gatlin, who was shucking off his rubber gloves and placing them on the body. "His name's Jude Marshall."

While Gatlin snapped on a fresh pair of gloves, Kit checked the bill compartment. "He's carrying eighty-two dollars."

"My own personal plan is to be broke when I die," Gatlin said, heading for the rear of the car.

"That's inconsiderate," Kit said. "When the cops get there, they might think you were robbed."

"When wouldn't that have been true? You checked the price of gas lately and coffee and toilet paper?" He pulled open the passenger door, popped the glove box, and began going through the papers inside. Kit checked the address on the license.

"He lives just off St. Charles on Octavia," she said.

"Yeah, same address on this receipt for an oil change," Gatlin responded.

"What's the date on that?"

Gatlin looked back at the top sheet in his hand. "August fifth."

"If this is a suicide, he obviously wasn't thinking about killing himself then."

"He didn't know then about Katrina."

"I suppose it'd be too much to hope there's a suicide note in that pile of stuff you're holding."

Gatlin riffled through the remaining papers. He looked at her. "Your stars must not be in the proper alignment." He put the papers back in the glove box, then reached over and snatched the key from the ignition. He carried the keys to the rear of the car and opened the trunk.

From where she stood, Kit couldn't see the contents, so she checked Gatlin's face for a reaction. He stared inside for a moment, then turned his eyes in her direction, focusing beyond her, his expression inscrutable.

Thinking he might have found another body, she hurried around to where she could see the trunk for herself.

Except for a couple of old, yellowed newspapers and some dried leaves, it held nothing.

She nudged Gatlin with her elbow. "Why didn't you say it was empty?"

He looked at her again, this time seeing her. "Guess my mind drifted." He stared off across the vacant park littered with branches. "I want the city back the way it used to be."

Not sure his wish would ever be fulfilled, Kit put a hand gently on his arm. "Everyone does. But that'll only happen if we all just keep doing our jobs the best we can."

He looked down at her and she could see the old Gatlin return. "Of course that's what it'll take," he said. "I'm surprised you ever thought otherwise."

Kit suppressed a smile at his comment. It was the first time since the hurricane hit that she'd found anything amusing … a small moment, but it gave her hope that one day everything *would* be back to normal. A scant second later, she remembered where she was, and she felt ashamed that, however briefly, she'd forgotten what had happened to Jude Marshall.

CHAPTER 3

Corpse 427 had not died from drowning. Broussard was certain of that because the lungs were normal in size and shape. When sectioned, they had contained no foam.

As he had expected even before opening the abdomen, the intestines had been extremely distended with decomposition gases. As he looked now at the uterus, he saw that it, too, appeared swollen, so its fundus sat well above the pubic symphysis, the line where the two hipbones are fused at the front.

He recited this finding aloud, and Jeff Lyons wrote it in the autopsy notes.

Most decomposition gases are produced by Clostridium, a bacterium common in the intestines and other locations, but uncommon in the uterus. For that reason and a sixth sense developed from over four decades of working with the dead, Broussard did not believe the appearance of this uterus had been caused by any postmortem changes.

He palpated the organ and his touch confirmed his belief that most of the bulk of this enlarged uterus was from a thickened myometrium, the muscle layer. This pointed to an extremely significant fact about the person who once inhabited the earthly vehicle containing this organ. Though convinced the conclusion he had reached was correct, he dissected the uterus free and carried it to the stainless steel work surface beside the sink, where he placed it in the pan for the hanging scales.

"Five hundred-fifty grams," he called out. This was nearly eight times larger than a normal uterus.

He removed the organ from the scales and placed it on the counter. With a long, thin knife shaped like the slim jim thieves use to open locked cars, he divided the organ.

And sure enough … "Myometrium thickened." There was absolutely no doubt now; around three weeks before her death, this woman had given birth.

Whenever Broussard awakened from those few hours of sleep he managed to squeeze into this long-running hell of an existence, he would pause a moment to repair his fragile state of mind with as much hope and optimism as he could muster so he could do his job. But even on his best days, the results had been little better than trying to repair a cracked engine block in one of his cars with spider silk. Today, the thought that some-where there was a newborn child whose mother now lay under his knife pulled mightily on the threads of his composure.

But he carried on. "Uterine appearance consistent with the view that this woman was three weeks postpartum."

He next turned to a search for the left ovary, which he found with no difficulty. Despite the deterioration of the rest of the body, the ovary was in fairly decent shape, allowing him to see that the fibrous capsule around the organ was thick and unblemished. The surface of the organ was smooth.

"Left ovary unremarkable. No sign of a recent ovulation."

With his big knife, he divided the ovary into five sections. Though decomposition had begun in the organ, it was not very advanced, so he was able to verify what he had seen from his initial observation: "Internal anatomy shows no evidence of a recent ovulatory cycle." In layman's terms, this meant it had been many months since this ovary had sent an egg into her oviduct, exactly what you would expect in a woman who had been pregnant until just three weeks ago.

"Corpus albicans of pregnancy not present."

When the egg that ultimately became this woman's child ovulated around ten months ago, it left behind, in the ovary of origin, a collection of cells that had grown until it formed a huge structure called a corpus luteum. For a while, this structure produced the hormones to maintain her pregnancy. Around three months after conception, when the embryo had taken over production of those hormones, the corpus luteum had turned into a scar called a corpus albicans. The fact there was no albicans in the left ovary meant he would find it in the other one.

Broussard placed the sections he'd just made into a small screw-top glass jar filled with formalin and replaced the lid. He returned to the body and began his search for the other ovary. When he found it a few seconds later, his interest in this case, already keen, sharpened, for where this one should have shown some external evidence of the large corpus albicans inside, the surface of the ovary had no bumps on it.

He relayed this information to Lyons and carried the organ to the counter. There, he sectioned it as he had the first.

In all his years doing this, he had not encountered such a situation before. "Internal anatomy of right ovary bears no evidence of a recent ovulation, nor is there a corpus albicans of pregnancy."

Before writing this down, Lyons said, "So she had a kid, but there's no evidence of that in her ovaries. What's going on here?"

Deep in thought, Broussard did not reply. Often, when he turned inward like this, he would rub the bristly hairs on the tip of his nose with his index finger to help him think. He tried to do that now, but his finger hit his face protector, jarring him back to an interactive state. "Sorry, what did you say?"

Lyons repeated his question.

"Only conclusion I can think of is she was a surrogate. She carried a child for someone else, conceived by *in vitro* fertilization and implanted into her uterus. Her eggs were never involved."

"What kind of woman would do that?"

"Most likely someone in need of money, or a relative of a couple who needed her."

"Is it easy for a woman, do you think ... giving up a child she carried inside her for nine months, even if it didn't come from one of her eggs?"

"I expect some think it'll be easy when they agree to do it, but then have problems later with their decision. At least the child she carried is probably in the arms of the family who contracted for her services and not cryin' somewhere over the loss of his mom."

"You said earlier, her lungs indicated she hadn't drowned. What killed her?"

"I'm not sure yet."

"When will you know?"

"Maybe after I look at corpse 428."

"So we're finished here?"

Broussard stood for a moment staring at the corpse of 427. In his life, he had probably autopsied over 500 decomposing bodies. He knew well the feel of tissue losing its architecture as dead cells digest themselves and bacterial enzymes induce putrefaction. But there was something about this body that wasn't right. He looked at Lyons. "Let's turn her over."

After they had the body turned, Broussard made a rectangular skin incision along the vertebral spines. He dissected the death-toughened hide of the corpse and reflected it, leaving one edge attached. He then dissected away and removed a block of the deteriorating superficial back muscles until he had worked his way down to the paraspinals, which were usually the last muscles to decompose. He cut a block of these fibers free and put it in a jar of formalin. He added another for good measure, then screwed the cap back on the jar.

Because there were so many bodies, all tissue samples from the St. Gabriel operation were to be sent to the Armed Forces Institute of Pathology in Bethesda for processing. But Broussard didn't want to wait the days it would take for the paraspinal samples to be cut and stained. Fortunately, Bethesda was not Broussard's only option. There was, on site, the equipment and hands for rapid microwave-assisted tissue processing in case a need arose to move quickly on a few samples. He looked at Lyons. "Let's turn her again and put her back in the bag."

When that was done, Broussard said, "Okay, return her to the cold room if you would and bring out 428."

While Lyons did that, Broussard stripped off his gloves and threw them in the discard box. He removed his face protector and put it on a clean part of the counter. He then picked up the paraspinal samples and headed for the admin area to get the processing underway.

CHAPTER 4

FOR DECADES, ST CHARLES Avenue in the garden district was
one of the most beautiful streets in America... A magical place
of huge mansions draped in wedding cake adornments, massive columns, tiered porches, and pierced fretwork, manicured
lawns and landscapes that would make even an escaped felon
find some measure of peace. But its crowning feature was its
trees: hundred year-old live oaks lining each side of the street,
their massive serpentine branches arching toward their brethren along the wide grassy median so they formed a leafy cathe-
dral along each lane. But those cathedrals had been horribly
brutalized by the storm. One after another of the noble trees
showed great gaping fissures in their trunks where two-ton
branches had been ripped loose. These huge limbs had fallen
into the street and made it impassable for days. It was a wonder
that with so few city workers available, a lane had now been
cleared in each direction from St. Charles to the park. But nothing had been hauled away, so as Kit followed Gatlin to Octavia
Street, they drove on asphalt layered with sawdust and passed
through a gauntlet of fallen boughs, their ends blunted by chain
saws.

Though all the physical circumstances surrounding Jude Marshall's death pointed to suicide, Kit's report would be complete only if she could document why he would have done such a thing to himself. So after contacting the FEMA central command for body collection and arranging for pick up and transportation of the remains to St. Gabriel, she and Gatlin were heading for Marshall's home to see what else they might learn about him.

The oaks lining Octavia Street were not as large as those on St. Charles, and they appeared to have suffered less damage. But fifty yards down Octavia, Kit saw one that had blown completely out of the ground and fallen on a car, crushing its roof. Skirting the stubs of that tree's branches, which had been sawed off to allow traffic to pass, she had to slow way down on the other side and carefully ease past a big metal awning that lay practically in the middle of the roadway.

Jude Marshall's home was on the left side of the street, a few doors before the Loyola intersection. It was a splendid one-story with a large porch and a beveled glass fan transom over a set of darkly-stained antique cypress front doors. On that porch were three ragtag-looking men. The tallest was carrying a big tree branch he was about to ram through one of the front windows.

Gatlin pulled to the curb and jumped out of his car. Gun in one hand, his badge in the other, he advanced on the three men. "Police ... drop that limb and get your asses off the porch."

For a moment, the men stood looking at Gatlin, expressions of cold hatred on their unshaven faces. They looked so dangerous and desperate Kit thought they might take their chances and rush Gatlin. She stopped her car in the street, reached down, and pulled her Ladysmith from its holster on her calf. Then she got out and joined Gatlin, her gun hand resting along her leg, where the three miscreants could see it.

The additional firepower didn't seem to have any effect on the men.

Good God, Kit thought. *Am I going to have to shoot someone?*

The standoff went on for an ice age, then the shortest of the three moved his left hand toward one of the pockets in the cargo pants he was wearing. In that pocket Kit could see the outline of what looked like a gun.

Gatlin fired a shot into the air. The man's hand stopped its advance. "Believe me," Gatlin said. "Nobody could be as honked as I am at what we're all having to go through because of the storm. Just drop the branch and leave. And we'll all live to be pissed off another day."

No one moved for a couple of seconds, during which Kit's nerves sizzled like frying bacon. Believing that the three men might take the offensive if they sensed how riddled with anxiety she was at the situation, she tried to look calm, whatever the hell a calm look was.

Finally, the guy with the limb threw it aside. "Another time, old man." He vaulted easily over the porch rail and headed off toward Loyola Street without looking back. The other two hustled down the porch steps and followed their departing comrade.

When the three thugs were far enough away that they no longer posed a threat, Gatlin looked down at Kit. "Thanks for the back-up. Would you have shot them if they came after us?"

"The guy who taught me to shoot also taught me that if you aren't prepared to use it, there's no point carrying a gun."

Gatlin nodded and pinched his lips together in an expression of agreement. "Good teacher."

They hadn't seen a single moving vehicle on the street since arriving. Even so, Kit returned to her car and drove it to the curb. She then joined Gatlin on the porch and rang the bell.

Already predisposed to believe no one was there, she didn't bother to press the bell again when no one answered, but opened the door with the house key on Jude Marshall's key ring.

Inside, lit by a large skylight directly overhead, an extremely wide, high-ceilinged hallway ran from the front door straight through the house. Under the skylight, in a small floor-level planter, a family of tree ferns and assorted other tropical foliage flourished in the natural light. Kit stepped onto the highly polished dark oak floor and announced herself. "Hellooo … Is anyone here? Hellooo …"

Receiving no answer, she moved further inside, Gatlin right behind her.

Beyond the skylight, the hall was dim. Forgetting that very little of the city had power, Gatlin reached for the switch by the door.

Miraculously, the ceiling came alive with recessed lighting that illuminated the many framed photos hung along each wall. Kit walked over to look at the first picture, which, though extremely colorful and appealing, was of a very unexpected subject.

"What *is* that?" Gatlin said from over her shoulder.

"A stained section of small intestine, I think," Kit said, drawing on what she'd learned in a long-ago college anatomy course. "The kind meant for viewing through a microscope."

"Yeah, that's what I always wanted on my wall … a picture of somebody's bowels."

Moving down to the next photo, Kit saw that this one was a connective tissue stain of the liver. She identified it for Gatlin.

"I don't even *eat* liver," he said. "So I sure don't want to see any pictures of it."

"I think it's kind of attractive. You don't see any beauty in it?"

"Rhetorical question, right?"

"Okay ..."

The remaining photos on that wall were sections of other organs. Kit looked at them without comment as she and Gatlin headed for the room at the end, which turned out to be the kitchen. She flicked on the lights and went into a welcoming space done in cherry cabinets and pale green onyx counter tops.

"This couldn't have been cheap," Gatlin said, following her.

While he ran his fingers over the nearest counter and inspected the rippling multicolored veins in the onyx, Kit went to a small plastic grocery bag by the sink and looked inside. There, she found a receipt showing the items purchased: two boxes of blueberries, two of strawberries, and some cottage cheese. The receipt was time-dated the day before at 4:40 p.m. She walked over to the refrigerator and opened it. Inside, along with a scant few other things, were the purchased items. The fruit was unopened. She inspected the cottage cheese and found it likewise, untouched.

Gatlin joined her. "What are you looking at?"

"Assuming no one else lives here, he bought that fruit and cottage cheese yesterday afternoon, but didn't open any of it. To me, that says when he bought the items, he didn't know he was going to kill himself."

"Otherwise, he wouldn't have bought two boxes of each kind ..."

"Yeah. Question now is, what happened between four-forty yesterday afternoon and when he threw that rope in the car and drove to the park."

"Over the years, I've had to inform a lot of folks that their husband or wife or parents have been murdered. I can't remember one of them who committed suicide after hearing the news."

"And your point is ...?"

"If a person is basically normal and well-adjusted, a sudden awful turn of events won't cause them to kill themselves. They somehow struggle through the horror and find a way to go on. Look at the thousands who went through hell when the flooding came. We've had maybe one report of someone being so strung out over what they lost, they decided to be dead. And this guy ... look at his house ... no damage. He's even got power. The storm hardly touched him. So whatever made him take his own head off, I suspect it was something that had been eating at him for a long time. This problem suddenly took a major turn for the worse. Having lived constantly with the fear of this thing for so long, he couldn't take it."

When they'd entered the kitchen and Gatlin had become enthralled with the countertops, Kit had wondered whether his mind was wandering again. But with this analysis, which was exactly what she believed, she saw he was all there.

"So let's see if we can figure out what that circumstance was," Kit said, leaving the kitchen.

"Won't be easy."

"Isn't that the way you like it?"

"Not so much lately."

From what Kit had seen so far, she was willing to bet Marshall had a profession, not a job. In her view, the best place in any professional man's home to learn about him was his study. They found Marshall's behind a door off the main hall, halfway down, between a photo of the gall bladder and a particularly colorful cross section of the esophagus.

The study was paneled in wood the color of weak tea. Kit didn't know much about decorating, but thought she'd seen pictures of similar paneling in magazines, where the style was referred to as Edwardian. The focal point of the room was a large fireplace surrounded by a simple but elegant mantel flanked by bookcases filled with leather-bound books. Above the fireplace, where Marshall could have put a large photo of the tongue or the trachea, he'd gone more traditional, choosing a large impressionist painting of women and children in old-style bathing suits playing at the beach.

"Look at this stuff," Gatlin said, over by another bookcase to the left.

Joining him, Kit saw as odd an assortment of objects as she'd ever seen in one place. On the shelf at eye level, an ornately carved replica of an old armoire about a foot tall was loosely flanked by more leather books. Artfully arranged on the left set of books were two white plaster casts of upper limbs, including the hands. To the right, a third cast was carefully balanced on its closed hand so the shoulder appeared to be coming out of the side of the bookcase. Below that shelf, supported by a pair of folding picture stands, sat two framed caricatures of human bodies with the skin removed. They were bracketed by identical plaster casts of a foot. Other shelves bore articulated manikins sitting on the edge of the shelf as though about to push off and make a run for it.

"He seems quite interested in the human body," Kit said.

"Too interested," Gatlin replied.

Then Kit saw why. Hanging above a nearby shelf with Marshall's name on it was a PhD degree in human anatomy from Tulane Medical School. Next to it hung another PhD in biomedical engineering. On the shelf below, there was a third, for molecular genetics. "Look at all these degrees. Was there anything this guy couldn't do?"

"Face life like the rest of us. I'd put that on the list."

Kit walked over to Marshall's big desk and picked up a digital camera by his computer. She turned it on and after a little fiddling, found the stored images, which were all dated. She scanned through them and handed the camera to Gatlin. "Here's what he did today, before going to the park."

Gatlin looked at the picture on the little fold-out screen. "It's just a photo of an area of the city that was flooded. From the look of those dilapidated stores and the shotgun houses in the background, it wasn't Lakeview."

"There are three more on there like that one," Kit said, moving around to the front of the desk, where she turned on Marshall's computer. "Maybe he's been in financial trouble for a long time. He could have had investment property there. When he saw what had happened to it, he knew he was ruined."

The computer played its happy little sign-on tune.

"Seems like he'd have to own an awful lot of that kind of property to be ruined by its loss," Gatlin said. "He was a smart guy ... he'd have had insurance."

The computer asked Kit for the access password. Having no faith she could guess her way in, she turned to Gatlin, who was looking over her shoulder. "Got any ideas how to bypass this?"

"Oh, sure. Sometimes I can't even get my car started. Why do you figure a guy would have his home computer password protected?"

"Makes you wonder doesn't it?"

"What's all this?" Gatlin said, moving to the other end of the desk, where there was a stack of DVDs in jewel cases. He picked up the top disc in the pile and read the information on the front. "Organogenesis Inc." He looked down at the next one, which bore the same words. Picking up that case, he saw an identical label on the disc under it.

"Let's put one in that player over there and see what it is," Kit suggested.

Gatlin handed her a disc, and she carried it to the player and TV on a nearby bookshelf. A few seconds later, Jude Marshall appeared on screen in a white lab coat. As he began speaking, Kit remembered his head lying in the grass. A shiver ran down her spine.

"I'm sure you have many questions about our service," Marshall said in a confident voice. "You have obviously contacted us because you know that many children in need of a liver transplant die before they can find one. With our service you will be assured of a liver. But that's not the only advantage we provide. The liver you receive will be an exact tissue match. That means there will be no need for your child to take any rejection-suppression drugs, which, in any other circumstance, would have to be used for the rest of their life. These drugs often have serious side effects. To be free of these dangers will ensure that your child will progress through life with no more health risks than the average little boy or girl."

"How can they do that?" Gatlin said.

"You're probably asking yourself how we can do this?" Marshall echoed. "It's possible because we are not an organ procurement agency. Instead, we will *create* an organ for you using cells taken from your child's bone marrow. In the marrow of everyone, there are cells that have the potential to form any cell in the body if given the proper instructions and environment. We alone know how to make these cells become the cell types found in a normal liver.

"Once we have created a population of each of the required cells, we place them in a modified ink jet printer, similar to the one you may be using at home or your office, except we fill the ink cartridges with the various cell types we have produced. A computer program then guides the printer so that the cells are 'printed' a layer at a time onto a flat surface. Gradually, as the printer makes many passes across the surface, a three-dimensional organ is constructed, complete even down to the blood vessels and bile duct system. What results is a perfect liver. Because it came from your child's own cells, it will be an exact tissue match.

"Here's a liver being made for a California client ..."

The picture shifted to a large glass box with a printer suspended on rails above a liquid containing a gray mass of tissue. The sound of a printer mechanism could be heard in the background.

Marshall's voice came back from off screen. "After each pass across the forming organ, the liquid level in the container is gently raised one cell diameter and the printer stops for thirty minutes to allow the seeded cells to spread and adhere to the tissues already laid down. Then another pass is made. In time, an entire organ will be constructed.

"One of the most difficult problems to be overcome in formation of organs in this manner is how to oxygenate and feed the cells deep in the organ. Because of proprietary considerations, I'm not at liberty to disclose exactly how that is accomplished, but I can tell you that what appears to be water in the container is something far different."

The camera cut back to Marshall.

"Organogenesis Inc. is a full-service facility. Once the organ is complete, our board-certified surgeons will schedule your child for transplantation. At present, there are over thirty happy, healthy children in the world who have benefited from our ability to create a new liver for them. If you feel this might be the right choice for your child, contact us and we'll discuss it. We can be reached in the following ways."

Just as the screen shifted to some printed contact information, the phone on Marshall's desk rang.

Kit picked it up. "Hello, Jude Marshall's residence. Who's calling, please?"

"His wife," an indignant voice said. "Who are you?"

Kit hesitated, trying to think of just the right words to tell her what had happened. Not finding any, she just plunged ahead. "Mrs. Marshall, I'm afraid I have some bad news for you. My name is Kit Franklyn. I'm with the medical examiner's office. I just came from Audubon Park, where ... I'm so sorry to have to tell you this, but ... your husband has passed away."

Nothing but silence came from the other end, then a choking sound. "What are you ... how ... what happened?"

There was no way Kit was going to describe the circumstances of Marshall's death to his wife over the phone. So she hedged. "We're not exactly sure, but at this point, it appears he may have committed suicide."

Hearing that a spouse committed suicide was often harder for the surviving member of the pair to deal with than to learn their loved one had died of natural causes or in an accident; it suggested to the survivor they had somehow failed to give the deceased the proper emotional support. Otherwise, this wouldn't have happened. Even though Kit had never met Mrs. Marshall, she felt for her.

"Mrs. Marshall, where are you now?"

"Houston. I've been visiting my sister here since the storm. But I need to come home right away ..."

"Because of the storm, there aren't any facilities here to serve your husband, so we've arranged for him to be sent to the FEMA mortuary in St. Gabriel. When you arrive, go there and they'll help you with further arrangements. I'm sorry to have to ask this, but do you know of anything that was bothering your husband to the point it would cause him to do this?"

"Absolutely not. He wasn't disturbed in any way. He was perfectly normal."

"Of course. I'm so sorry for your loss. I'll see that your husband's keys will be with his other effects at the St. Gabriel facility. If you have a pen, I'll give you the number there ..."

After a short interval while Marshall's wife rounded up something to write with, Kit gave her the mortuary number. She then hung up and looked at Gatlin. "That wasn't fun."

"You did it as well as anyone could have. I guess she didn't know of any reason for her husband killing himself."

"No."

"What now?"

"I'm going to take a ride over to Organogenesis Inc. and talk to them about Marshall. Maybe someone there knows things his wife doesn't." She ran the DVD back to the company's contact information and wrote the address and phone number in the little note pad she always carried. She then looked at Gatlin. "Thanks for coming over here with me."

"It was interesting. You gonna be at Andy's birthday party at Grandma O's tonight?"

"Wouldn't miss it."

CHAPTER 5

Uh-oh ... Broussard stood looking at the sectioned right ovary of corpse 428, the second of the three bodies found together in the lower Ninth Ward brush tangle. Like 427, this one had *not* drowned. Moreover, she also had given birth about a month before her death, yet her ovaries showed no signs of a corpus albicans of pregnancy.

It was not hard to believe that two women, both of whom had served as gestational surrogates, might have been living together in the lower Ninth before the flood. But then to find both dead and wearing nothing, neither one with water in her lungs, both with what appeared to be antemortem bruises around their mouth and nose ... Broussard's skullduggery sonar was now squealing.

And, like 427, the consistency of this body didn't feel right.

Despite all he was doing that was right and clever, Broussard had been insensibly snared in a trap baited by his provocative findings on 427. Becoming too focused on looking for those same features on the second corpse, he had once again failed to notice what he had also missed on the face of the first.

At that moment, the drapes parted and a young redhead leaned in. "Dr. Broussard, those samples you wanted processed are ready. Should I hold them until later?"

"No. I'd like to see them now." He looked at Lyons. "I'll be right back."

Broussard took off his gloves and face protector and followed the redhead down the draped hallway to the tissue processing area, where when he entered, his eyes went directly to a microscope equipped with a TV camera and monitor on a table. A slide was already on the scope so the monitor screen was filled with images of skeletal muscle fibers.

"Is that slide from what I sent down?"

"Yes. I was checking the section for staining quality and just left it on there."

Broussard was a man of many passions. He had read nearly all 110 books written by Louis L'Amour. He owned fifteen paintings of sheep by six different Old Master Dutch painters. Though the supply he'd brought to St. Gabriel had run out days ago, he usually carried a cache of cellophane-wrapped lemon balls in his pants pocket. He firmly believed his six 1957 T-Birds were a reasonable number and that one more would make him an eccentric, but whenever one drove by that he didn't own, he watched it with envy as long as it remained in sight. To his mind, mankind's greatest accomplishments included French cooking and anything written by Tchaikovsky. These were among the things that had shaped his existence and given his life meaning for much of his adult life.

But he could hate as well as love. And nothing incurred his wrath more than the arrogance that made one person believe they had the right to kill another. Now, that familiar anger began to sweep over him, engulfing him in a tsunami that made his face flush, for the muscle fibers displayed on the monitor were full of holes obviously caused by ice crystals forming in them.

Corpse 427 had been frozen before she was found.

Coupled with the antemortem bruising he'd seen around her mouth and nose, there was no doubt whatever in his mind that this woman had been murdered and her body hidden away in a freezer before hurricane Katrina had somehow liberated it. Though he hadn't yet seen sections of muscle from 428, or even autopsied 429, he was equally certain they had the same history. But it still had to be documented.

He looked at the tech. "Good work. I can already see what I was lookin' for. In a few minutes, I'd like you to process a few more samples. Will you be available?"

"That's why I'm here."

This changes everything, Broussard thought as he headed back to the autopsy room. Before he'd known they'd been frozen, he'd assumed all three women had died at roughly the same time, most likely within a day or two after the flooding began. But now, he had no idea when they'd been killed. A month ago? Three months? A year? That meant they could have been killed not at the same time, but at widely-spaced intervals.

This was going to make catching the killer extremely complicated.

For the first time in nearly a month, Broussard's mind became engaged at a level that, for a moment, lifted his veil of depression.

CHAPTER 6

ORGANOGENESIS INC. APPEARED TO be the only occupant of a one-story, monolithic cement building with little rectangular windows that made the place look like it was squinting. Inside, the sprawling lobby was decorated like an art museum, its white walls hung with bright, happy impressionist paintings whose colors danced in the light focused on them from canister fixtures in the ceiling. The similarity in feeling to the long hall in Jude Marshall's home was striking.

The cry of a child drew Kit's attention to a couple sitting on a sofa in a waiting area along the back wall. A baby was in the woman's arms, and she was speaking to it and stroking its face. Beside the sofa, a receptionist behind a French writing desk was working at a computer.

Kit crossed the lobby and approached the receptionist, an older, light-skinned black woman with thinning hair and suspicious eyes that reminded Kit of her high school algebra teacher. She was even wearing a big, gold brooch like the kind Mrs. Claymore wore every single day to school.

How many times when returning one of Kit's test papers had the imperious Claymore looked down over her glasses and said, "Young woman, I'm afraid you're not going to amount to much in this life." Now, for the first time since graduating from Speculator High, as Kit looked at the baby being comforted by its mother, her own childless state made her feel that Claymore might have been on to something.

Reaching the receptionist, Kit spoke first. "Hello, I'm Dr. Franklyn from the New Orleans medical examiner's office."

This mention of her affiliation had no effect on the woman. Marshall's wife must not have called the company and told them what happened. Not wanting to divulge the reason for her visit to someone this low in the corporate hierarchy, Kit phrased her next words carefully. "It's my understanding that Dr. Jude Marshall works here. Is that correct?"

The receptionist's already cold eyes seemed to ice over. "He's one of the owners, but he's not in just now."

"You said *one* of the owners. How many are there?"

"Two."

"Who's the other?"

"Dr. Quentin Marshall."

"Jude's brother?"

"I'm not comfortable with this conversation."

"Then perhaps you'd tell Dr. Quentin I'd like to speak to him."

"He's very busy today. And these folks are next. *They* made an appointment before coming."

Kit looked at the couple on the sofa. "I'm sorry to ask, but would you mind if I spoke to the doctor very briefly, before he sees you? I know your business with him is extremely important, but I have some information for him that he needs to hear."

The husband, a guy wearing the mustache and goatee that seems to be required of men who shave their head as he had, said, "Yeah, I do mind. My son was born with a liver that doesn't work right. Without Dr. Marshall, he's not going to grow up. He'll die. Is your business here more important than that?"

His wife, an attractive blonde with her short hair swept back from a face that showed the strain of their child's condition, put her hand on her husband's arm. In a gentle voice, she said, "They're not going to give Adam a new liver today, or even tomorrow. This is going to take a little time. We have to understand that." She looked at Kit. "You go ahead. We'll wait."

"Thank you. I'm so sorry your child isn't well. I know how hard that is." *No you don't*, a voice in Kit's head responded. *How could you?*

"I'll tell Dr. Marshall you're here," the receptionist said, reluctantly.

She made a call, listened to the voice on the other end, and said to Kit, "He'll see you in his office … through that door."

Inside, Kit was met by a nurse wearing her black hair in a style that resembled coiled springs.

"Hello," the nurse said, her smile convincing. "Down this hall, second door to your right. Dr. Marshall will be with you in a moment."

A few seconds later, Kit saw that Marshall's large office was a homage to his collection of carved jade, which occupied every available surface. The largest was a complicated dragon figure at least four feet tall in a glass case.

She walked over to see it better. As she bent to study the exquisitely detailed scales around the mouth, a voice from behind her said, "That was made from a single piece of serpentine jade, the largest ever mined in China."

Kit turned and saw a tall, tanned man with a long face and prematurely silver hair. He was wearing rimless glasses and a white coat so starched it probably could have stood up all by itself. But the thing that made Kit's voice catch in her throat as she tried to answer was the last time she had seen that face it had recently rolled in the grass at Audubon Park without its body.

"You and Jude are twins ..." she said, confiding a fact he had likely been aware of for several years.

"So you know my brother?"

"Not exactly." The receptionist had relayed Kit's name and affiliation to whomever she'd spoken to on the phone, but Kit thought maybe that information hadn't made it to Marshall. She began to introduce herself.

"My receptionist told me who you are," Marshall said. His expression shifted from one of curiosity to apprehension. "Why are we talking about Jude?"

Normally, by the time Kit spoke to any relative in one of her cases, they'd already been told by the police what had happened. Her brief conversation with Jude's wife had, therefore, been an aberrant event. Yet, here she was doing it again.

"Wish I didn't have to tell you this, but his body was found this morning in the park near the New Orleans zoo. At this point, it looks like a suicide."

Quentin Marshall's reaction to this news seemed odd. His lips thinned and his brows dipped, making him look angry rather than shocked.

"Selfish bastard," he muttered, for the moment existing somewhere inside himself. Then his eyes flicked back from that hidden place. "I'm sorry. Of course, I didn't mean that. It's just that we've got transplants scheduled Tuesday and Wednesday of next week, and I'll need him during surgery."

"You create the livers and also perform the transplants?" Kit said.

Quentin's eyebrows went up. He rocked his head to the side in a show of feigned modesty. "We pride ourselves on seeing our clients completely through the process." His face again grew dark. "But now Jude's put that in jeopardy. And with two sick children depending on us. Where am I going to find another surgeon to assist me on such short notice?"

"I'm aware your brother was a very accomplished man, but I didn't know he was an MD."

"He wasn't. I taught him what he needed to know for our surgeries."

"How would you describe your personal relationship with him?"

"Amiable, comfortable, mutually supportive."

"And professionally?"

"The same. You said he committed suicide. How?"

Kit explained the circumstances.

"Never do things the easy way. Did he leave a note?"

"No." Kit saw the shadow of another unexpected expression pass briefly across Quentin's face. "If he'd left one, I'd probably already be writing up my report. I'm here in hopes you might be able to tell me why he'd do such a thing. Was he facing some kind of personal crisis?"

Quentin mulled over her question, then said. "He was very despondent over what the storm did to New Orleans. Didn't think it would ever be the same again."

"I've seen his home. There's no damage there at all. Did he have some uninsured property in areas that were flooded?"

"I don't think so."

"Then why would damage from the storm weigh so heavily on him that he no longer wanted to live?"

"Maybe it was the thought of how much others had suffered."

"But a moment ago, you said he was selfish."

Anger flared on Quentin's face. "Why are you working so hard to find discrepancies in what I've told you?"

"It's my job to make sure what appears to be a suicide, really is. When the decedent doesn't leave a note, one of the factors helping me decide if I *am* dealing with a suicide is determining whether there was some event in the person's life that could have been behind such an extreme act. It has nothing to do with you, but everything to do with your brother. I'm simply trying to get an accurate picture of him before his death. I'm sorry if in doing that I've offended you."

Quentin's expression softened. He raised his palm and waved his hand as if to erase what he'd said. "I'm the one who should apologize. I'm not thinking very clearly right now. Jude gone ..." He shook his head. "It doesn't seem possible."

"How was your brother's marriage? Were he and his wife getting along?"

"Could anyone but them answer such a question?"

"Did he ever say anything to indicate they were having problems?"

"I've always believed marriage dilutes a man's focus in his work. Jude knew that, so we never spoke about his home life."

"Yet your own work is dedicated to helping children, the product of a relationship between a man and a woman."

"You think I'm inconsistent?"

"I do."

"So maybe I should tell those people out in the waiting room to go home, because you find my work inconsistent with my views on marriage. Should I do that? Should I?"

"Of course not."

"Then perhaps you'll allow me to get on with my day."

"Good idea for both of us."

Kit whisked past him and headed for the door to the lobby.

Outside, she went to her car and sat for a moment thinking about the conversation she'd just had. Talk about inconsistency ... For a guy dedicated to helping children, he seemed surprisingly cold and unsympathetic. Had Jude been the same way? After all, they *were* twins. If he *was*, then Quentin's comment about Jude being despondent over the plight of all the people who had lost their homes in the flood didn't track. And that momentary look on Quentin's face when he'd asked whether Jude had left a suicide note ... It was almost as though he'd been relieved to hear there wasn't one. What was that all about?

Still ruminating over the Jude-Quentin axis, she started the car and left the premises.

A few minutes later, her mind turned to the party tonight. It had always been impossible to know what to get Broussard for his birthday. Now, with many stores closed even in unflooded areas because its employees had lost their homes, and stores that were open choked with people who seemed to need *everything*, she castigated herself for not dealing with this sooner. What the devil was she going to do?

She'd about decided to just give up and plead exigent circumstances at the party when she had a thought. That shop a block from her apartment was still open. And considering the circumstances, wasn't doing much business. Maybe that was the answer ...

CHAPTER 7

K<small>IT PULLED INTO THE</small> parking lot of Grandma O's a little after 6:00 p.m. Broussard and Gatlin's cars were already there. She parked by the FEMA trailer Grandma O's kitchen help was living in, picked up Broussard's gift from the seat next to her, and headed for the front door.

Located on Poydras Street, a location that had kept it out of the floodwaters, Grandma O's was Broussard's favorite restaurant. Though it sat in an area still without power, the business was running on the big propane generator Grandma O had the foresight to install a year before the flood. It was not the first time the old Cajun had shrewdly anticipated trouble and had taken steps to avoid it. Some believed it was more than cleverness, that she used some kind of magic to see the future. While Kit found such a thing hard to believe, the old gal was such an enigma Kit wasn't able to completely dismiss the possibility.

From the doorway as she entered, Kit saw the birthday boy sitting in the back at his permanently reserved table. On his right was Phil Gatlin, wearing the same clothes as when he'd gone with her to Jude Marshall's. Bubba Oustellette, grandson of the proprietor and the mechanic that kept Broussard's fleet of T-Birds running, sat to Broussard's left. As usual, Bubba was wearing a blue T-shirt, blue coveralls, and a green baseball cap bearing a Tulane logo. Grandma O was there as well, distributing drinks. There was apparently a dominant gene in Oustellette DNA for constancy in clothing choice, because Grandma O was dressed as always in a black taffeta dress that swelled her already considerable bulk to incredible proportions. As she put down the tray with the drinks and came to greet Kit, her dress swooshed over Bubba's head and pulled his cap off.

"You runnin' a little late tonight chil'," Grandma O said, the gold star inlay in her right front incisor flashing. She wrapped a big arm around Kit's shoulder and gave her a hug, crushing Kit's face against her chest. If the greeting had lasted a moment longer than it did, Broussard would have had his first death by taffeta suffocation.

"You ain't missed much," Grandma O said, lowering her voice. "Jus' city boy complainin' about us makin' such a fuss over him. But he don't really mean it."

She ushered Kit to the table, where Broussard said, "Now look … she brought a gift, too. I don't know why you are all actin' like this is a national holiday. It's not as though I haven't had more …"

Grandma O leveled a finger at Broussard. "You jus' calm down. You might a had a lot a birthdays already, but you ain't had dis one before. An' dis one is ours as well as yours. So pipe down."

Broussard took a breath to respond, but Grandma O shook her finger at him in warning. "Don't sass me."

Broussard sank back in his chair, folded his arms over his chest, and obeyed her warning.

Gatlin looked at Kit. "Don't know about you, but this is about the best birthday party I've ever been to. Have a seat and join in."

Grandma O pulled out the chair next to Bubba, and Kit sat down.

Behind the little Cajun's heavy black beard and mustache, he grinned broadly at Kit, his teeth arctic perfection. He turned to Gatlin and Broussard. "So, turns out *I* got da best seat."

"I'm guessin' you'd like a glass a white wine," Grandma O said to Kit.

Kit looked up at the mountain of fabric and flesh towering over her. "I would, thanks."

Grandma O handed Gatlin the remaining glass of wine still on her serving tray. Before leaving, she cycled back past Kit and snatched up the gift Kit had placed on the table. "I'll jus' put dis with da others and we'll open 'em later."

Broussard leaned forward and picked up his own glass. Settling back in his chair with it, he said to Kit, "Heard you and Phillip had an interestin' mornin'."

"You mean the headless guy in the park?"

"If there was somethin' else you'd rank before that, I'd love to hear what it was."

"No, I'd say that was number one. But a conversation I had with the victim's twin brother was pretty strange, too."

"In what way?"

"When I told him his brother had died in an apparent suicide, his first reaction was to call the deceased a 'selfish bastard.'"

"Had they been estranged?" Gatlin asked.

"What's dat mean?" Bubba said, his eyes wide with interest in the conversation.

Had the little Cajun not been so completely trustworthy with a confidence and had he not been a lifelong friend of Broussard, those present might have had some qualms discussing any case in front of him. As it was, no one gave it a thought.

"If you're estranged with someone, it means you don't like each other anymore," Gatlin explained.

"Nice word," Bubba said. "Go ahead."

Kit continued. "When I asked him to describe his relationship with his brother, he said, 'amiable, comfortable, and mutually supportive.'"

"Sounds a little distant to me," Broussard observed.

"Jude, the deceased, was married," Kit said. "But his brother, Quentin, didn't believe in marriage. So they never discussed Jude's home life."

"Yet Quentin thinks they were mutually supportive," Broussard said.

"Exactly."

There was a commotion at the front door as three men and a woman all wearing camouflage pants and black T-shirts with a skull and crossbones on the chest came inside. From their dress, they were obviously part of the weapons of mass destruction team sent in for body collection. One of them pointed at a table near the window, and they all headed toward it. If anything, the woman had more swagger in her movements than any of the men, and that was saying a lot.

Grandma O appeared from the kitchen, put a glass of white wine in front of Kit, and went over to serve the new arrivals.

Broussard leaned forward and lowered his voice so the WMD group couldn't overhear. "Why'd Quentin say his brother was selfish for killin' himself?"

"It had to do with their work," Kit replied. "They grow livers for kids who need a transplant."

"That's what Phillip said. I didn't know such a thing was possible."

"Neither did I. Anyway, Quentin also is the primary transplant surgeon. Jude was his assistant. They've got some transplants coming up soon, and Quentin was upset that he wouldn't have Jude's help."

"So maybe he loves kids more'n he did his brother," Bubba suggested.

"Then why doesn't he marry and have some?" Kit said.

Bubba's brow furrowed, and his eyes rolled upward in thought. After a few seconds, he said, "I got to think about dat one awhile."

"You sayin' you don't think the case really is a suicide?" Broussard asked.

"It probably is. I just don't know yet why he did it."

"Seems to be the day for interestin' cases," Broussard said. "Today, I discovered that three female bodies collected from the same brush tangle in the Ninth Ward had all been frozen at some point."

Everyone else at the table sat for a moment in shocked silence.

Gatlin made a sour face. "That's not good."

"So they were all murdered," Kit said.

"Unless you all can come up with some other explanation," Broussard replied.

"That means there's no way to even know *when* they were killed," Gatlin said. "Or where."

"Same thoughts I had," Broussard said.

Gatlin asked, "*How* were they killed?"

"They all had blisters in lines that radiated away from the corners of their mouth. I think somebody put a plastic bag over each victim's head and pulled it tight around their mouth so it pinched the skin."

"So dey couldn't breathe," Bubba said, wide-eyed.

Gatlin leaned closer to Broussard and gave him a hard look. "Have you sent a report on this to Homicide?"

"It's in my car. Figured it'd be best if I gave it to you directly."

"Got an ID on any of the victims?"

"Not yet."

"Their descriptions and your conclusions about how the killer works need to be sent to the state police and to VICAP," Gatlin said, the acronym he mentioned being the FBI's Violent Criminal Apprehension Program. "With the disarray our department is in, we might not get the job done in a timely manner, so you should probably follow up personally with those agencies and make sure the information gets there."

Broussard looked at the old detective over the tops of his glasses.

"I'm just trying to help," Gatlin said. "Occasionally, you *don't* think of things before I do."

"Name three times where that happened."

Gatlin leveled a finger at Broussard. "Aha! If it wasn't true, you would have said, 'name *one* time.'"

Kit shook her head. This was the way it was with these two. Close friends for most of their lives, Broussard was even the namesake for Gatlin's son, Andy, who'd died at three of rheumatic fever. Despite their long history together, most of their conversations became sparring events in which each would try to make a salient point before the other.

"Well, this isn't one of those times," Broussard said.

"What did you do?"

"Sent all the information to both places myself."

"That was a good idea. What time frame do you have for the victims' disappearance?"

"Had to guess, obviously, so I chose the last three years."

"Might be wrong."

"Had to start somewhere."

"What kind of descriptive information do you have?"

"The usual … prints, dental x-rays, sex, height, hair color and length. And one of them had a silicone chin implant."

"That last one should really help," Kit said. "There can't be too many missing persons with one of those."

"Still might come up with bupkis," Gatlin said.

"How come?" Bubba asked.

"In most departments, unless the national press gets hold of it for some reason, missing person's cases for adults are something you pretend to work on, but don't ... not really," Gatlin said. "At least half the missing persons reports filed never get to VICAP or even state records. They just get buried in the shit storm of paper from cases where you know a crime has been committed. Missing kids ... that's another story. You get all over those. But adults ... how do you know they didn't just want to disappear? There's often no way to know if there was even a crime involved."

"Now you all know why Phillip's nickname in Homicide is 'Sunshine,'" Broussard said.

"Just a reality check," Gatlin replied, raising his wine to his lips.

"No, here's the reality," Broussard said. "Whoever did that to those three women has to pay for what he did. And I'm gonna do whatever it takes to see he does."

Broussard's hatred of murderers was well-known among everyone at the table. But they had never before heard him make such a pronouncement. They all sat in surprised silence until a few seconds later Grandma O appeared with a large tray and sat it in the middle of the table.

"Nymphs a L'Oustellette," she announced. "You all can nibble on dem while I get da main course ready." She then went back to the kitchen.

On the tray was a large rectangle of pale golden jelly on which there rested, between tarragon leaves and some other material that together resembled water grasses, four long rows of slippery looking ...

"Nymphs," Kit said, looking askance at the display. "What is that really?" she whispered.

"Frog legs," Broussard said.

Across the table, Gatlin was rolling his eyes at Kit, apparently trying to send her some kind of signal. She glanced back toward the kitchen and there was Grandma O watching, a stern look on her face. Well aware of the consequences of not eating everything Grandma O put before you, Kit said in the old Cajun's direction, "Actually, one of my all-time favorite foods." She reached for one of the legs. Trying not to recoil at its cold, clammy feel, she forced the thing toward her mouth, while everyone else at the table sensing her discomfort, tensed, fearing this was not going to end well.

Suppressing a shudder, Kit's teeth bit delicately into the soft frog meat, and she pulled some of it loose from the bone. She let the meat drop onto her tongue and … a flavor that seemed to carry her from the room to another world overwhelmed her senses.

She looked back at Grandma O. "This is incredible."

The old Cajun smiled with satisfaction, her gold inlay glinting off the overhead lights. Beside Kit, Bubba sighed with relief.

Watching until he was sure Grandma O was truly gone, Gatlin then whispered, "For a minute there, I was afraid you were gonna get us all killed."

The nymphs were followed by the main course: sole poached in white wine and mushroom cooking liquor, served under Nantua sauce and garnished with crayfish tails and truffles. For a vegetable, they had an artichoke bottom-asparagus tip pyramid coated in Mornay sauce a culinary triumph under normal circumstances, a miracle under these.

When they had all finished, Broussard sat back in his chair and folded his chubby fingers over his now greatly expanded belly. He looked up at Grandma O, his expression one of sleepy contentment. "What would it take to get the recipes for everything we had tonight?"

Grandma O seemed to think about that a moment, then she said, "If we was married, dat might do it."

Broussard's little eyes popped to full open and his mouth gaped.

Grandma O hooted with laughter, a sound that would make a safari camper wake in a cold sweat and reach for his gun. "Relax, city boy," she said. "It was a joke. You ain't ever gonna get my recipes. Now it's gift time."

She went over to the bar, where she'd put the packages, and carried them back to the table. She handed Broussard Kit's gift first.

"This is too much fuss for a natural biological event," Broussard said, looking at everybody.

Grandma O put her hands on her hips. "Jus' open da package."

Broussard proceeded to slowly and meticulously unwrap the gift.

"Way you pickin' at dat thing, looks like you expectin' to use da paper again," Grandma O said. "I better not see what you give me for *my* next birthday wrapped in it."

He finally got the package open and took the lid off the flat rectangular box inside. He removed the contents and let it unfold so he and everyone could see what it was: a huge, blue T-shirt with yellow lettering across the chest that said, *WITHOUT FRIES IT'S JUST NOT ESCARGOT.*

Other than disposable autopsy attire, and a hospital gown that time he nearly died with Congo-Crimean hemorrhagic fever, no one at the table had ever seen Broussard in anything but a starched white shirt and a bow tie, not even when he was helping rescue people caught in the flood. The thought that he might find the pairing of escargot with fries appealing seemed equally preposterous. So everyone applauded Kit's choice.

Though he tried to hide it, Kit saw a flicker of a smile tug at the old pathologist's lips as he folded the shirt and placed it back in the box. Then he looked at Kit. "The perfect thing to wear next year when I run the Boston marathon."

"By the way," Kit said. "Teddy says happy birthday." She was referring to Teddy LaBiche, her long-time boyfriend, who ran an alligator farm in Bayou Coteau.

Broussard shook his head. "This just isn't the kind of news that should be affectin' folks that far off."

"Dis one is from Phillip," Grandma O said, handing Broussard a box wrapped in a Piggly Wiggly grocery sack and tied with twine.

"It's so beautiful I hate to open it," Broussard said.

Gatlin nodded. "It *is* one of my finest works."

Broussard pulled off the wrapping, looked at what was inside, and held up a water-stained box to the rest of the table.

Grandma O ripped off another safari laugh and pounded the table with a big hand. "You got him, Phillip ..."

Gatlin had given Broussard a used thigh-master.

"Cause I know how much you like to stay in shape," Gatlin said.

Broussard turned the box and looked again at the front. "Awww, it's not the professional model. I'll wear this one out in a week."

Grandma O handed Broussard the last gift. "Dis is from Bubba an' me." She turned to the kitchen and nodded to one of her staff waiting by the door.

Broussard quickly shucked off the white wrapping paper and red ribbon. Inside was a certificate in a plain, black frame.

"We're not mind readers," Gatlin prompted. "What's it say?"

Broussard began to read aloud. "Whereas, the ignition within the New Orleans city limits of such flammable materials as would constitute a major fire hazard requires the presence of a fire marshal, and whereas, Dr. Andy Broussard has reached the age at which the collective candles on his birthday cake will constitute such a hazard, he is hereby granted the title of honorary fire marshal for as long as it takes for him to blow out said candles."

"In case you're wonderin', Kit helped write dat," Grandma O said. She took a small bell from her pocket and rang it.

This brought two of her staff from the kitchen, one carrying a large, square cake with candles ablaze and a second person with a tray of plates and silverware.

The cake was set in front of Broussard, and Grandma O said, "City Boy, you better blow dose out 'fore I have to get a hose after 'em."

It took Broussard three separate breaths to extinguish all the candles. When they were out and he sat down, red-faced from the effort, everyone applauded.

"I was afraid for a minute dere, you might lose your teeth on to da cake," Bubba said.

Everyone had another good laugh.

Broussard started to reply, but before he did, a loud voice rose from the WMD table.

"I'd think with all the death and destruction in this city, you all wouldn't be quite so happy."

Everyone turned to the table by the window.

Puffing up to where she appeared to double in size, Grandma O walked over to the other group. "Who said dat?"

"I did," a guy with a crew cut and bony features said.

"Where were you when da hurricane hit?" Grandma O asked.

"Kansas City."

"Not exactly in da storm's eye were you?"

"No, but ..."

"We was all *right* here. You see dat woman over dere?" she pointed at Kit. "She could a evacuated, but she stayed to make sure da paralyzed old woman in da apartment next to hers would be okay because da woman's wheelchair had a respirator on it to help her breathe an' it was all too bulky to move. When da power went out, dat respirator stopped workin'. An' da backup battery turned out to be dead. So with da phone out, dis woman, who could a gotten herself to a comfortable hotel miles away to wait out da storm, stayed behind and used a hand-pump respirator to keep dat woman alive. She pumped dat respirator for twelve hours until her hands cramped up so bad she jus' couldn't squeeze it anymore. As her hands failed her, she prayed for help, but none came. When she couldn't pump another lick, dat old woman died ... right dere in front a her."

Grandma O lowered her voice to spare Kit what followed. "Can you imagine what dat's like ... watchin' life seep out a someone so close you can see da fright and da plea for help in dere eyes ... thinkin' you could save 'em if only your hands would work. But dey won't work and because a dat, da light in dat old woman's eyes went out for good.

"An' dose three men ... dey worked for forty-eight straight hours pickin' up folks stranded on top a their houses and bringin' 'em by boat to dry land and tellin' 'em how to get here. Dey rescued a hundred an' fifty people. But you know da one dey remember ... da one dey'll never forget ... da chil' dey found on a roof beside a small hole chopped through from da attic. Dere wasn't room for an adult to get through, so da momma must a pushed her baby up dere to save him. What happened to her, no one knows. But da chil' sat up dere all alone for a long time. Finally, dose men found him ... he was still alive den, but not by much.

"Seein' how weak and blue he was, dey headed back to dry land hopin' dey might run across a paramedic team with some oxygen and an IV rig dey could use to give him liquids and food, all da while knowin' dey probably wouldn't find such a thing … But at least if dey could get him to me, he could be warm, and I'd get food and water into him some kind a way.

"But five minutes from dry land … he stopped breathin'. An' even though dat man at da head of da table dere is a doctor, he could do nothin' to save dat chil's life. Dat little boy died in his arms.

"I'm not discountin' da pain your job is causin' you; I jus' want you to understand. Dis is our home and we've lived through more hell dan you can imagine. We're *still* livin' it. And no one knows when it'll end. Da only way any of us can go on is to find a glimpse of what normal is wherever we can. Dis party tonight was one a dose moments. If we wasn't laughin' here together tonight, we'd be alone wonderin' if it was worth da struggle to keep goin'."

When Grandma O finished, the guy who'd made the remark sat for a moment looking at his plate. Then he stood, pushed his chair back, and walked past her to the party table.

"I don't know why I said what I did. With all the death we've had to deal with and all we've seen in the last week, our whole group is barely holding it together. Guess that made me forget about what you might have gone through. I know it doesn't do any good to say it, but I'm sorry I spoiled your evening."

Everyone at the table murmured some words to the effect that they understood, then Grandma O laid her big hand gently on the guy's shoulder and said, "Now why don't you an' your friends help us eat dis cake."

It was only the force of Grandma O's personality that kept everyone there until they'd all had coffee and cake as she had planned. But the color had drained from the room, leaving a sepia-tinted tableau in which no one felt like talking. So, after a lethargic quarter hour of relative silence in which the only sounds were fork and plate noises, the now-somber gathering broke up.

For MANY YEARS, BROUSSARD had lived across the river in the Algiers section of Orleans Parish, where he'd inhabited a concrete, insect-proof home he'd built when the ancestral Broussard mansion had succumbed to a huge colony of Formosan termites. Three years ago, he'd sold that replacement home and the surrounding land to a developer for enough money to buy the place he'd always wanted on St. Charles Avenue in the flood-free garden district, which meant, unlike many in the city, he still had a home to return to.

Until the guy at the other table at Grandma O's had spoken up, Broussard had been enjoying his party, all the more so because he'd done a good job of hiding that fact from everyone else there.

Now, as he headed down St. Charles, he thought again of the baby they hadn't been able to save. If only they'd gone in his direction to begin with, they could have found him hours earlier. Why had they chosen to go the other way? Sure, they hadn't wasted their time. They'd picked up lots of other folks in need, but none that tiny and that close to death.

Then he caught himself.

Stop it. It's over. Reliving it won't change anything.

For the next block, the old pathologist's mind sat in neutral. Then he flashed on the dirt-encrusted ponytail of the corpse with the chin implant.

The bodies all frozen ... That indeed made time of death for any of them impossible to determine. And the actual crime could have occurred anywhere. But the bodies had all been found together in the same brush tangle. So they had probably been stored somewhere near where they were found, which meant the killer was a frequent visitor to the city or lived there.

But where was he now? Had he fled the storm, or was he still around? He'd kept the bodies all in one place. Why? Why not dispose of them in some back bayou where the gators would get them? Should have asked Kit about some of these things at Grandma O's.

Broussard tried to imagine what the killer looked like, but, of course, could come up with nothing but a faceless specter. That was natural. The killer is always the last piece of any case to take form. But he had no trouble visualizing the victims. Those images were seared so deeply into his brain, he could still feel the heat of them inside his skull.

That was the way to the killer … through the victims. Where had they crossed his path? How did he choose them? What did they all have in common? Know those things and the way becomes easier. But how can you possibly answer those questions when the victims hadn't even been identified?

You don't.

You can't.

Phillip was right about missing persons cases being routinely ignored by police. Would that scuttle any progress in solving this thing? Was the world so perverted those bodies would remain forever as Jane Does? There was a time when he would have bet against it. But tonight, fresh from being reminded how he and Phillip and Bubba had arrived too late to save that baby, he believed the odds were probably in favor of that outcome.

The city now seemed even more desolate than it had a moment earlier.

At that moment, Broussard's cell phone rang.

He retrieved it from his pocket and flipped it open. "Broussard."

"Hey Andy, Tim Morgan here."

Broussard's heart gave a little lurch, pushing the buttons on his shirt a little harder against the T-Bird's steering wheel. Morgan was an old friend who was in charge of the VICAP program at the FBI. After submitting the data on the three corpses, Broussard had called Morgan and asked to be informed the moment the database produced any hits. Morgan had promised to check it regularly, which he could do even from home.

"Yeah, Tim. What's up?"

"The vic with the chin implant ... Her name is Jennifer Hendrin."

CHAPTER 8

GRANDMA O'S KITCHEN SKILLS and a full night's sleep in his own bed pulled Broussard back from the brink of exhaustion. By the next morning, he pictured himself as an old T-Bird with a new engine.

Before Katrina, the Orleans Parish morgue and medical examiner offices had been in Charity Hospital. With the morgue destroyed by floodwaters and the hospital still without power, Broussard had set up temporary facilities in a former auto upholstery business across the river in Gretna, where they had both electrical and phone service. When Kit checked in a little after 8:00 a.m., he was at his desk in one of the small rooms in back signing death certificates.

"Hi there," she said. "I'd like the carpet in my car replaced with a green shag the color of a leprechaun's hat. How long would that take?"

Broussard looked up. "Next time you see that leprechaun, grab him for me, will you? I could use some luck."

"Couldn't we all."

"Actually, the scales tipped a bit in my direction last night. On the way home I got a call from my friend at VICAP. They've identified one of the victims I told you about at the party."

"That *is* a break. What do we know about her?"

"Her name was Jennifer Hendrin. She was a student at Louisiana Technical College in Houma. Her parents reported her missin' thirteen months ago. I was about to head over to Thibodaux, where they live, and talk to 'em."

"Forgive me for saying this, but isn't that a bit beyond our sphere of responsibility since the evidence points to homicide?"

"I spoke to Phillip this mornin'. Homicide is so short-handed and focused on sortin' out seven incidents where policemen shot civilians durin' the storm, they'd welcome our help. Phillip has been assigned the case and will step in when he's able. Meanwhile, we're to keep him informed of anything we learn."

Kit had never known Broussard to move so clearly beyond the defined role of a medical examiner in a case. He'd always detested murderers, but had confined his efforts to providing the forensic evidence that would bring them down. This was something different.

Coupled with his impassioned comment at the party last night about making sure the killer of those women paid for what he did, Kit believed there was more going on here than she could see, more than Broussard simply lending Homicide a helping hand. Out of respect for his privacy, she didn't ask for an explanation, but simply said, "Do the Hendrins know their daughter's been found?"

"Not yet. Police chief over there thought he could get someone out to tell 'em later today. I can't wait that long."

"So you're going to do it."

"Not exactly."

"Then who ...?" Suddenly getting it, she threw up her hands. "Oh no. Yesterday, I had to tell Jude Marshall's brother and wife about him. I like to spread that sort of thing out. Say, do it twice every lifetime. Oh, that means I'm all caught up. How do you know someone will even be home? It could be an hour's drive for nothing."

"Chief in Thibodaux said her father's an architect who works out of his house."

"Doesn't mean they'll be there. Call now and see."

"Can't do that without gettin' into what we know. Rather not tell 'em that kind of news over the phone."

"Sometimes you can be sooo stubborn."

"Like someone else I know. Help me out here. This requires a woman's touch. I need you."

Kit had so much respect for Broussard, she regularly longed to hear him say things like that. Technically, all he'd just said was he needed a woman's touch, not specifically hers. But it was close enough. "Okay … I'll do it."

He handed her a manila envelope. "Here's a copy of the report that was filled out when the Hendrins contacted the police about their missin' daughter. The Houma PD sent it over electronically a few minutes ago. I just printed it out. You can read it on the way. Won't take long. It's pretty sketchy."

Kit accepted the folder. "They didn't send any notes of the subsequent investigation?"

"They been havin' some computer problems. Said we're lucky to have that."

Riding somewhere with Broussard meant Kit could see in detail the technique he used to get so much bulk into such a little car. But it was always like watching a great illusionist. You saw the results, but had no idea how the trick was done. Securely wedged now behind the wheel, Broussard plucked two cellophane-wrapped lemon balls from his shirt pocket and offered one to Kit. He used to carry unwrapped ones he bought in bulk, but after realizing she found those unsanitary, he'd begun carrying imported wrapped ones just for her. With that history, how could she not take one when offered? Thus, they got underway each with similar lemony bulges in one cheek.

"Did the Houma PD send over any pictures of this girl?" Kit said when she'd finished reading the report a few minutes later.

"They did. I just didn't print 'em."

"What did she look like?"

"Blonde ... attractive."

"There's no mention in here of her pregnancy. Wonder if her parents even knew about it?"

"We'll ask 'em."

KATRINA, AND LATER, RITA had each dealt Thibodaux only a glancing blow. Even so, the storms knocked down a lot of trees and left a number of homes with damaged roofs now covered with blue tarps. The Hendrins lived in a two-story red brick Georgian with an oval portico. Their roof and all their trees appeared intact, but the obviously professional landscaping was very unkempt and overgrown. It looked like a place of sorrow so great, living with the pain was a full-time job.

"I'll ring the bell and do the introductions," Broussard said as they stepped up onto the porch. "Then you take over. Ready?"

"Does it matter?"

He pressed the doorbell, and from inside they could hear a two note chime.

Kit hadn't yet decided what she was about to say, so she spent the time waiting, going over a few more possibilities.

They heard a key turning. The door opened and a nicely dressed, matronly woman with silver hair and sloping, heavily-lidded eyes looked out at them through the storm door.

"Good mornin'," Broussard said. "I'm Dr. Broussard and this is Dr. Franklyn. We're from the Orleans Parish medical examiner's office. I'm afraid we have some bad news for you."

Her face sagged noticeably. She opened the storm door. "Is it about my daughter?"

Broussard looked at Kit.

"May we come in?" Kit asked.

The woman moved back and opened the door.

As they stepped inside, a voice came from a room beyond the French doors off the foyer. "Who was at the …"

A balding man with double dark bags under his eyes appeared in the interior doorway.

"James," the woman said, emotions flickering over her face like candle light. "It's about Jennifer." Her lower lip began to quiver. "They said it's bad news."

James turned and disappeared. As he departed, he said, "I don't want to hear this."

The woman went after him, but remained where Kit and Broussard could see her. She called out angrily to her husband. "James … you will not make me bear this alone. Come back here."

She stared in the direction her husband had gone. Soon, he joined her and wrapped his arms around her. They stood there hugging each other for a long time, while Kit and Andy waited patiently for them to gather the strength to continue. Finally, they released each other and turned to hear what else had to be said.

"We should all sit down," the woman said. "Sitting would be better."

Andy and Kit followed her and her husband across a large reception hall decorated with French gilded furniture and fake palm trees into a comfortable parlor with the feel of a fine English antique shop. The woman motioned Andy and Kit into matching striped chairs on either side of a huge mahogany secretary. The couple then sat together holding hands on one end of a long sofa upholstered in a nappy red fabric. The room smelled of dust and felt as though it had not held any occupants for a very long time. To Kit the entire place reeked of hopelessness, and she imagined that the private parts of the house were a shambles.

The woman spoke first. "You haven't actually said the words. We're ready now."

Kit responded. "I'm very sorry to have to tell you that Jennifer is dead." Inwardly, Kit cringed. After considering dozens of ways it might be said, she'd decided simple and direct was the best. Hearing the words aloud, her choice seemed cold.

James threw his head back and closed his eyes. His wife just stared at Kit. Oddly, her eyes were dry. But there was no mistaking her grief.

She took a breath, then said, "Do you remember that film, I forget the title, where this entire town has no color in it? All the houses, the people, everything in it is black and white. Then these two kids arrive and gradually transform the place, so that things start to have color, just a little at a time, until finally the whole place is vibrant and beautiful. That's how Jennifer was. Until she arrived, we were black and white. She brought us color."

As Kit looked at the sad couple, she could almost see the color drain away from them, not just from their faces, but even their clothes and the sofa they sat on seemed to fade to gray.

"She must have been a wonderful girl," Kit said.

James wiped at his eyes with the back of his hand. "How did she die?"

This part was going to be even harder. Since the direct approach hadn't worked so great a moment ago, Kit chose to camouflage the truth. "It appears her life was taken."

"I don't understand," James said. "What does that mean?"

Now she had to deliver. "Indications are she was murdered."

The news seemed to accelerate the color sink around the grieving couple.

"Who would do such a thing?" James said.

"We don't know," Broussard chimed in. "But I aim to find out."

"Where was she found?" James asked.

"In a pile of brush that collected in New Orleans floodwaters."

"You're sure she didn't drown?"

"Positive."

"Then how ...?"

"That's less clear."

"When did it happen?"

Broussard leaned forward, put his forearms on his thighs, and folded his hands. "I don't know."

James shot to his feet. "What the hell *do* you know? You come in here and tell us our daughter's dead, our only child, and you can't answer any questions about what happened. Why should we even believe she's really dead?"

"Mr. Hendrin," Kit said. "Don't take refuge in our ignorance about the circumstances. That'll just hurt you more and keep the wound fresh."

"You don't know anything about me. What makes you think I *could* hurt more?"

"Sit down, dear," Mrs, Hendrin said, putting her hand gently on her husband's arm. "They're just trying to help."

Reluctantly, James returned to the sofa. "I'm not asking you to tell me the exact minute she died, or the hour. I can understand how that might be difficult to determine. The day ... what's your best guess as to the day?"

Broussard looked him in the eye. "Mr. Hendrin, in murder cases, there are always facts that must be withheld, so when a suspect is taken into custody, those unreleased details can be used to determine if the suspect is guilty. Sometimes they help to obtain a confession. In this instance, one of the facts in that category has caused us to have no idea at all when your daughter died."

"Are you saying Jennifer's body was …"

Broussard interrupted. "Please don't probe me about me that. As I tried to explain, I can't talk about it."

"I have to know … was she … complete?"

Broussard hesitated. Then, seeing the haunted look in James Hendrin's eyes, he caved a bit. "She was complete."

To help get the conversation off that sensitive point, Kit said, "Do you feel up to answering a few questions about Jennifer that might help the investigation?"

"I think we'd rather be alone right now," Mrs. Hendrin said.

"I do understand, but the quicker we talk, the sooner we can find the person who took her life."

"Then we'll talk," James said. Apparently anticipating an objection from his wife he looked hard at her. "We *will* talk." He turned to Kit. "What do you want to know?"

"I understand from the missing persons report that she was attending Louisiana Technical School in Houma at the time she disappeared."

"It was actually a month before she was to begin her second year. She wanted to be a practical nurse. Some would say she was setting her sights too low. In fact, a few people we thought were our friends *have* said it, right to our faces. I didn't see it that way. She was doing what she wanted, and it was an honorable ambition."

"She had her own apartment in Houma …"

"Yes. She wanted to be independent. She could have commuted, but she wouldn't hear of it. And wouldn't take any money from us. Wanted to earn her own way. That's the kind of child we have …" His face fell as he considered the verb tense he'd used. "The kind of child we … had." His eyes became vacant as he looked inward. Under his breath he said, "But we don't have her any more … not any more …"

"How often did you see her when she lived in Houma?" Kit asked.

James was still lost somewhere inside himself and didn't seem to hear the question. So his wife answered.

"At least once a week. She'd always come to Sunday dinner. And sometimes I'd drive over to Houma and we'd go shopping." Now *her* eyes glazed over. Voice dropping almost to a whisper, she said, "I didn't know it then, but those were some of the best times in our lives."

"Then you knew about her pregnancy."

Mrs. Hendrin didn't appear to hear the question, but it snapped her husband out of his conversational vacation. "Unselfish, that's what it was. Sure, she got paid for it, but the service she provided some lucky couple was worth far more than what she earned."

"You didn't mention any of that to the police …"

"It didn't seem pertinent. They were mostly interested in ways to identify her. She had the child three weeks before she went missing. So that was no longer a part of her. And she hardly gained any weight from it. Still looked like her pictures. Were we wrong to leave that out?"

"Not at all. But I am curious about it now. You're probably aware she had to undergo some hormonal preparation in order to be implanted …"

Mrs. Hendrin had apparently rejoined the proceedings, because she nodded and said, "She mentioned that."

"Do you know where she went for the treatments?"

"Somewhere not far away, I think," Mrs. Hendrin said.

"Can you remember the name of the place?"

Mrs. Hendrin searched her mind. "I don't think Jennifer ever said." She looked at James. "Did she?"

"I never heard her say so. I would have remembered. It was a fine thing she did for them though. I know that. A fine thing ..."

Kit said, "The report mentions that Jennifer's best friend was Cindy Babineaux. Do you think she would know where the clinic is?"

"I have no idea," Mrs. Hendrin said. "But they did a lot of things together. Jennifer may have spoken to her about it."

"There was no address or phone number for Cindy in the report. Do you have either of those?"

"We never knew them, or we would have given them to the police. But now that you ask, I think Jennifer once mentioned that Cindy worked for a vet in Houma."

"Do you recall which one?"

"It had something to do with a nursery rhyme ..." Mrs. Hendrin bowed her head and looked at the floor, as though the name was stitched somewhere into the carpet. "Jack Horner Veterinary," she said, lifting her head.

"There was no mention of a boyfriend in the report ..."

"Pretty as she was, she didn't date much," Mrs. Hendrin said. "Probably because her standards were so high. Young men these days have a lot wrong with them."

"You've got to catch the person who did this," James said. "He took our little girl ... ripped the heart out of our lives. People shouldn't be allowed to do that." He wiped at his eyes with the

back of his hand. "I can't talk about this any more. I'm sorry."
He got up and left the room.

"We need to be alone now," Mrs. Hendrin said.

"Of course," Kit said, standing.

"When can we pick up our daughter's ... remains ... for the funeral?"

Broussard struggled out of his chair. "There are some details yet to be arranged. I'll call you as soon as they're complete. I'm so sorry to have brought you such pain."

"You didn't," Mrs. Hendrin said. "Jennifer's killer did that."

"WHY AREN'T YOU READY to release the body?" Kit asked Broussard when they reached the car.

"There's somethin' about it that bothers me, and I can't figure out what. I want a little more time to think about it." He started the car, and they set out for Houma to find Cindy Babineaux.

"I feel so bad for the Hendrins," Kit said a few minutes later. "But at the same time I envy them, too."

"What do you mean?"

"The love they had for their daughter ... What happened was horrible, but to have experienced that kind of bond with a life you brought into the world. There can't be another feeling like that."

"Maybe not just like it, but there are many kinds of love."

This was not a subject Kit had ever heard Broussard expound upon. And she was greatly interested in what he had to say, mostly because over the years, she had grown to love him like a father. She was pretty sure he thought of her as the daughter he'd never had. Otherwise, why would he have started carrying cellophane-wrapped lemon balls just for her, instead of those old dirty ones that used to rattle around in his pocket with all the lint? Why had he gone so far out of his way to restore her confidence after she'd been humiliated by those two bottom-feeding kidnappers? The time he had her office painted to make her feel wanted ... that was significant. And she wasn't the only one to sense his feelings for her. Even that killer who left scrabble letters on his victims had gone after *her* because he wanted to take someone Broussard loved.

But none of those events proved anything. They were merely signs subject to interpretation. What she needed was to hear it directly from the source. Today seemed like the day that might finally happen.

She waited a moment for him to follow up on his comment about there being many kinds of love, but he gave no indication he had any intention of continuing.

Pressing the issue, she said, "It's customary, when one puts forth such a statement as you just did, to provide some examples."

With a puzzled expression Broussard said, "Of what?"

"Many kinds of love other than that shown by a mother for her child."

"Did I say that?"

"Don't pretend you didn't."

"I spoke without thinkin'."

"Come on. I've never known you to say a word that wasn't careful and considered."

"Guess my mind was on ..."

Kit waited expectantly, like a fisherman feeling for a second tug on his line.

"There's no way I can truly know what the Hendrins are goin' through, but when I think about what's happened to New Orleans, I feel like somethin' has been ripped out of me. I've heard analysts on TV say it's all gonna be okay because the best parts of the city never flooded. The garden district and the Quarter are fine. But they don't understand ... New Orleans isn't just those spots; it's Lakeview, and Bywater, and the Ninth Ward, and Gentilly. It's not only the trees along St. Charles ... it's all the trees and all the people. Did you notice how down in the Ninth, where the trees sat in brine for weeks, they're all dead ... gone, like the people there who've lost everything they owned. New Orleans was a state of mind as much as a place ... an attitude ... a spirit. And it's vanished. Two hundred years of cookin' and simmerin' until it had a thousand flavors that could be sensed, but not described. Then, in the space of a few hours, erased. And I don't know if it can ever be resurrected."

Broussard's pain layered on top of the Hendrins' made Kit's concern about his feelings toward her suddenly seem so petty she vowed not to let herself get distracted like that again.

CHAPTER 9

Halfway to Houma, Broussard suddenly checked the rearview mirror, slammed on the brakes, and pulled onto the shoulder. Appearing agitated, he oozed out of the car.

"What's going on?" Kit asked.

"Minor emergency," Broussard said, shutting the door.

Through the windshield, Kit watched him hustle along the shoulder toward some distant point. Having seen this behavior before, she knew what to look for. Sure enough, about fifteen yards ahead there was a dark-colored object in their lane on the highway.

When Broussard drew even with the object, he ran onto the highway and scooped it up.

It was just another example of Broussard's personal turtle rescue and relocation service. He deposited the animal in the brush beside the shoulder and returned to the car.

"Was he grateful?" Kit asked as Broussard got in.

"He was so choked up with gratitude he couldn't speak."

The Jack Horner Clinic looked like it was in a remodeled Taco Bell. The sign out front said, *If you're not satisfied with our service, we'll go sit in a corner.*

"Little Jack Horner sat in a … I think they'd be better off just offering a refund," Kit said as Broussard pulled into a lined parking place on the right. Two other cars occupied slots nearby. Four more vehicles, most likely belonging to the help, were huddled near the back of the building.

"How about you handle the tough part this time?" Kit said as they prepared to get out.

Broussard nodded. "That's fair."

On the way inside, they passed a small, grassy area needing the diligent application of a pooper scooper. A pair of otherwise healthy boxwoods in the space had lost all their lower leaves.

Inside, the place was a typical vet operation. A rack of bagged and canned animal food stood along the far wall. In front of the rack, a couple of flimsy plastic chairs flanked a little plastic table piled with animal magazines. Flyers touting the virtues of animals needing a home decorated a bulletin board on the left wall. The smell of disinfecting chemicals was a pervasive presence. Behind an enclosure to the right, a young woman was typing something into a computer from a chart.

"Be right with you," she promised without looking up.

While waiting, Kit wandered over to the bulletin board, where she saw a picture of a bright-eyed Jack Russell Terrier. Under the photo, a caption said, *TALKING DOG, $2500. SPEAKS 5 LANGUAGES. DEMONSTRATION UPON REQUEST. IF NOT COMPLETELY SATISFIED WILL GIVE YOU THE DOG ABSOLUTELY FREE.*

The keyboard clatter stopped, and the person who'd been making it said, "Now, how can I help you?"

"We're lookin' for Cindy Babineaux," Broussard said, as Kit joined him.

The girl stood, an inquisitive look in her large, brown eyes. "I'm Cindy."

Her flowered scrubs didn't make for a particularly attractive outfit, but with her smooth, olive complexion, long brown hair, and perfect features, Kit doubted any man who saw her would deduct points for it.

Broussard introduced Kit and then himself, this time adding his title. When Cindy heard the phrase "Medical Examiner," her full lips parted and she took a quick breath.

"Jennifer Hendrin's parents told us you might know where the clinic was that handled her pregnancy," Broussard said.

But Cindy's thoughts had become snagged on Broussard's title.

"Medical examiner," she said. "You work on dead bodies … Is that right?"

"Yes."

"Has Jen been found?"

"I'm afraid so."

Cindy's eyes widened. Her hand went to her mouth. "Oh my God. I'm not ever going to be able to talk to her again, am I?"

"No."

She shook her head as though trying to clear her mind after a punch in the face. "I don't know what to say. How did she die? Was it … did she have pain?"

"I'm so sorry you've lost your friend. But please understand, I'm not free to discuss any of those details. Just know that by talkin' to us, you'll be helpin' her a great deal."

"You're not free to discuss … You're investigating a crime, aren't you?" She made a faint moaning sound and said, "Oh my God. Jen was murdered. Do you think the clinic had anything to do with it?"

"We're just tryin' to fill in some details of her life prior to her disappearance."

She appeared to recall something worth telling. "Did you know Jen went over there asking to see her baby a few weeks after she gave it up?"

"We hadn't heard that," Kit said. "What did they say?"

"They told her she'd signed a contract giving up all rights to the child, and she couldn't even see him."

"How did Jennifer take that news?" Kit asked.

"She was mad as hell."

One of the examination room doors on the left opened, and an old woman whose lipstick had bled up into the wrinkles around her lips came out with a poodle straining on its leash. The vet, a slight man with sandy hair, followed. He handed a charge sheet to Cindy and turned to the old woman.

"You put that solution in Sam's ears like I said and keep an eye on him. If in a few days, he's still scratching up there, we'll take another look."

He went back into the room he'd come from, and Cindy turned her attention to running the client's credit card. Watching the young woman work, Kit thought she seemed nervous and unsure of herself, not surprising considering what Broussard had told her.

While Sam's owner was occupied with paying the bill, the little dog mounted Broussard's left leg and began humping it. Apparently accustomed to Sam's indiscretions, the woman looked down to check on him. She jerked his leash, pulling him free. "Bad Sam. Bad boy."

Her pale skin flushing, the woman turned to Broussard and sputtered an apology.

"I like dogs," Broussard responded. "And, as you can see, they're also quite fond of me."

To ensure that Sam behaved himself, the old woman picked him up and kept him in her arms until she'd signed the credit card slip and was out the door.

Broussard restarted his conversation with Cindy. "A moment ago you told us Jennifer was angry at the surrogacy clinic. We'd like to know more about that."

Cindy shrugged. "Nothing more to tell, except that Jen was thinking about getting a lawyer and challenging the contract she signed. Giving up her baby turned out to be harder than she thought. I'm not surprised. Even though it wasn't technically hers, she carried it inside her for nine months. How could anyone just walk away and forget that?"

"Unless you're cold as stone, I don't see how you could," Kit said.

"Do you know where the clinic is located?" Broussard asked.

"Morgan City."

"I don't suppose you know what street it's on."

"No, but I recall the name. It's called Surrogacy Central. I remember because I thought it sounded like a hardware store."

KIT LOOKED AT BROUSSARD as he fired up the T-Bird's engine. "So Jennifer was angry at the clinic. That could be a motive for her killing one of the employees there, rather than the other way around."

Broussard backed the car into a tight turn. "Wonder if the other two victims were surrogates for that clinic."

"There's still no ID on either of them?"

"No." He put the car in first and nudged the gas.

"Then I don't see any way to find out. Showing people at the clinic photos of the victims the way they look now isn't going to jog any memories."

"I'd like to hear their version of Jennifer's reaction when they told her she couldn't see her baby."

"Morgan City is what ... forty miles from here? Do you have time to do that?"

"Things are slowin' down in St. Gabriel. And I've got enough volunteers to cover for me. We'll drive over to Morgan City and check a phone book for Surrogacy Central. Ask 'em where they're located."

"Not necessary," Kit said, digging in her purse. She pulled out her cell phone and flipped it open. "I'll find out where they are and get us a map from the internet."

Broussard shook his head. "Pretty soon we'll be able to enter a victim's name into a cell phone, and it'll tell us who the killer is."

"Wouldn't *that* be great?"

"Peachy."

MORGAN CITY IS DIVIDED by the Atchafalaya, a waterway that, were it not for the control gates north of Baton Rouge, would become the new route for the Mississippi River. Some who live there worry that one day, when the Mississippi is so full it threatens to engulf even more of New Orleans than Katrina took, the water will be diverted into the Atchafalaya, thereby sacrificing Morgan City to save the greater treasure. Apparently, the owners of Surrogacy Central were among those not bothered by this possibility, because they had located their business on Fairview Drive, where a well-cast buzz bait launched from the roof would plunk into the Atchafalaya.

The business was housed in a white, single-story antebellum home with a columned porch and green shutters. The place was made to look larger than it was by a second, smaller columned porch that extended forward as a dormer from the sloping roof. But the most interesting feature was the FOR RENT banner being taped over the Surrogacy Central sign by a pear-shaped guy in a gray suit.

Broussard pulled into the oyster-shell paved parking area, and he and Kit got out and trekked across the grass to the man working on the banner. He turned as they approached, picked up a cane leaning on the sign, and hobbled toward them.

He was about five foot seven with curly hair in bangs over his forehead. Seeing him up close, he reminded Kit of a chubby female impersonator she'd once seen in a Bourbon Street club.

"Duke Delcambre at your service, folks," he said, giving them a little salute. "You have a good eye for real estate, I can already tell that about you. Ad won't even be in the paper until tomorrow. And here you are. A nose for a bargain ..." He chuckled. "Actually two noses. Let me show you around inside before we talk money. What business you two in?"

"Does that sign mean the clinic is closed?" Broussard asked.

"They moved everything out two nights ago."

Broussard and Kit exchanged a quick glance.

"Had no idea they were leavin'. Rita blew a tree down over there ..." He pointed at an uprooted stump. "I came over to see if the guys I hired to cut it up and haul it away did the job. That's when I realized the place was empty. Still had a year and a half left on the lease. When I rented it to 'em, there were other people interested. But the clinic promised they'd be here long term. So I let 'em have it. It's a dandy property ... roof came through the storms just fine ... no leaks at all."

"We drove over here hopin' to talk to the owner of the clinic, or at least to someone in charge," Broussard said.

The guy's face fell. "Oh ... Guess I shouldn't have expected to rent it again that easy. I'd give you the owner's name, but it wouldn't do you any good. I called the unlisted contact number I had for him and learned the phone's been disconnected. I'm thinkin' now he probably didn't even use his real name."

"What *was* his name?"

"Arthur Loftin. Bet he wasn't even a doctor like he said. I should have listened to my conscience when they wanted to set up here. Payin' women to carry someone else's baby ... That's not Godly. Knew it at the time. But I needed to get some income from the place, and I went with the long-term prospects. Legally, they owe me for eighteen months rent. Care to guess what my chances are of collectin' it?"

"What about employees of the clinic ... Any of them live in Morgan City or close by?" Broussard asked.

"They all commuted. From where, I don't rightly know."

"WHAT DO YOU THINK about that clinic now?" Kit said as Broussard pointed the T-Bird toward New Orleans.

"Would you see if you can get someone on the line for me with your cell phone?"

"I can try. What's the number?"

"Don't know. But the person I want is Dr. Allen Howell, University of Mississippi Medical Center in Jackson. If he's not available, have him paged."

It took Kit four minutes to get Howell's office on the phone. He returned their page in two. Kit handed the phone to Broussard.

"Allen ... Andy Broussard here ... Yeah ... It was and still is a bad situation all right, but we're copin'. I'm callin' to ask if you've ever heard of a Dr. Arthur Loftin ..."

Kit watched Broussard's face for some indication of what Howell was saying, but saw nothing there to read.

"Okay, thanks very much. Say hello to Claudia for me." Broussard handed the phone back to Kit. "Allen Howell has an encyclopedic knowledge of everyone in reproductive medicine. He's never heard of Arthur Loftin."

"This is all so suspicious … the clinic closing as we learn about its connection to Jennifer … the director likely using a false identity …"

"I'm not likin' the smell of it either."

"What do we do now? Try to locate this Arthur Loftin?"

"If it's an alias, as it appears to be, that could be a sinkhole."

"This clinic is a real lead. We can't just let it die."

Broussard didn't reply, but instead withdrew into one of his famous episodes of silent nose stroking while he considered the options before them. Knowing she'd have to wait until he emerged from this cocoon on his own, Kit turned her attention to the passing scenery.

Two minutes later, the butterfly crawled from his chrysalis and said, "When we get back to New Orleans, let's take a ride down into the Ninth Ward and see where those three bodies were found."

"Is it dry enough to do that? Last I heard the reflooding from Rita wasn't entirely pumped out."

"Let's try."

CHAPTER 10

KIT CHECKED THE GPS receiver. "We're getting very close ..."

To avoid any remaining standing water from Rita, they'd entered the Ninth via St. Claude, which ran along the relatively higher ground near the Mississippi. With their credentials, they had no trouble getting past the St. Claude National Guard checkpoint, one of many set up on the Ninth's perimeter to keep out looters.

From the checkpoint they'd taken Caffin Street to LeDoux. Still seeing no standing water, they'd proceeded east on LeDoux, against the direction all the floodwaters had come from the breached industrial canal.

"Bet that's the spot right there," Broussard said, pointing to the right, through the windshield of the white T-Bird he was driving.

Kit looked in the direction he was indicating and saw a large mound of debris, piled up against a short, chain-link fence that ran from the sidewalk toward the backyards of the houses on either side.

Broussard went past the pile, pulled to the curb, and shut off the engine. He opened his door and maneuvered to get out of the car. Being more nimble and not wedged behind the steering wheel, Kit was already waiting on the mud-caked sidewalk by the time he'd shed the vehicle.

Together, they walked to the large brush pile that extended all along the fence up to where it passed between the adjacent houses. "Yeah," Kit said, looking at the receiver, "… this is it." Wrinkling her nose at the stench, she put the receiver in her pocket and looked at all the stuff caught on the chain link.

Much of the pile was composed of tree branches. Among the other things embedded in that structure were a lot of little sticks, an old tire, a muddy teddy bear, a kid's tricycle, and a lot of black bags, presumably filled with garbage. Down about three feet from where she stood, she saw what appeared to be the maggoty carcass of a cat mingling with the remains of a large fish. It was kind of hard to tell what they were because both were covered with a black, undulating carpet of flies. In addition to smelling of death, the area was just as still. They hadn't seen a single person since they'd left Caffin Street.

"What we need to know is where those bodies came from," Broussard said. He turned and looked in the direction of the canal breach. "Obviously, it was up there. But how far?"

"Can we ever know that?" Kit asked.

"All depends …"

"On what?"

"C'mon." He headed for the car.

When they were both settled in their seats, Broussard sent the T-Bird slowly up the street. Kit didn't ask again what they were looking for because she'd figured out on her own what one of the items might be. A block and a half of filth later, she spotted a likely candidate a moment before he did. "There," she said, pointing at a large white object lying on the sidewalk.

He stopped the car and they both got out.

The object was a large chest freezer lying on its side, the lid slightly ajar.

Broussard walked over to the freezer and grabbed hold of a still-wet, mud-caked mattress partially covering it. "Help me pull this out of the way."

They dragged the mattress into the yard of a yellow shotgun house with a brown watermark on it just below the windows.

Broussard went back to the freezer. "Let's get it up on its legs."

Sweat glistening on their foreheads, they rocked the freezer back and sat it upright. Broussard lifted the lid and looked inside.

Empty.

"It's definitely big enough to hold three bodies," he said.

He turned his attention to the locking mechanism in the lid. After examining that part of it, he briefly studied the half embedded in the upper rim of the chest. Then he looked back at the lid.

Finally, he turned to Kit. "The lock is ripped loose. Somethin' hit the lid hard, right here," he ran his hand along a small dent, "and forced it open. Can't know for sure, but could be why the bodies fell out. Locked freezer floats into the street, tips over on its side … somethin' rams into it right under the lid, lock tears loose, bodies roll out into the water."

"Other than the broken lock, why should it be this freezer?"

"Hard to get three bodies into an upright. Chest is the best choice." He looked farther up the street. "Don't even see any other freezers. C'mon."

Kit followed him back to the car.

A few minutes later, he stopped the car at a large tree that had fallen across the road. On the other side of it, two cars still on their wheels, and another, upside down, were jammed into its branches. With the road and the sidewalk fully blocked by the tree, a garbage dump of debris had piled up on the far side.

"Not much doubt now that the three bodies originated somewhere between here and where they were found," Kit said.

"I'd say between here and that freezer."

"What's next?"

"We could try to find out from the manufacturer of the freezer who bought it."

Kit nodded. "We could. It's a long shot though. If the buyer didn't register the warranty, they won't have the name. And most people these days just throw registration papers away. I do."

"Me, too."

Kit looked at Broussard. "So I didn't just tell you anything you weren't already thinking."

"No, but I enjoyed hearin' you say it." He turned and studied the desolation around them. "You feel up to pokin' around out there and see if we can turn up anybody who might know where that freezer came from?"

"I'm willing. But everyone who lived here is supposed to be evacuated. What are the chances anyone is still around?"

"Immeasurably small. But we're not really riskin' much to try. And the gain, if it pays off, could be huge."

"Let's go then."

"Get the flashlight out of the glove box. I've got another one in the trunk."

Broussard popped the trunk lid, and they got out of the car. Kit met him at the trunk, where he picked up the second light.

"Should we split up?" she asked.

"Got your gun?"

"Always."

"Then I'm stickin' with you. Might as well start right here."

The house in front of them was a dingy, blue clapboard shotgun with the door standing open and the usual orange cross spray-painted on the siding beside it. The numeral 1 was spray painted in the quadrant indicating the number of bodies that had been found inside.

At the walk leading to the porch, Broussard hesitated and looked down. Wondering what he was doing, Kit did the same.

She saw a lot of footprints in the dried mud going to the house and back.

"Don't care for this," Broussard muttered.

"Why not? Isn't that what we're looking for … someone to talk to?"

"I count five different shoe treads. The same five are down there where we moved the mattress. They go in and out of that house, too."

As many times as Kit had seen the old pathologist demonstrate his ability to observe things others didn't, she was still surprised he'd managed to gather that information at the other house without her even noticing. "Maybe they belong to the crew that checked the neighborhood for bodies."

He gestured to the marker painted on the house. "There's the date they were here. This area was still flooded then. These footprints have sharp edges. They weren't made by somebody wadin' in water. I believe a pack of human jackals has recently been down here huntin'."

Kit took a nervous look around. "Think they're still here?"

"Don't know. Stay alert." He headed for the blue house.

A moment later, he stepped onto the porch. Under his great weight, the soggy floorboards sank an inch. He looked over his shoulder at Kit. "Better wait there."

Worried there might be another body inside, or a band of thugs waiting to jump them, Kit didn't argue the point.

Though the boards sagged ominously as he moved across the porch, Broussard reached the front door without falling through. He knocked on the doorframe. "Anybody here? Anyone in there?"

He waited for a response, but got none. He turned and carefully made his way back to where Kit waited. "You think it smells bad out here, it's worse in there."

Wincing, Kit said, "You don't think ..."

"It's not the odor of human decomposition. Believe me, I'd know."

Having once seen him locate a submerged body in a lake by simply sniffing the air over the water, Kit had no reason to doubt him.

Over the next half hour they worked their way down that side of the street until they were just a few houses from the freezer they'd found. The sun, already hot and high in the sky when they'd arrived, had continued heating the air, pushing it into the low 90s. The hotter it got, the worse the area smelled. Kit tried pulling a lock of hair under her nose so the smell of her shampoo would block the stench. That worked for a while, but eventually, in the heat, the hair against her skin became so irritating, she gave that up.

Though Broussard's white shirt was now soaked with sweat, he didn't even bother to loosen his trademark bow tie.

The odor across the street was every bit as strong as what Kit and Broussard were experiencing, and the heat was just as oppressive. But the furtive figure who had been watching them since they'd found the freezer was so absorbed in their movements and what they were doing, he didn't notice.

CHAPTER 11

KIT AND BROUSSARD WERE now standing in front of the tallest house on the street. It was also the largest. Even above the brown water line, there was almost no paint on the weathered gray clapboards, many of which were split and curled away from their nails. Oddly, the Victorian ball and spindle beadwork that connected the tops of the porch posts was completely intact. The orange X bore a zero in the body discovery quadrant. A large pile of moldy carpeting, upholstered furniture, insulation, and broken sheetrock stretched along the gutter in front of the house.

Kit looked down at the mud on the sidewalk. The usual cluster of footprints they'd seen leading up to all the houses they'd checked so far was missing, replaced by two distinctive sets, different from all the others. One set was very tiny, the other, huge. The big set had come and gone many times while the mud was drying. It was the first home they'd seen in which the door wasn't gaping open. The lower sashes in all the windows, however, were fully raised.

"Think someone's in there?"

"Too hot to speculate," Broussard said, heading up the sidewalk.

This porch was sturdy enough that both of them could stand on it at the same time, so they approached the front door together.

Broussard rapped loudly on the door and swatted at a fly that had landed on his nose.

He waited a few seconds and knocked again.

No response.

"Guess it's empty," Kit said, turning to go.

Out of the corner of her eye, Kit saw Broussard reach for the doorknob. As she turned back toward him, he pushed the door open.

"Anyone home? I'm Dr. Broussard, the medical examiner. Is this home occupied?"

Kit suddenly understood why the predators who'd left footprints on the walks to the other houses had avoided this one. The largest man she had ever seen loomed out of the darkness inside and filled the doorway.

He was seven feet tall if he was an inch, and he probably weighed three hundred pounds. He had skin the color of a roasted coffee bean, but with a sheen on it as though he had been lightly varnished. His enormous head was completely bald and he had no eyebrows. He was wearing dirty, blue shorts and a dingy, gray, sleeveless T-shirt that showed upper arms the size of an ordinary man's thighs. Beads of sweat studded his brow and scalp. In his enormous left hand, he carried a piece of two by four with a hand grip crudely carved into it.

"What do you want?" His deep voice set the floorboards under Kit's feet vibrating. He apparently wasn't happy to see them.

Showing no sign he was worried about the club in the guy's hand, Broussard said, "After this area flooded, three female bodies were found in front of a house two blocks east of here. I'm convinced they all were murdered. My colleague, Dr. Franklyn," he looked at Kit, "and I want to find the person responsible. We believe the bodies were kept for a time in that freezer on the sidewalk across the street. Do you know where that freezer came from?"

The guy scowled at Broussard for a few seconds, then turned and gave Kit the same treatment. He looked back at Broussard. "Why do you care what happened to those people? Because it's your job?"

"No, I took the job because I care."

"What color were they ... the victims?"

"White."

"And you're white."

"I'd be just as upset if they were black."

"Why should I believe that?"

"Why shouldn't you?"

"You want somethin' and you'd say anything to get it."

"I do want something. I want justice. You should want it, too."

"Justice ..." he snorted with indignation. "Look around you, man. You see any justice?" He raised his club. "This is my justice."

"It shouldn't be that way," Broussard said.

"Well, it is. And it's been like that down here long as I been around."

"That needs to change."

"Well, it won't ... ever."

"I can't accept that. And you shouldn't either."

"I don't exactly have much choice."

"You have one now. I think you know somethin'. You can turn us away without tellin' us what that is and maintain the same situation you say has always existed here, or you can take a stand and move things a little in the other direction."

He scowled at Broussard for an eternity, then raised the club in his hand. "Maybe I'll just whup you upside the head and call it a day."

Without flinching, lips set, Broussard said, "You can try."

Thunder clouds rolled across the giant's face.

The color drained out of Kit's cheeks. *Jesus, what was Broussard thinking?* Fearing for his safety, not to mention her own, she reached down for her gun. Before her hand could find it, a rumble started in the chest of the colossus in the doorway. The rumble became a roar. Kit was afraid the first swing of the club was on its way.

But her gun was still under the fabric of her pant leg.

The roar became bellowed laughter. "You just ain't afraid of pain, are you?" the giant said. He turned his massive head and spoke to someone behind him. "Momma, come and tell this crazy white man what you saw."

The monster in the doorway stepped back, and a tiny, sinewy old black woman came out of the darkness. It seemed incomprehensible to Kit that the behemoth with the club had come from her body. She turned her sad, wizened eyes first at Kit and then Broussard. She lifted her hand and pointed a long, thin finger at the old pathologist.

"What I'm about to tell you, I'm only gonna say this one time. Don't think someday you can make me go to court and I'll say it again, cause I'll not only deny I ever spoke to you, I'll say I never saw you before. You understan' me?"

"I do," Broussard said.

The old woman looked at Kit.

"Message received."

"When the water came, we had to go up on the second floor. An' I spent a lot a time lookin' out the front windows, tryin' to figure out how bad it was gonna get. An' you know, despite how terrible it was, when the wind went away, it was kinda pretty, all that water jus' sittin' there quietly with the sun reflectin' off it. Never seen anything like it before. It was a lot later it got the oil and gasoline slick on it. But that ain't what you want to know about.

"We got a gang a hoodlums down here, been givin' people trouble for a long time. When the water was about two feet deep, they come sloshin' down the street whoopin' and carryin' on, generally makin' fools a themselves and lookin' for trouble. When they got to that little strip a stores over there across the street, they started kickin' in doors an' goin' inside to see what they could steal.

"Firs' they went into that abandoned store. Wasn't no reason to believe there was anything of value in there, all run down and boarded up like it was. But they go in anyway an' come out a few minutes later with nothin' jus' like you'd expect. Then they go next door to Tookie's Beauty Den.

"They tried to kick her door in, but it's steel, so it ain't so easy. One of 'em gets an idea an' they all go back to the first store. They come out pushin' that freezer you asked about. They floated it over to Tookie's place and started rammin' it into her front door. But it don't do them no good, so after a couple tries they give up."

"The freezer came out of that first store," Broussard said.

"Didn' I say that?"

"Thanks very much. You've been a big help."

The old woman's thin eyebrows crept together. "Don't you want to hear the rest? You should."

"I'm sorry. Of course. Please go on."

"The freezer floats out into the street and bobs around while the water rises. Then the water starts comin' fast like somethin' big gave way. The freezer gets caught in a whirlpool and for a long time jus' spins 'round and 'round. Things start hittin' it an' it tips over. Then a big limb smacks it hard, an' I see the lid pop open. That's when them bodies floated out."

CHAPTER 12

"Do you know who owns that buildin'?" Broussard asked the old woman.

She shoved out her lower lip and shook her head.

"Ever see anybody goin' in and out?"

"Not through the front door. An' if they went in the back, couldn't see that."

"Thanks very much. You've been a big help." Broussard reached in his pocket and took out his wallet.

"What are you doin'?" the big guy said from behind his mother.

"You helped us, I want to help you."

"Then get the damn levees fixed so this don't happen again."

The guy gently pulled his mother back and slammed the door.

"What on earth were you thinking when you challenged that monster to fight?" Kit said a moment later, hurrying to keep pace with Broussard as he headed for the boarded-up store across the street.

He glanced back at her. "Figured if I got in trouble you'd shoot him."

They reached the store's kicked-in front door a few seconds later. Flashlight on, Broussard went in first, Kit following closely.

Inside the store, they played their flashlight beams around the dank interior. At first, they saw nothing but mud-caked floorboards and walls pockmarked with starbursts of mold, then Kit's light picked up a chain hanging from the ceiling. Following it up, she saw it was attached to a large screw eye. Walking her beam back down the rope, she discovered a large metal hook on the other end. By now, Broussard was looking at it too.

"What do you suppose that was used for?" Kit said.

"Hangin' somethin'."

"What?"

But Broussard had already turned away to see what else might be found. His light located some twisted chrome rods and a pair of loose wheels that, together, were probably once a rolling wardrobe trolley. It didn't take much detective work to arrive at that conclusion because the chrome wreckage was lying on a clot of muddy clothing. With Kit supplementing his light with hers, Broussard walked over to the clothes, knelt, and began pulling at the matted, muddy mess to see what kind of clothes they were.

The first piece to come free was apparently a dress. He reached down and worked another edge free.

A much brighter light than either of the ones they carried suddenly blasted them from the doorway. They both turned to see who was there.

"Look," a mocking voice said. "Looters. I don't think there's a lower form of humanity than people who would take advantage of a catastrophe for personal gain. We should instruct them and set them on a better path."

"The woman's a major babe," a second voice said.

With the light shining in her eyes, it was hard to see through it, but Kit thought there were only two of them.

Were they carrying guns? She couldn't tell. If she reached for hers and pointed it at them, the natural response would be for them to start shooting. If she was going to produce the Ladysmith, better to just start blasting away with it. But what if they weren't armed? And maybe they're just kids. Could she live with killing an unarmed kid? Damn it.

The two moved inside. The one with the light shifted it onto Broussard.

"What are you dressed up for old man, Halloween?" the second voice said. "Couldn't you afford a real tie?"

"I'm the medical examiner," Broussard said. "I do a lot of my work bendin' over examinin' the dead. I found early in my career that a long tie gets in the way. Kind of like what you're doin' right now."

With the light out of her face, Kit played her own light over the two so she could see their hands.

"Ohhh, get him," the second thug said. "He ain't scared. But you oughtta be, old man."

The thug slipped his hand into his pocket and brought out an object. There was a snicking sound, and Kit's light caught the glint of a knife blade. She saw no guns.

Before she could reach for the Ladysmith, she was grabbed in a bear hug from behind, pinning her arms. Her flashlight clattered to the floor. Instinctively, she threw her head back, hoping to drive her skull into her captor's face, but he must have been expecting that because he moved his head to the side.

"Your hair smells great," he said breathing into her ear. "I'll bet your pussy smells even better."

His breath curled around to the front of her face and went into her nose. Though the odor in the store was bad, his breath was worse. One of his hands slid down between her legs, and his fingers began probing.

She stamped on his right foot as hard as she could. But her soft deck shoes didn't have any effect. She drove her left foot back into his kneecap. That didn't accomplish anything either. Running out of options, she leaned into him and drove herself backward. He gave ground and they began to move, slowly at first, then faster as she continued to dig in. They hit the back wall a moment later with a thud. She heard the air rush out of him, but he didn't loosen his hold.

The guy with the knife advanced on Broussard.

"He likes unusual ties," the guy with the light said. "Cut his throat and pull his tongue through the opening. See how that suits him."

Kit watched with horror. They were both in trouble, but it was Broussard she was worried about. They were going to kill him and she couldn't do anything about it. If she could just get free for a second ... She struggled in the grip of the cretin holding her, but he was too strong.

Broussard shoved his flashlight into his back pocket. Fists raised, he edged forward in a crouch to meet the guy with the knife. The thug moved in closer, his hands making circling motions, trying to confuse Broussard about the direction the attack would come. He lunged.

With surprising quickness, Broussard knocked the knife hand to the side with his left hand. He took a step forward and brought his right fist around in a looping motion that caught the thug hard on the side of the head. Stunned, the thug staggered sideways, turned, and fell on his ass. But he didn't drop the knife.

"I could be wrong, but I think you missed him, Chato," the guy with the light said. "Try again."

Chato got awkwardly to his feet. Grinding his teeth and growling, he charged again. This time he swung the knife from Broussard's left to his right in a huge, underhand slicing motion.

Broussard leaned back so the knife barely missed his face. He grabbed the thug's arm and used the momentum of the guy's charge to spin him around. Broussard then sent him sprawling onto the floor with a kick in the glutes.

The guy with the light played the beam over his embarrassed lackey, then turned it back onto Broussard. "You're not an easy mark, I'll say that for you, old man. And I've enjoyed your performance. But now it's time you were dead. Chato … again …"

"I'll help him," the guy behind Kit said. He pivoted to his right and hooked his right foot around Kit's legs, then loosened his grip and pushed her to the floor. The guy with the light hustled toward her, cursing. "Damn it, Roach, did I say let her go?"

Kit rolled over and rose into a sitting position.

Ignoring the rebuke from his buddy, Roach headed for Broussard, knife in hand. At the same moment, Chato closed in on Broussard from the front.

Before the guy with the light could reach her, Kit bent down, pulled up the leg of her slacks, and yanked the Ladysmith from its holster. She raised the barrel to the ceiling and fired once.

The sound echoed through the empty room. Plaster fell from the ceiling. The guy with the light played it directly on Kit, all of them staring at the gun.

"Who wants the next round?" she asked angrily. She looked from thug to thug. "Any volunteers?" None of them moved. "No? Then get the hell out of here."

Slowly, the three men moved toward the door. Broussard pulled out his flashlight and lit up their departure.

The leader of the three was the last one out. He paused in the door and looked back. "You two don't belong down here. *You* get the hell out."

Then they were gone.

Keeping her gun in play, Kit bent down and picked up her flashlight, which was still lit. She walked over to Broussard. "Lot of good those security checkpoints just did us."

Broussard shook his head. "Too big an area to monitor effectively."

"I didn't know you could move like that."

"Neither did I."

"I doubt that."

"Okay, I kind of knew." What he meant was, he *used* to be able to do that kind of thing, but those dizzy spells in St. Gabriel had him wondering if he was still capable of defending himself.

"You should feel proud of yourself."

"Why?"

"If it wasn't for you handling that first guy like you did, the one holding me wouldn't have let go."

Broussard wasn't pleased at her compliment. He'd felt so much better since returning home, he'd pushed those thugs partly to test himself. It was reassuring to know he could still pass such an exam, but it had been a foolish act. "Should have been able to *talk* 'em into leavin' us alone. But I didn't even try. And when they first came in, I got tough with 'em." He shook his head. "Just sets their kind off … like kickin' a mad dog. If anything, I owe you an apology for puttin' your life at risk."

"That's just nuts." Kit did not like to hear this kind of talk from Broussard. He was the standard by which she measured all other men. In the years she'd known him, he'd shown hundreds of times that he had impeccable instincts for doing the right thing. She'd never before heard him question himself. It was very unsettling. "We should leave before they come back with better weapons," she said. "Assuming they're part of the gang that left all those footprints you saw, there could also be two more of them."

"I want to take that clothing."

Broussard went over to the muddy clothes, shoved his flashlight in his back pocket, and gathered up everything in the pile. Kit led the way out. At the doorway, she paused and checked to see if any of the thugs were out there. "Looks clear."

And it was.

On the way to the car, Kit said, "Now that we know where the freezer came from, we could find out from the city tax records who owns the building. That could lead us to the killer."

"I hope it's that easy. The office housin' the computers with those records was under water. Those files may all be lost."

"What a pessimistic view."

"So I'm nuts *and* pessimistic."

"Well, just on the two issues we discussed."

At the car, Broussard put the clothes in the trunk and shut the lid. A few seconds later, they were sitting in the car, engine running, blessed cool air blowing over their sweaty bodies.

"Boy, that feels good," Kit said.

"I used to believe concrete was the most important technology ever devised," Broussard said, putting the car in reverse. "Right now I'm leanin' toward air conditionin'."

While Kit craned her neck around to see if the three thugs were lurking close by or running toward them, Broussard backed the T-Bird into a tight turn, then headed toward Caffin Street. As they neared the building they'd just left, Kit saw it from a fresh angle.

"Stop the car," she shouted.

Broussard hit the brakes. "What's wrong?"

"The suicide I told you about last night … I found a camera in his study that contained a lot of pictures taken just hours before the owner killed himself." She pointed across the street, "And most of them were of that building."

CHAPTER 13

Broussard stopped the car and looked at Kit. "You're sure ... there's no doubt in your mind? Because if Jude Marshall took pictures down here the mornin' he committed suicide, that's pretty strong circumstantial evidence he was involved in the death of those three women."

"I know what I saw. But if he *was* involved, that would suggest he also had some connection with the surrogacy clinic ..." Kit's eye's widened even further. "I wonder if *he's* Arthur Loftin."

"I've got to head back to St. Gabriel and make sure everything is runnin' smoothly over there, so I'm gonna need you to follow up on this."

"Guess you're about to suggest I get a photo of Jude Marshall from motor vehicles and ask Duke Delcambre in Morgan City if that's Loftin."

Broussard took his foot off the brake and gave the T-Bird some gas. "Always a pleasure to work with people who see the big picture."

"I'll also check and see if you're right about the tax records being destroyed."

"You mentioned earlier that Jude Marshall was married. If the tax records can't be accessed, maybe you could find Mrs. Marshall and ask her if her husband owned that buildin'."

"She might not know. I could also try his brother. On my first visit to his business, Quentin said he didn't think Jude owned any property that was flooded, but my question was very brief and very general. Now that we have a specific building and a street address, it might be worthwhile to ask him again."

They drove in silence for about ten seconds, then Kit said, "Why would Jude Marshall kill those three women?"

"Could have somethin' to do with all those dresses in the trunk."

"I don't get it."

"Maybe he liked to play dress-up with dolls as a kid."

"Oh, that's sick."

"Can't find any fault with *that* view."

THEY GOT BACK TO the office in Gretna a few minutes before three o'clock. That didn't leave Kit much time for all she needed to accomplish by the end of the business day.

First, she needed to obtain a copy of Jude Marshall's driver's license from the DMV. Believing as Broussard and Gatlin did that the New Orleans PD computer network wasn't very reliable at the moment, she made her request by phone, through the Baton Rouge PD. While waiting for the license to arrive by e-mail, she did a computer search for the phone number of Duke Delcambre Realty, the company name she'd seen on the "For Rent" banner at the clinic.

She jotted the number on a piece of scratch paper, then did a search for the New Orleans tax assessor's web site, where the owners of any piece of property in the city could usually be found by just entering the address. She had no trouble finding the link, but when she clicked on it, the server couldn't locate the site.

Score one for Broussard.

She lugged out the New Orleans phone book the previous business had left on the premises and turned to the city government listing.

A half hour later, having been unable to contact any of the city departments she'd called, she hung up the phone and checked her e-mail.

Still nothing from Baton Rouge. And it was getting late.

To see if she could hurry things along, she made a follow-up call, stressing the importance of a timely response to her request.

Assured that she'd receive what she wanted within the next fifteen minutes, she hung up and sat back to wait. As she did, her thoughts went to Jennifer Hendrin's parents and how much they loved their daughter. Suddenly, she realized she still didn't even know what the girl looked like. Remembering what Broussard said about the Houma PD sending over some photos of her along with the missing persons report, she got up and went to his office.

Broussard had his computer password protected. But he had given her the password in case, in his absence, she needed to check any of his records for her own work.

She sat behind his desk, turned the chair to the table bearing his computer, and switched the machine on. When asked for the password, she typed in "L'Amour," a choice she thought far too obvious if you knew Broussard at all.

Looking over his list of documents, she quickly found a folder labeled *ST. GABRIEL*. Inside were two sub folders, *UNIDENTIFIED* and *IDENTIFIED*. In the folder containing information on bodies that had been identified, victim information was arranged alphabetically, so she had no trouble locating Jennifer Hendrin's files. She clicked on the missing persons report.

Along with the document she'd already seen, there were two photos in the folder. She chose the first one listed.

The image that appeared was a full-figure shot of a vibrant, beautiful blonde with soft, shoulder-length hair. She was wearing rose-colored bell bottoms and a long-sleeve, off-white pullover with rose threads woven through it. The bosom of the pullover bore a large, rose-colored, Asian symbol. The girl's broad smile, accentuated with rose lipstick, looked entirely natural, as though she was having a great time.

Looking at the photo, Kit remembered how Mrs. Hendrin said Jennifer had brought color into their lives. She could definitely see that in the picture. Whoever took this girl's life had made the world a darker place. In that moment, Kit hated him for it.

She clicked on the second picture. When it came up on the screen, she saw a slightly different close-up shot of Jennifer in the same pullover.

Thinking she might have some use for a hard copy of Jennifer's picture as the investigation unfolded, she sent the close-up to the printer. She then closed the photo file and exited the entire missing persons report.

Her eyes fell on the next folder: COLLECTION AND AUTOPSY PHOTOS.

The thought of what might be in there made her mouth an arid place. No way she wanted to see any of that.

But her hand slowly moved the mouse cursor to the folder. She paused a moment, then clicked the folder open. There appeared a series of preview images so tiny she couldn't make out any detail. A part of her wanted to close the folder and leave, but another part, one she didn't fully understand, moved the cursor to the first image. Almost against her will, her finger clicked on the image.

A photo appeared showing three nude and bloated bodies floating face-down among a pile of debris caught against a fence. Presumably, Jennifer Hendrin was among them, but it wasn't possible to tell which one she might be. Kit's rogue hand moved the cursor to the next picture.

A grotesque mockery of a once-human face appeared on the screen. A bad taste filled Kit's mouth, as though she'd bit down on some turgid, bitter insect. Her breathing became labored. It seemed incomprehensible that the monster before her could actually be Jennifer Hendrin. She wanted to make the image go away, but instead she stared at it, studying every mottled nuance, every blackened, distended vessel, each bloated inch of what was once the Hendrins' beloved daughter. Revulsion at what she was seeing abruptly trumped curiosity. With a final shudder, she closed the file and shut off the computer.

She sat for a moment, thinking about why she'd looked. There was a time in her life when she wouldn't have. But that Kit was gone. She was now someone who would choose to look at the decomposing face of a dead young girl. But at least she had been disgusted by what she saw. Would there come a time when she would be unaffected by something like that? Standing and grabbing the living-Jennifer's photo from the printer, she sincerely hoped that would never happen.

Returning to her own office, she checked her e-mail.

Hah. There it was.

She downloaded the replica of Jude Marshall's license and made a digital copy. Using Photoshop, she cropped all the license information from the copy and saved both files.

Now we'll see who you've been pretending to be, she thought, pulling the phone closer.

Her call was answered promptly by a female voice. "Delcambre Realty, we know Morgan City."

"Mr. Delcambre, please."

"I'm sorry, he's out showing a property at the moment. Would you like his cell number?"

Kit took the number and called it.

"Duke D speaking ..."

"Mr. Delcambre, this is Kit Franklyn. We met this morning in front of the surrogacy clinic and spoke about Dr. Loftin ..."

"I remember. Did you find the rascal?"

"I'm not sure. I'd like to send you a photo of someone I believe may be him. Would you take a look at it and tell me what you think?"

"Absolutely. If it *is* him, I'd appreciate knowin' how to reach him. How you gonna send the picture?"

"As an e-mail attachment, if you'll give me the ..."

Without waiting for her to finish, he gave her his e-mail address, which she added to the scrap of paper with his phone number. Then, more faintly, she heard him say, "I believe the roof was reshingled just last year." Turning back to the phone, he said, "Gotta go. I'll let you know."

Frustrated that she didn't know how long he'd take to respond, or how he'd choose to get back to her, she hung up. A minute later, with her e-mail to him probably already at its destination, she sat back to see if maybe he'd pick up the message on his cell phone and answer right away.

Five minutes passed with no phone call or no incoming e-mail. It was now three-thirty. She couldn't just sit around any longer. With the business day nearly gone, she decided to drive over to Organogenesis Inc. before trying Jude's wife. Wishing she'd called Delcambre on her cell phone so he'd have that on his caller ID, she left the office and went to her car.

It would have been much easier to simply call Quentin Marshall and ask him about the LeDoux Street building, but considering the terse conversation they'd had earlier, he might not even come to the phone. And, of course, there was her rule that, whenever possible, all substantive questions should be asked in person so she could see the respondent's face as they answered.

She pulled into the Organogenesis parking lot a little after four o'clock. Looking toward the front entrance, she saw the husband of the couple she'd met on her earlier visit come out of the clinic and pause to light a cigarette. He then strolled around to the side of the building where, through a wrought iron gate, there appeared to be a garden.

Kit parked her car, got out, and headed for the garden.

She found the man standing by the far brick wall of the garden watching water bubble out of a lion's mouth and cascade into a shell before it spattered into a pool at the fountain's base. She walked over to him. "How's Adam?"

He turned, obviously surprised anyone else was there. "He's a sick little boy who's not going to get better until he receives a new liver."

"I've been thinking about you all since we met here yesterday. I'm sorry you're going through such an ordeal. But I sense great strength in both you and your wife."

"I'm sorry ... you're Dr. Frankum?"

"Franklyn."

"Of course, sorry ... I don't feel very strong. If I was, I'd be in there now. But I just couldn't bear to see them stick such a big needle into my son." He took a pull on his cigarette and exhaled smoke to the side so it wouldn't blow in Kit's face. He looked back at her. "Adair, that's my wife ... I'm John ... John Munson.

Adair says I'll have to quit smoking, that it'll be a bad influence on Adam as he ..." his voice broke. "...as he grows up." He turned and stubbed his cigarette out on the top edge of the pool. He looked around for a trash can to dispose of the butt. Seeing none, he dipped the butt in the pool, squeezed out the water, and shook the moisture from his hand. He put the butt in his pants pocket.

"I guess that big needle you mentioned is how they get the bone marrow cells they need," Kit said.

Munson nodded. "From his hip."

"How was Adam's liver damaged?"

"The channels that drain the bile didn't develop right. They don't know why ... it's not a genetic disease. If we had another child, there's no reason to believe it would happen again. And even if Adam was conceived and developed at another time, it probably wouldn't happen. It's just one of those shitty sticks life hands you once in a while. Without those channels, the bile backed up and killed some of his liver cells. When the doctors realized something was wrong and figured out what it was, Adam had an operation to buy him some time. They hooked a piece of his intestines up to his liver to make a bile channel. It kind of worked, but the channels inside his liver were also poorly formed, so he wasn't cured, which is apparently the usual situation. Most of the kids with the condition, even if they also have the operation, will eventually need a new liver. It's the most common cause for liver transplants in kids. Adam doesn't have much time left."

"How long will it take for the people here to make him a new liver?"

"*Too* long. They've got a lot of clients ahead of us and can only make a few organs at a time. We offered to pay more if they'd move us up the list. But Dr. Marshall said he couldn't do it ... that if he did, it wouldn't be fair to the other children they're helping. I know it was a selfish thing for us to do, but ... Do you have kids?"

"No."

"If you did, you'd understand."

Kit reached out and touched Munson's sleeve. "It's going to work out for you."

Munson looked at her, and his eyes teared. Chin trembling, he said, "Wish I could believe that."

Kit turned and left the garden. As she headed for the front entrance, she remembered a quote she'd always viewed as hogwash: *until you've had kids, you aren't truly part of the human race*, or something to that effect. Was there more truth in that than she realized?

A few seconds later, she stood in front of the same receptionist who had been there on her previous visit. "I'm Dr. Franklyn. You may remember me from yesterday."

Today, the woman was wearing glasses. She made a big show of taking them off before speaking, as though she was throwing down some kind of receptionist gauntlet, "I remember."

"Once again, I'm here with no appointment and would like to see Dr. Marshall."

"He's with a client."

"I know. I'll wait. Just let him know I'm here."

Grudgingly, the receptionist got up from her desk and went through the door leading to the rest of the clinic.

She soon reappeared, wearing a contented expression. "Dr. Marshall said he's much too busy to talk to you today."

"And I'm much too busy to come back. Tell him I'll wait … until hell freezes over if necessary."

CHAPTER 14

"You're a tenacious woman," Quentin Marshall said from behind his desk. "That's actually a trait I greatly admire. Is there something more you wanted to know about Jude?"

"The last time we spoke you said you didn't think he owned any property in the flooded area of the city. I'd like you to give that a little more thought. Did he ever mention buying a building in the lower Ninth, maybe on LeDoux Street?"

"That's a very specific question. You apparently believe he did."

"Does that street ring any bells?"

"No."

"You didn't think very hard about it."

"Why, because I didn't clench my fists and close my eyes while grinding noises came out of my brain? I have an excellent memory. If we had ever had a conversation about a purchase in such an area, even if LeDoux Street wasn't mentioned, I'd remember. Can't you find out the answer to your question by checking the tax records?"

"They aren't available right now."

"Jude's wife then. She might know."

"That's where I'm headed next."

His brow furrowed. "You came all the way back here just to ask me whether Jude owned property in the Ninth Ward? What's going on?"

Kit sat and looked at him for a few seconds, then reached into her bag and took out the headshot of Jennifer Hendrin. "Have you ever seen this person before?"

He took the picture, examined it, and handed it back. "It's no one I know. Who is she?"

"Her name is Jennifer Hendrin. Did Jude ever mention her?"

"Not that I recall." Then he sarcastically added, "Sorry I didn't take longer to answer. Was he involved with her?"

"I'm not sure what their relationship was, if any. She was once paid by a clinic in Morgan City to serve as a surrogate mother for some of the clinic's clients. To your knowledge, did Jude have anything to do with that clinic? It was called Surrogacy Central."

"I've never even heard of it. If Jude was connected in any way with it, he never said so to me. Can't imagine what interest he'd have in such a thing, unless it was a business investment. You should understand: Jude and I weren't very close. We didn't get together socially … I've never even been to his home. So you probably shouldn't read too much into my ignorance of all the things you've brought up. But I am wondering what all this has to do with his death. Are you thinking it wasn't a suicide?"

"I have no reason to believe otherwise. I'm still just trying to get a clearer picture of what factors might have driven him to kill himself."

"How close are you to finishing your investigation?"

"Most likely I'll wrap it up in the next few days."

Back in the car, Kit reviewed her conversation with Quentin Marshall. During their talk, there was no indication he was shading the truth. If Jude had killed himself because he was worried the three bodies released by the flood would somehow lead to his arrest as their killer, Quentin didn't seem to know anything about it.

Speaking of which …

Kit took out her cell phone and called her office to check her messages.

Nothing.

She navigated to the e-mail function on her phone.

There it was: Delcambre's response.

She opened the message and consumed the contents: *Never saw this guy before.*

Kit sagged in her seat. Her hand dropped to her lap. Damn. She would have bet enough for the loss to hurt that Jude was Arthur Loftin.

Almost as quickly as her spirits had been dashed, they rallied. Okay, so that idea didn't lead anywhere. He's still a good suspect.

Then a grimy cloud rose in her sky.

When she was around Broussard, it was always her intention to appear strong and decisive. Thinking back to the moment when he'd asked if she was sure the photos on Jude's camera were of the building where those three bodies had been stored, she might have sounded a bit more confident than she should have.

Of course she was right. She just needed a little booster to prove it to herself. When she saw Mrs. Marshall, she'd ask to see the camera again. And it would confirm what she already knew.

Kɪᴛ ᴛᴜʀɴᴇᴅ ᴀᴡᴀʏ ꜰʀᴏᴍ the Marshall's front door. She'd been standing there waiting for someone to answer the bell for over two minutes. Thinking this was one visit where she could reasonably have called ahead before driving all the way over there, she crossed the porch to the front steps and started down.

As she reached the bottom step, a silver sedan pulled to the curb and stopped. A slim brunette in a tailored black suit over a white blouse got out of the car and headed for the sidewalk. The woman's high forehead showed her puzzlement at who might have just come off her porch.

"May I help you? I live here," the woman said.

"Then you're Mrs. Marshall."

"That's right."

Jude's wife was a striking woman who actually wasn't very pretty. Appearing to be in her mid-forties, her skin was good and her hair, which she wore in a page boy, had a healthy sheen to it. But her eyes were small and her large nose had a distinct downward drift to the tip. Her lips, particularly the upper one, were quite thin. Overall, once you got past her well-chosen clothing and polished way of moving, she resembled a predatory, yet elegant bird.

Kit offered her hand. "I'm Dr. Franklyn. We spoke when you called home yesterday."

They exchanged a brief handshake in which Mrs. Marshall seemed a hesitant participant and didn't offer her first name.

"I'm sorry to have brought you such sad news," Kit said.

"Sorry because you drew the dirty duty?"

This comment put Kit on instant alert because it signaled to her that Mrs. Marshall was a shrewd woman who could clearly see to the heart of a matter. She was likely also able to discern when the truth was being hedged. So Kit gave her a forthright answer. "Honestly, that was part of it, but my feelings also went out to you."

"You drove over here just to tell me that?"

"No. I'm still trying to piece together what would cause your husband to take his own life. I was hoping you could help me."

"I'm not keen on discussing my husband with a stranger."

"I understand. I do. But a report will have to be written. Wouldn't you rather it contain information you gave me rather than second-hand gossip from people who didn't know him like you did?"

Mrs. Marshall considered this a moment, then retreated to a wicker chair that had somehow not blown away during the hurricane. She inspected the cushion, pulled it loose, and beat it on the back of the chair to clear it of debris. She replaced the cushion and sat down. Settling her bag in her lap, she folded her hands over it and looked at Kit. "So talk."

Kit pulled a companion chair around so it faced Mrs. Marshall. She sat down without inspecting the seat and said, "Did your husband have a financial interest or any other connection with a business called Surrogacy Central in Morgan City? It was a clinic that provided surrogates to carry fertilized eggs for couples who couldn't have children on their own."

This question obviously caught Mrs. Marshall by surprise. "Where did that come from? Who told you that?"

"I haven't heard it from anyone. It simply cropped up as a possibility."

"Did his brother say it?"

"No."

"I've never even heard of … what was it … Surrogacy Central."

"Who controlled the finances in the family … paid the bills, did the taxes?"

"I did. Before we were married, I was an accountant."

"What about property in the Ninth Ward? Do you own any?"

"No, why?"

"The day I picked up the phone when you called home, I was in your husband's study. There was a digital camera on his desk that contained some photos of what I believe was a building on LeDoux Street in the Ninth Ward. The date on those photos indicated they had been taken that morning. So his trip to shoot those pictures was one of the last things he did before … what happened to him. I have to wonder if that photographed building had anything to do with his death."

Mrs. Marshall's face shifted to a naked expression of distrust. "What's going on? From what you just said, you know the exact building supposedly in those pictures. How do you know that?"

Kit hesitated, trying to find a safe path through this dangerous territory. Unable to see one, she simply forged ahead and hoped for the best. "Late yesterday, I was working on another matter that took me down to the Ninth Ward. I happened to see the building then."

"What other matter?"

"I can't discuss it."

"So you saw some pictures on my husband's camera and they made such an impression on you that you were just driving around the Ninth Ward and recognized the building as the same one."

"Something like that."

"You're a terrible liar. I think the building in question is tied to some crime, and you believe because my husband had pictures of it on his camera, he was a party to the crime. And that's why he committed suicide. Accurate statement?"

"Honestly, I'm not even sure the pictures I saw truly were of the same building. I looked at them so quickly, and it wasn't a distinctive kind of structure. I could be mistaken about the whole thing. I was hoping I could take another look at those photos. That could clear up the whole matter."

"What crime are we talking about?"

"Why go there when I'm not even sure now it's an issue?"

"My husband was an honest man. Whatever you think he did, I can tell you you're wrong."

"I probably am. Let's look at the pictures and prove it."

Mrs. Marshall's face turned hard. "No. You can't see them."

Kit was shocked at her reaction. "If it can prove what you say, why not?"

"If I let you see them, it means I think you may be right. I don't believe that. So forget it."

"Don't make me play hardball with you."

"Meaning?"

"I can get a search warrant for the camera."

"Go ahead. But before you get to the corner as you leave, those pictures will no longer exist."

"You could be charged with aiding and abetting if you did that."

"I doubt it. You've already admitted you don't even know if the building in the pictures is the one you're interested in. So what I will have destroyed is, in all probability, meaningless. Then too, what proof do you have this conversation ever took place? I could just inadvertently delete the pictures. I had no idea they were important."

"You've got this all backward in your mind. If you really believe your husband had nothing to do with this other issue, you'd welcome the chance to clear him."

"That's not the way I see it."

Kit felt like pulling out her Ladysmith, marching Mrs. Marshall into the house, and taking the camera by force. Any evidence obtained by such an act would, of course, be inadmissible in court, but if Jude Marshall *had* killed Jennifer Hendrin and the other two women, there wouldn't be any murder trial. So this was more about knowing the truth than doing things by the book.

But was it only about truth?

Wasn't it at least partly about her intense desire to avoid telling Broussard she wasn't as sure about the contents of those photos as she'd led him to believe? Seeing it in that light, the idea of using force lost its appeal.

She decided to play her hold card. "All right. You win. No search warrant." She opened her bag and took out the photo of Jennifer Hendrin. Getting up from her chair, she walked over and showed the picture to Mrs. Marshall. "This young woman was murdered. Her body was, for a time, kept in the building we've been discussing. Ask yourself, as I have, why your husband would have taken photos of that building the morning of his death. Ask yourself if you're really as sure of him as you've said. Do you want to go through the rest of your life wondering if you were right? I couldn't live that way. But it's your choice." Kit withdrew the photo and put it in her bag. She located a business card and a pen in there, crossed out the number of her office in the now defunct Charity Hospital, and wrote the Gretna number above the old. She put the card on the armrest of Mrs. Marshall's chair. "If you change your mind, give me a call."

Mrs. Marshall plucked Kit's card from the armrest, stood up, and flicked it into the shrubbery. She gave Kit a smug look and turned to let herself into the house.

Unable to do anything else, Kit went to her car and got in. There was no doubt in her mind that Mrs. Marshall wasn't hiding anything. The woman was utterly convinced of everything she'd said. Kit was equally confident she was, at that very moment, heading for Jude's study to delete the photos on his camera.

Kit started her car and pulled away from the curb, heading for St. Charles Avenue. It might have been the fact she had been denied the opportunity to see the Ninth Ward photos again, but whatever it was, she was now even less certain they contained pictures of the building where the three bodies had been stored.

Damn, she hated having to tell Broussard that. But she couldn't think of any …

Wait a minute …

Maybe …

She took out her cell phone and punched in a number.

CHAPTER 15

With Police headquarters destroyed from the flooding, the Homicide squad had set up temporary offices on the cruise ship Ecstasy where most of the detectives were now living. When Gatlin came down the ship and stepped onto the timbers of the wharf behind the convention center, Kit was waiting for him.

"I'm not sure I can help you on this," Gatlin said by way of a greeting. "I only got a quick look at one of those pictures on the camera, so I …"

"You already told me that when I called."

"I just don't want you to get your hopes up."

On the way to Kit's car, she filled him in on what she hadn't told him over the phone.

In the car, as Kit headed for LeDoux Street, Gatlin said, "Sounds like you've made some good progress."

"Won't amount to much if I'm wrong about Marshall and that building."

"The link to that surrogacy clinic will still exist."

"A clinic that's no longer there."

They drove for a while in silence, then Kit said, "You've known Andy a lot longer than I have. What do you make of his wish to push his involvement in this case beyond just the forensics?"

"You really don't know?"

"No."

"He's depressed over the baby who died in his arms. He couldn't save that child, and he can't fix any of what's happened. There are close to a thousand bodies in St. Gabriel, and he can't bring any of them back to life. He's hurting and needs desperately to feel he's doing something to make a difference. He doesn't see that just by doing his job, he's helping. Right now, he needs more."

Of course. Hearing it from Gatlin, it was so obvious. "I spent four years in graduate school majoring in psychology. Apparently, I didn't learn much."

"Don't beat yourself up. I've spent thirty years majoring in Andy Broussard. I've got a little advantage on you there. And I was in the boat when that baby died."

Fifteen minutes later, they arrived at the building on LeDoux Street, and Kit pulled to a stop so Gatlin could see it from the same angle as when she'd recognized it.

"What do you think?"

Gatlin got out and looked at the building over the top of the car.

He stayed out there for half a minute or so, then got back in and said, "I'm sorry, I just don't know."

KIT DROPPED GATLIN OFF at the wharf and watched him walk toward the ship. Still smarting from the psychology lesson he'd given her about Broussard, she let that spill over into her doubts about the pictures on Jude Marshall's camera. Now, she was even less sure they were of the LeDoux Street building.

There was no way around it. She'd have to tell Broussard how she'd misrepresented her level of confidence in what she'd seen. Knowing she'd likely sit around all evening and mope about it later, she made another call, long distance this time, to her boyfriend, Teddy. By the end of the call, her prospects for the evening were much brighter.

KIT LOOKED AT HER watch … 6:55. Night had settled over Grandma O's parking lot ten minutes ago, and the lights were now on. Before leaving for St. Gabriel that afternoon, Broussard had mentioned he was planning on having dinner at Grandma O's around seven, and they could meet there to discuss whatever progress she'd made on the investigation. He hadn't been worried about the clogged expressway interfering with that time frame because he could always get a state trooper to escort him there and back in the breakdown lane.

Kit thought about waiting for him inside, but since she was planning on having dinner elsewhere and didn't want to hurt Grandma O's feelings by having to admit that, she'd decided to just wait where she was.

Another fifteen minutes crept by, then Broussard's familiar red T-Bird pulled into the lot and parked beside her. She quickly got out and knocked on his passenger window. He popped the lock and she got in.

"You must have good news to be so eager to talk," he said, his optimism evident.

"I've got a dinner date for later, and I didn't want to have to explain to Grandma O."

Broussard nodded and gave a little laugh. "She *can* be a handful sometimes."

Rather than crush his hopes with a flat-out statement that her part of the investigation had fizzled, she decided to itemize. "First of all, I couldn't even raise anyone to ask about the tax records."

"That's understandable."

"I got in touch with Duke Delcambre and sent him Jude Marshall's driver's license photo ..."

Even in the poor light, Kit could see the hopeful look on Broussard's face. "He's not Arthur Loftin. In fact, Delcambre didn't recognize him at all."

Broussard emitted a little grunt. He looked down and rubbed his temples with the thumb and forefinger of his left hand. Then he looked back at Kit. "Well, if it was easy, it wouldn't be any fun. What did Marshall's wife say ... she know anything about him ownin' that buildin'?"

"She said not and she handles all their financial records, so she would probably know. I'm convinced she was telling the truth."

"But if he bought the place to store dead bodies, he wouldn't leave any paper trail around for his wife to see."

The time had now come for Kit to tell him what she dreaded to say. "That building ... I'm not as sure about the pictures on Marshall's camera as I said I was earlier."

Broussard's mouth dropped open.

"I know how much you were counting on Marshall being our man. And that's my fault. I'm sorry."

"Surely you looked at the pictures again when you talked to Mrs. Marshall."

"She wouldn't let me ... thought it would be a demonstration of disloyalty and distrust toward her husband. I'm pretty certain that when I left her, she deleted the pictures."

"Did Phillip see any of the photos when you were both in Marshall's study yesterday?"

"I thought of that too, and I took him over to LeDoux Street a few hours ago to get his opinion on the match. But he couldn't say one way or the other."

Broussard turned and stared out the windshield at the brick wall in front of the car. The index finger of his right hand began to stroke the bristly hairs on the end of his nose.

After a long, silent interval in which Kit waited patiently for him to speak, he slowly turned to her. "Chances are Jude Marshall is the guy. He killed himself over somethin' he couldn't bear, and he did take those pictures, which, despite your second thoughts, you probably identified correctly. So we could just say case solved. And I hope to God it is, because that means the man who took the lives of those women is dead, as he deserves. But there's still the unexplained connection with Surrogacy Central. Without knowin' what that's all about, there's always gonna be a piece of me that thinks maybe we're wrong. I don't want to be caught short there. Because if we *are* wrong, other women who have served as surrogates could be at risk."

"I told Phillip everything we've learned. Now that we know several other cities beside New Orleans are involved, Phillip is updating your report to Homicide and personally making sure it all gets to the state police."

"Good idea. Their crime lab ought to take a look at the clothing we found as well as the interior of the place we found it. They might also want to pick up that freezer. In the mornin' I'll make a few calls."

"Anything more I can do?"

"Let me sleep on it."

Fʀᴏᴍ Gʀᴀɴᴅᴍᴀ O's, Kɪᴛ headed for her apartment in the French Quarter, relieved that Broussard didn't attach much significance to her doubts about those pictures. But he was aware now that her word wasn't always reliable when she vouched for what she knew. And that was bothersome.

Kit lived in an apartment behind a photo gallery on Toulouse Street. One of the perks of living there was it came with a parking space in an old wooden garage, three blocks away on Dauphine. Even on a normal night when the Quarter was full of life and lights, she kept one hand on her key ring Mace canister as she navigated from the garage to the gallery. Tonight, with no tourists in town and most of the shops and restaurants closed, there were many more dark doorways than usual, so as she walked, she felt isolated and vulnerable.

Turning onto Toulouse, where only a few of the streetlamps were working, she faced a shadowy gauntlet of black storefronts and dim recesses where danger might lurk. Picking up the pace, she moved quietly forward into the waiting gloom, her Mace out and ready.

She'd walked about ten steps when she caught movement out of the corner of her eye at the junction of the sidewalk with the building to her left. As she jerked her head down to see what it was, two rats the size of small nutrias scuttled across the sidewalk and into the street. Feeling a shudder ripple down her spine, she resumed walking. But as she swung her right foot forward, another rat ran into her path. She accidentally kicked it hard, the toe of her shoe sinking deeply into the furry body before she sent it squeaking into the air.

The rat hit the pavement two feet away and let out another squeal. It righted itself, sat up, and glared at her for a moment before scuttling after its brethren.

At the Bourbon Street intersection half a minute later, the landscape brightened. In contrast to Toulouse, Bourbon was an oasis of life. That's not to say it was anywhere near normal. Compared to its pre-Katrina status of permanent mayhem, the dark shops liberally dotted among those open for business gave it a struggling third-world look. Among the places bustling with activity was Bunny's, a bar and grill that had been open around the clock for over a dozen years, including the hours during the height of Katrina's fury when Bunny had to serve up burgers cooked on a camp stove.

Looking at Bunny's neon sign, Kit was reminded again that if she had only been able to get word down to Bunny's while she was struggling to save Mrs. Lucas, she could have gotten help to squeeze that respirator bag. But there had just been no way ... no way at all.

She changed direction and angled across the intersection, heading for the bar. As she drew near, she heard "Okie from Muskogee" spill out the front door and into the street from Bunny's jukebox. After the dark isolation of Toulouse, Kit followed the sound like an amoeba seeking light.

Inside, the place was dimly lit. Most of the tables and the seats at the bar were occupied. These days, Bunny's customers consisted of a few regulars who lived in the Quarter and had refused to evacuate, supplemented by off-duty national guardsmen and construction workers trying to repair the levees and put the city back together. The clientele was exclusively male. Seeing Kit in the doorway, they made her the focus of their attention.

Bunny came from behind the bar and headed her way.

"Hello Darlin," Bunny said, embracing her. She let go and took a step back so she could see Kit's face. "Can you feel the testosterone spotlight, babe? ... 'Cause you're standin' in it."

"I feel it."

"How you doin'?"

"Not too bad. Business looks good."

Bunny leaned close and lowered her voice conspiratorially, "But they aren't really havin' fun. Guess too many of 'em are away from home."

Looking at Bunny with her double chin, it was hard to believe she had once been Bunny LeClaire, one of the hottest exotic dancers on Bourbon Street. But she had pictures of herself in costume all around the place to prove it. Kit was one of only a few who knew her real last name was Lefkowitz.

"Can I throw a burger on the grill for you?" Bunny asked.

"Can't stay. Just stopped in to say hi and soak up a little civilization after coming down Toulouse."

"Hope you're careful walkin' in those dark areas."

"I try to be. A few minutes ago, I accidentally kicked a rat."

"I've kicked a few in my time, mostly the two-legged kind and always on purpose as they hit the road."

"Someday you'll find the right guy."

"They always seem right at first. Why is that?"

"Protective camouflage. Lots of predators use it to get close to their prey."

Bunny picked up Kit's hand and slapped it affectionately. "Girl, you got a way of goin' right to the heart of things. Protective camouflage ... I have to remember that."

"It's not often I get a chance to leave the impression I'm clever. I better go before I ruin it."

"Oh, that Westie breeder friend of mine in Mississippi called today. The litter we've been waitin' for has been born. And there's one healthy male unspoken for. If you want him, we should let her know ASAP."

Bunny had been working on Kit for months trying to convince her to get a puppy to replace her dog, Lucky, who had died of old age in June. Kit had been resisting because she felt it dishonored Lucky's memory to replace him so quickly. But after talking to the Hendrins and John Munson, she could no longer ignore the empty feeling growing inside her.

"Tell her I want him."

Bunny's eyes glistened with approval. "I'll call her tonight."

On the way out the door, Kit ran into an attractive redhead that lived in one of the two apartments above Bunny's place.

"How's the crowd?" the redhead asked.

"Not bad ... all male, so get ready for a lot of stares if you're going in."

"You say that like it's a bad thing."

It was far from obvious, but the redhead was actually a man in drag Kit knew only as He Daisy. Daisy had many wigs, but usually favored the flaming red one he was now wearing. He wasn't into soliciting men, but simply liked to dress as a woman. By trade, he was an artist who supplemented his trust fund income with sporadic sales of his paintings. Though he had an unusual lifestyle, he was a gentle, kind man Kit counted as a friend.

"Does this color lipstick make me look like a tart?" Daisy asked.

"Not at all."

"Too bad. I was hoping it did." Daisy laughed. "Well, I'm going to get something to eat and go upstairs and work. You have a good one."

As Kit walked back to Toulouse, crossed over, and went another half block to the photo gallery fronting her apartment, she wasn't sure at all that a little Westie puppy was big enough to fill the hollow space in her heart.

Tourists comprised most of the business that came through the doors of the Nolen Boyd gallery. No tourists equaled no business. So Boyd had decided to take a long European vacation while the city got back to where it could once again entice enough visitors for him to justify reopening.

Mace canister in hand, Kit walked past the dark front of the gallery and stepped up to the eight-foot tall, heavy cypress door leading to the back courtyard. She took a quick look around.

Seeing no one lingering or approaching, she quickly keyed the lock and opened the door.

The gallery and the adjacent building formed a long passage leading to the rear courtyard, where Kit's apartment was located. The passage had a lattice ceiling on which a hundred-year-old wisteria had spread its branches. During the day, this made the passage a delightful, light-dappled avenue. But at night, the wisteria would have caused it to be a very dark twenty-foot stretch were it not for the little lights Boyd had rigged along the left wall.

Above the big cypress door, Boyd had installed a coil of razor wire to keep anyone on the outside from climbing over the door. So as the door shut and locked behind her, the tension Kit felt from being on the Quarter's dark streets flowed out of her.

Even though she was now safely home, she kept her Mace ready.

Walking toward the courtyard, which was brightly illuminated by a dark-activated mercury vapor light, Kit remembered how happy Lucky always was to see her, his little tail wagging furiously, his mouth open in an expression of pure joy. How she missed that little varmint.

But what to name the new one? Lucky II? That's no good.

She reached the end of the lattice ceiling and stepped out from under it. Suddenly, she heard a sharp, scratching sound from the lattice. Before she could turn to see what it was, a soft object hit the top of her head. Something heavy thudded onto the ground behind her. At the same instant, the thing that had hit her seemed to be melting over her hair.

As she struggled to complete her turn to see what the hell was going on, the melting liquid slid down over her face … It covered her eyes … so thick she couldn't see through it.

Down it went over her nose and mouth. And it was making a crinkling sound.

She lifted her hands to wipe the stuff away.

That's when she discovered it was not liquid.

It was a plastic bag.

CHAPTER 16

Mouth gaping in surprise, Kit took a sharp breath. The flow of air sucked the plastic against her nostrils and tented it over her mouth. She turned to the rear, but her assailant moved as well, twisting the plastic bag tight against her neck. She cocked her elbow and sprayed Mace blindly over her right shoulder.

Hearing no scream of pain, she kept her finger on the button and cranked her arm around as much as the awkward angle permitted. This changed nothing. The bag remained tight against her skin.

She kicked backward, but didn't connect with anything.

Already the lack of oxygen was affecting her … the exertion making it worse. Her head felt light and her lungs were burning. She had to do something … NOW.

She dropped the Mace canister and clawed at the bag, trying to tear a hole in it.

Her nails found a purchase on the skin of the bag and she dug in.

No good …

The damn thing was impenetrable.

The lack of air was making her queasy. Any moment, she was going to pass out. She screamed, but the sound, puny without adequate breath to support it, was muffled by the bag.

In desperation, she threw her legs out from under her and dropped to the ground, hoping to surprise her attacker and cause him to loosen his grip. But he went to the ground with her and held on.

Unwittingly, she had given him greater leverage. She felt him twisting the bag tighter, pressing the plastic hard against the skin around her mouth.

Strobe lights began stroking the indigo sky inside her head. In an instant, that changed to the most beautiful sunset she'd ever seen: turquoise and blue and red and orange marked with a patchwork of glowing contrails. Then the sun suddenly dropped beneath the horizon, leaving a starless firmament. Her struggles ceased.

Outside, on Toulouse Street, Teddy LaBiche, Kit's alligator farmer boyfriend, who'd just driven the two hours from Bayou Coteau to have dinner with her, stepped up to the big courtyard door and paused.

What was that? Did he just hear a muffled scream from inside?

Teddy thrust his key in the lock and opened it. He pushed the big door out of his way.

It took a moment for him to understand what he was seeing, but then it sank in … a figure on the ground, another kneeling beside the first. Then he saw the plastic bag.

Kit …

Screaming in rage, he began running.

The kneeling figure leapt to his feet and took off, heading for the left side of the courtyard.

By the time Teddy reached Kit's limp body, her assailant was running up the outside stairs leading to the second floor of the rear wing where Kit's apartment was located. Teddy wanted desperately to run after him, get hold of him, and beat him senseless, but he couldn't. He thought about reaching for the chrome .22 he always carried so he wouldn't be without it in the alligator pits. But there was no time for that either. His first priority was Kit.

He dropped to his knees where she was lying on her side, facing away from him. Cursing, he yanked off the plastic bag and gently let her head return to the ground. He ripped off his shirt and crumpled it into a cushion that he placed beside her head. Then he gently rolled her over so her head was supported by the shirt.

No ...

In the harsh mercury light, her skin had the pallor of death. And she didn't seem to be breathing. The hairs on the back of Teddy's neck stiffened. Trying to be calm, he put two fingers against the side of her neck.

No pulse.

At the top of Teddy's visual field, he caught a glimpse of the fleeing assailant as he went up the ladder on the second floor walkway to the roof.

Rage against her attacker and fear for Kit's life battled for control of Teddy's mind. Knowing if he gave in to either, he would be of no use to her, he focused on bringing her back.

What was it you were supposed to do first if a person wasn't breathing ... chest compression? Breathe for them? Damn it, which was first?

Four first ...

The phrase came to him in a rush. Four what?

Breaths ... it was breaths.

Supporting himself with his elbows on the ground, he pinched her nostrils shut with one hand and pulled on her lower jaw to open her mouth with the other. He bent down and placed his lips over hers. He exhaled into her. Her chest rose. He drew back and her chest fell.

Without waiting to see what effect that might have produced, he did the same thing again. "Breathe for me, baby." He waited a moment to see if she would. But she remained still. He thought her color looked better, but in the harsh light, it was hard to tell.

He made another transfer from his lungs to hers. As he drew back, she suddenly sucked in a huge lungful of air on her own and bucked upward at the waist. Her eyes opened and she coughed.

"Kit ... baby, it's me, Teddy."

She dropped her shoulders back to the ground, and Teddy scrambled to make sure his shirt was under her head. Eyes closed, she drew two more gasping breaths, then began to breathe more normally. Teddy squirmed around so he was sitting beside her. He reached out to stroke her hair, but as he made contact, she screamed and swung wildly at him with her right hand.

He caught her gently by the wrist. "I'm Teddy. He's gone. You're in no danger now. It's okay."

Her eyes opened and she stared at him for a moment. "Teddy ...?"

"I'm here. He can't hurt you now."

"I want to sit up."

Teddy leaned forward and took her by the shoulders. She came up and fell forward into his embrace all in one motion. Her arms went around him and they sat there on the ground, clinging to each other.

CHAPTER 17

KIT SAT ON HER sofa, feet drawn up, arms hugging her knees, trying to become as small as she could manage. On the end table next to her was a cup of hot chai Teddy had made, but which she had so far not touched. Her mouth was sore, and her right arm ached from the awkward way she'd bent it trying to spray Mace in her attacker's face. She also had a headache. None of those pains was as bad as they had been thirty minutes ago, so the two aspirins she'd taken were helping. But her feelings of anger and stupidity showed no signs of diminishing.

Attacked just yards from her apartment … inside the courtyard she had believed was safe. How could she have been so naive? And she'd been able to do nothing to save herself. If Teddy hadn't come when he did …

She shivered at the thought that she could now be lying on the ground outside, her corneas already clouding over, her body growing cold, possibly lying in her own excrement.

And it might not be over, because whoever had attacked her had escaped. Teddy got a quick glimpse of him and he'd seen that the creep was dressed all in black and was wearing a ski mask. Beyond those few details all Teddy could tell Gatlin was that he was of average height and build. Big deal. The handful of cops Gatlin had assembled, and who were now combing the Quarter looking for him, were too few and too late. Gatlin knew that as well as she did.

"Okay, keep looking," Gatlin said into his two-way radio to the cop in charge of the search. He shoved the radio into his pocket and looked at Kit, who had heard the negative report as clearly as he. "It's still early in the search."

She responded with a small nod. At least he hadn't insulted her intelligence by promising something he couldn't deliver.

Gatlin resumed pacing.

Broussard had been sitting quietly in the armchair across from the sofa. Now he spoke. "We all know who did this."

Gatlin turned and looked at him skeptically. "We do?"

"The same person who killed those three women. Look at her ..." he gestured to Kit. "Those bruises around her mouth from the bag ... same as what I saw on the three bodies. Except on them, it was worse because he carried the act to completion."

"You don't mind if I bring up a few problems with that idea, do you, just so we see the whole landscape?" Gatlin said.

"I'd be disappointed if you didn't."

"All the evidence points to Jude Marshall as the killer of those women. But he's dead. If this guy tonight was the real killer, why the hell would he advertise the fact he's still alive by using the same method on Kit he used on them? Why not just let us believe Marshall's our guy?"

"There's obviously a twist to this thing that so far eludes us," Broussard replied. "And by the way, all that evidence you referred to is actually not much evidence, more a hunch," he added.

"Let's say this *was* the real killer," Gatlin said. "Why'd he choose to come after Kit? How'd he know *she* was working on the case?"

"Maybe it was someone she interviewed about it," Teddy suggested.

"Okay, let's follow that thought," Gatlin said, taking no offense a civilian untrained in police work had made the suggestion. "I'm sure we can all agree that Jennifer Hendrin's father can be ruled out right off the top." He looked at Kit. "From the questions you asked Quentin Marshall about the building on LeDoux Street, if he knew about the bodies being stored there, he'd have concluded you believed Jude put them there. But suppose Quentin actually did it. The best thing he could do under those circumstances would be nothing. He'd have no reason to attack you. That leaves only this realtor in Morgan City, this Delcambre character ..."

Sitting there listening to him, Kit was impressed with his grasp of the case.

"Let's say Delcambre was watching the surrogacy clinic, saw the three victims going in and out, and decided to do them harm. Wait a minute ... he walks with a cane, I believe you said." He looked at Kit, who nodded. "Kind of hard for a man with an infirmity to overpower three women, kill them, *and* exhibit the mobility this guy tonight showed. But maybe the cane is just a ploy to make people think he's gimpy." He pretended to think a moment. "Oh yeah, he's also very much overweight." Gatlin looked at Broussard. "Not that I think folks of girth are immobile, but Teddy said our guy tonight had an average build." His eyes still on Broussard, Gatlin turned his palms upward inviting a response.

"I think you're right. It isn't any of them," Broussard said.

"Then who?"

Before Broussard could speak, Kit said, "Someone who doesn't live in the real world ... who thinks that if I were dead, the investigation would stop."

Gatlin looked back at Broussard to see what he thought of her comment.

Broussard raised his right hand, fingers lightly curled into a fist until it touched the side of his nose. He uncurled his index finger and wiggled it at Kit. "She's got it."

"So it's someone who's nuts," Gatlin said.

"Depends on your definition of nuts," Broussard said. "He's functional enough to have figured out where Kit lives, and he knows how to plan."

"We've just eliminated every person we know of that's connected to the case," Gatlin said. "How'd he even find out an investigation was underway and who was involved? Hold on … the reports we filed … who knows how many people have seen them?"

"It's a possibility," Broussard said.

"Let me see if I can get a list together." Gatlin shook his head. "I don't like the idea that somebody in law enforcement may be behind this. But I'll admit I've known more than a few captains who should have been committed."

"We also need to find out who owns the buildin' where the bodies were stored," Broussard said. "With that name, everything might fall into place. If only we knew a good detective …"

"You just never let up, do you?" Gatlin said. "I'll take care of that too."

"How?"

"I'll *detect*. Meanwhile, until this whole thing is wrapped up, Kit shouldn't be left alone."

Kit bristled at the assumption she couldn't take care of herself. Then, considering what had just happened, his suggestion didn't seem like a bad idea.

"Don't be concerned about that," Teddy said. "I'm not letting her out of my sight until we know it's safe." He looked at Kit. "If that's all right with you."

"Did you bring your gun?"

"I've got it."

"Then you can stay."

"I'll put a cop down in the courtyard, too," Gatlin said.

"You should take some time off," Broussard said to Kit. "However long it takes until you feel like workin' again. And don't worry, we'll find this guy."

WHEN BROUSSARD AND GATLIN were gone, Teddy turned to Kit, who was standing behind him.

"What do you say we get in my truck and get the hell out of here. Come and stay with me until this is over. I think you'll feel better with a hundred miles between you and this place."

Kit shook her head. "Far too risky. We'd be on the road where we can't control things. With a cop downstairs and you with me, I'm safer right here."

Teddy nodded. "You're probably right. In any event, it's your call, whatever will make you feel safe. With all that's happened, I'm sure not hungry. What about you?"

"Me neither." She looked into his brown eyes. "You saved my life."

He took her into his arms and pulled her to him. Against her ear, he whispered, "If you had died, my life would have been over, too."

She drew back and looked hard at him, trying to see deeper into him than she ever had.

"What?" Teddy asked.

There was nothing about Teddy she didn't adore ... His fine features, his straight black hair, his lithe, slim body, his gentle good humor, the way he could find all the places on her body that made sex with him a transcendent experience. She adored it all. For most of their relationship, she had been content to just enjoy being with him and had not worried about any long-term prospects, mostly because she was still discovering who *she* was. But tonight, everything had nearly ended. And if it had, she would have left nothing to show she'd once lived. She truly loved Teddy. But she would have never experienced the kind of love the Hendrins had for their daughter and the Munsons for their son. That frightened her. She needed to tell Teddy how she felt, but as she looked at him, waiting for her response to his question, she was reluctant to reveal how she felt. This shouldn't come from her. He should be the one to initiate that discussion. Otherwise, he'd just be reacting to pressure.

"Nothing," she said.

"You sure?"

"Positive."

CHAPTER 18

"WHEN ARE YOU GONNA get a new car?" Broussard said, looking at the cracked fake wood on the instrument panel of Gatlin's Pontiac as they drove deeper into the lower Ninth.

"Why you ragging me about that?" Gatlin said. "All *your* cars are over fifty years old."

"They're vintage. This one is just old."

"It's barely broken in."

"It's got nearly three hundred thousand miles on it."

"I got more than that on me, and *I'm* still functional."

"You might want to reconsider that statement. Since you picked me up, you've pumped enough methane into the air to raise the temperature of the northern hemisphere three degrees."

"Sorry, I was hoping you hadn't noticed," Gatlin said. "I'm having a little problem this morning."

They were in the Ninth Ward because Gatlin had managed to obtain the name and address of the owner of the building on LeDoux Street. Knowing that finding anyone there after the flood was a long shot, they decided they still had to try.

Gatlin slowed for a stop sign, looked both ways down the empty cross street, and turned right.

"You didn't come to a complete stop," Broussard said.

"I'll sign myself up for traffic school later today."

They drove for another half a block with neither of them saying anything, then Gatlin glanced at Broussard. "Were you happy with your behavior last night at Kit's apartment?"

"What do you mean?"

"You didn't seem very upset at what happened to her ... even made a little joke about wondering where we could find a good detective."

"If she'd been killed, I'm not sure I'd ever be the same."

"You didn't show it."

"What did you expect me to do?"

"Show a little emotion for once ... let her know you care. Would that be so hard?"

Broussard considered the question for a moment, then said, "I'll sign myself up for emotion school later today."

"You should."

"I guess the bag the guy used on Kit is on its way to the state crime lab?"

"I sent it with a lieutenant who went up there this morning to get a statement from a witness in one of the shootings we're working. But if Teddy was right about seeing rubber gloves on the guy, it's not gonna be any help. We talked about that last night."

"I know. I just want so badly to make some progress on this thing, I'm grabbin' at any possibility."

A few minutes later, they pulled to the curb, between two piles of trash nearly as high as the car.

"There it is," Gatlin said.

He was referring to a narrow shotgun duplex painted pink with blue trim on one side and yellow with green trim on the other. Above the high water mark, the paint on both sides was fresh. Below, it was as grimy as all the other houses in the area. The doors on both sides stood open.

"Doesn't look like anyone's home," Gatlin said.

"Let's take a look."

They both got out and walked up on the porch. Gatlin knocked on the doorframe. "Hellooo ... Anyone there? Visitors here ..."

He went inside and Broussard followed.

The place smelled of mold and rot. All the walls were sprouting Rorschach patterns of mold and fungus. The silt was so thick on the floor nothing could be seen through it. But there were a lot of footprints, so they had hopes the owner might yet be found.

As they moved through the house, something crackled under Broussard's feet. He looked down and saw he was standing in an area where the floor had a droop in it. When the water receded, it had apparently left a temporary puddle there, because the sound had come from a school of tiny minnows that had been caught in it, subsequently drying into fish crispies.

They went through the entire silent, decaying house and found no one. But when they reached the kitchen and looked past the open back door through the dirty haze of a closed screen door, they saw an old black man picking through a heap of debris piled against the side of a rickety garage. The bulldog with him was lifting his leg on a disgustingly filthy mattress propped on a dead tree.

The hinges on the screen door squealed as Gatlin opened it and stepped onto the small porch. The sound caught the old man's attention. He turned toward the house. The bulldog looked, too, but kept peeing.

"Sorry to bother you," Gatlin said. "Are you James Bolden?"

"What you want Jimmie for?"

Thinking this guy might *be* Bolden, Gatlin tried to put him at ease. "He's not in any trouble."

"He might disagree."

"Why do you say that?"

"Go over to the Three Pines nursing home and talk to him. Then you'll know."

"Does he work there?"

"Go see him."

Back in the car, Gatlin said, "Why can't people ever give you a straight answer? Everything's gotta be a big puzzle. Got any idea where this nursing home is?"

"I think it's in Harahan. If my memory is accurate, it's right on 39."

"So where are the pines?" Gatlin said, looking at the low brick building with the wheelchair ramp leading up to a side entrance.

"I remember hearin' that this is a satellite facility," Broussard replied. "The main operation is in Baton Rouge. That one probably has the pines."

"How the hell hard would it have been to plant three here, too? I don't have a lot of confidence this is gonna produce anything, but we're here, so let's go in."

The front entrance opened onto a small space with an institutional terrazzo floor and cold, white walls that emphasized *Nursing* more than *Home*. Broussard noticed that the fake palm near the door needed a good dusting.

The two men walked over to the glass-enclosed administrative cubicle and stepped up to the counter, where an overweight woman whose breasts probably entered a room a full second before the rest of her came over to see what the two men wanted.

"Is there a James Bolden here?" Gatlin said.

"What's the nature of your interest?" the woman asked.

Gatlin flipped out his badge. "NOPD Homicide. We'd like to talk to him."

"Have a seat over there. I'll get him."

"We'd rather this not be a public conversation."

Giving Gatlin a stern look, she said, "Then you'll want to keep your voices down."

"I like your perfume," Broussard said to the woman. "It's Obsession, isn't it?"

Suddenly beaming, the woman said, "That's exactly what it is."

"Very nice."

She picked up the phone and put her fat finger on one of the buttons across the bottom of the keypad. After a brief interval in which she stared at Gatlin with pursed lips, then shifted her eyes to Broussard, whom she favored with a much fonder look, she said into the phone, "Would you bring Mr. Bolden to the front? He has some visitors."

Gatlin and Broussard moved to the opposite side of the small room, where there was a sofa and two chairs all constructed of strips of fake brown leather slung over a chrome frame. They formed a sterile, unfriendly grouping that didn't beckon either of them to sit.

Making sure he couldn't be overheard, Gatlin leaned close to Broussard. "Obsession … How the hell did you know that?"

"Knowin' smells is part of my job."

"All I could smell was disinfectant."

"Maybe you should also sign up for nuance school later today."

After a short wait, a tall fellow in a white uniform came from the back of the facility, pushing a wheelchair containing a wizened old black man with close-cropped hair the color of dirty cotton. Looking at Bolden, both Gatlin and Broussard saw what the guy in Bolden's backyard meant when he said Jimmie might disagree about being in trouble.

The right side of Bolden's face looked like it was melting, an obvious sign he'd had a stroke that paralyzed him on that side. His right arm lay limply in his lap. His left held a wadded tissue.

The attendant pushed the chair over to the two men. "This is Mr. Bolden. I'll leave you all alone so you can talk."

As the attendant left, Gatlin introduced himself and Broussard. Believing a handshake might be difficult for Bolden, neither extended the offer of one.

Gatlin said, "Mr. Bolden, we understand you own the property at 523 LeDoux Street. Is that right?"

"I can't see you with you standin' up like that," Bolden said, slurring the words because of his paralysis. "You gotta sit. Pull those chairs over and put your asses in 'em." He dabbed at the drooping corner of his mouth to blot at the saliva escaping there.

When everyone was at eye level, Bolden said, "That's better. How'd you know where to find me?"

"We tried your home," Broussard said. "A man in your backyard told us you were here."

"He have a bulldog with him?"

"Yes."

"He's the biggest liar in the neighborhood. You shouldn't listen to a thing he says."

"But he did send us here."

The old man looked puzzled at this response. He dabbed at the corner of his mouth with the tissue, then said, "How's my house? Is it ruint?"

"It's gonna need a lot of work," Broussard said.

Bolden let out a long breath. "I was about to put it up for sale just before the storm … to help pay for livin' here. Guess I can forget that …" His mood suddenly improved. "… unless the gov'mint is buyin' everybody out. Heard anything about those plans?"

"Sorry, no."

Hope still evident on the working side of his face, he looked at Gatlin, who shook his head.

Bolden lowered his eyes. "It figgers." He looked at Broussard. "Ever notice how when you're down, up is not a possibility?"

"I have indeed," Broussard said.

Bolden touched the tissue to the drooping corner of his mouth. "And you know, I can't even get a little rice puddin' here. They say it's not available from their supplier. And God forbid they should actually *make* somethin' in the kitchen. Take my advice … don't ever get dependent on other folks. You won't like it. Yeah, I own that property on LeDoux Street. Worst decision I ever made. Couldn't rent it … nobody else was stupid enough to buy it from me. It's just been a tax drain ever since I took it on."

"So you never leased it to anybody," Gatlin said.

"Couldn't. It needed to be fixed up inside. I didn't have the money, and nobody else wanted to risk theirs in that neighborhood. I once tried to talk the owner of that beauty shop next door into expandin' into my area, but she's barely holdin' on as it is. So at least the flood didn't hurt me over there any morn' I was already hurtin'."

"Ever give anyone a key to the place?" Gatlin asked. "… A realtor … a relative …"

"I wouldn't use a realtor. They cost too damn much. And I wouldn't give any of my relatives the sweat off my nuts."

Heading back to the car, Gatlin said, "Maybe it's just me, but I have a hard time seeing that guy sprinting across Kit's courtyard and running up that ladder to the roof."

"Know what I think?"

"Usually, but not at the moment."

"We need to go back to LeDoux Street."

CHAPTER 19

Broussard came back into the main room and walked over to Gatlin, who was kneeling on the mud-covered floor fiddling with the electrical outlet that served the freezer where the bodies had been stored. "There's also a deadbolt on the backdoor that can only be locked from the inside."

"How come you didn't notice that when you were here the first time?" Gatlin replied, standing up and brushing off the knees of his pants.

"We were a little occupied keepin' a band of thugs from killin' us."

"Yeah, but how long could *that* have taken?"

In truth, Broussard, too, was wondering why he hadn't noticed that earlier. After the thugs had gone, he could have spent another minute or two looking around a bit more, but he hadn't.

"This outlet has been spliced into the wiring for the business next door," Gatlin said. "So *they* were paying for running that freezer. Any lights he needed when he was here could have been run off the other plug."

Feeling his cell phone vibrate, Gatlin took it out of his jacket pocket and flipped it open. "Gatlin."

Broussard could hear the caller on the other end, but only faintly.

"Okay, thanks," Gatlin said a moment later. He pocketed the phone and looked at Broussard. "This just gets better and better."

"What do you mean?"

Gatlin told him what the caller had said.

"We can't keep all this from Kit. She has a right to know."

Gatlin passed him his phone. "You do it."

D<small>ESPITE THE PRESENCE OF</small> the cop in the courtyard and Teddy by her side, there was no way Kit could sleep after what happened. So she and Teddy spent the night fully dressed on the sofa, apparently watching the TV but comprehending very little of what they saw. For the first few hours, Kit went to the door every half hour and checked to make sure it was locked. She would then go to the window and look for the cop downstairs. Feeling she needed this reassurance, Teddy did nothing to interfere with her ritual. Eventually, as dawn washed over the French Quarter, Kit's eyes closed and she slumped against Teddy's shoulder, finally sleeping.

Teddy pulled a couple of pillows from the far end of the sofa into his lap. Carefully, he moved down and lowered Kit's head onto the pillows. There they remained for the next several hours until the phone rang.

The sound jolted Kit awake. She was up and on her feet in an instant. Her hands went for the Ladysmith.

Teddy bolted from the sofa and gently touched her on the arm. "It's okay. You're safe. It's just the phone."

She gave him a disoriented look. She turned and stared at the still-ringing phone.

Teddy said, "Want me to get it?"

"No," She slowly ran her hand through her hair. "I'll do it." She crossed the room and picked up the receiver.

"This is Kit."

"It's Andy. How you doin'?"

"I'm okay. Did you catch him?"

"Not yet. Look, I'm with Phillip. We just came from talkin' to the owner of the buildin' on LeDoux Street."

"The owner ... it's *not* Jude Marshall?"

"No. A guy named James Bolden. Phillip got his name from the tax rolls. Anyway, he's an old man in a wheelchair from a stroke. He obviously has no connection with what happened. Right now, Phillip and I are standin' inside that buildin'. Both doors have had deadbolt locks installed on the inside so no one on the outside could get in by usin' a key. Phillip found that the freezer was run by hijackin' power from the shop next door. All that means the person we're after didn't have any connection to the place. He was just an opportunist who saw it was empty and moved in."

"Then I guess it's like you suggested; he probably picked up my name from the report you sent to the state police."

"Could be."

"Any good prospects there, or is it too early to know?"

Broussard didn't answer right away.

"Hello?" Kit said. "You still there?"

"About those other prospects ... There are six people whose duties require them to have handled that report. Five are women and one is a 61-year-old male with emphysema. Apart from that, the report could have been viewed by an untold number of others in the system."

"What are you saying?"

"I'm sorry, but ... we've hit the wall here."

Kit couldn't believe it had come to this. Broussard had promised they would catch the guy who attacked her. Broussard ... the man who could always see what others missed, the man whom she believed could do the impossible, was saying he was beaten. There was no one in custody or even under suspicion. The guy was totally free to try again. The thought made her feel cold and helpless. A shiver ran down to the small of her back. Her arms erupted in gooseflesh.

"Of course, we're gonna keep after it," Broussard said. "There has to be a thread somewhere that'll get us cookin' again. And I'm gonna find it. Meanwhile, Phillip will keep a uniform in your courtyard around the clock. And Kit ... you and Teddy need to be careful."

Kit responded mechanically. "We will."

"Believe me, I wish I could offer more."

"I do believe you. Let me know if you make any progress." She hung up.

"What'd he say?" Teddy asked.

"They're out of leads. They have no idea what to do next."

"How is that possible?"

"Same thing I thought when I heard. They're going to keep a cop downstairs."

"So they think the guy may come back?"

"I'm sure they don't know. It's a precaution."

"I'm staying, too."

"What about the alligator farm?"

"I got somebody who can look after that. I'll call and let them know I'm going to be here awhile."

"I'm sorry to be so much trouble."

Teddy moved closer and took her in his arms. "I'd never think of being with you as trouble."

Kit drew her head back. "I'd like to get cleaned up."

"Okay, you take a shower, and I'll make us some breakfast. I won't find the fridge bare, will I?"

"I've got everything you'll need."

"See you in a few minutes then."

Kit gave him a kiss on the cheek and headed for the bathroom. When she reached it, she pushed the door open and paused on the threshold. Suddenly, she felt once again the plastic bag over her head … and even though the bag wasn't really there, she couldn't get her breath. It was all happening again. She inhaled as deeply as she could, making an audible gasp that Teddy heard in the kitchen.

Leaving the fridge standing open, he darted across the hall to her side, where he took her by the shoulders. "What's wrong?"

At his touch, the horror diminished, but didn't leave. "I had a flashback to last night. Felt like I couldn't get any air."

"You okay now?"

She inhaled deeply and let it out slowly. "I think so." She looked into the bathroom. "I know it's crazy, but … would you pull the shower curtain back for me?"

"Sure."

She stepped aside to let Teddy pass. He went inside and swept the curtain along the rod. He turned toward her. "See, nobody there."

She let him back into the hall.

"I'll be right over there in the kitchen," he said. "No need to worry."

She looked at the tub without moving. Her gaze shifted to the small window high on the wall opposite the door. The thought of being alone and naked in the bathroom was more than she could handle. "Would you mind staying in here while I shower? I'll do it fast so it doesn't get steamy and uncomfortable for you."

"Of course."

The bathroom was small and didn't easily accommodate two people, but with Teddy seated on the commode, it gave Kit enough room to maneuver. The first item she removed was the Ladysmith, still on her calf. Reluctantly, she laid the holster on the sink, arranging it so the butt of the gun faced the tub.

She undressed and hung her clothes on the hook beside the tub. She pulled the shower curtain partially closed, then leaned in and turned on the water. A few seconds later, with the water at the proper temperature, she glanced at her gun. She wanted to do a quick practice move to see how fast she could yank it from the holster, but not wanting to appear any more paranoid to Teddy than she already had, she turned back to the tub and stepped in.

She drew the shower curtain fully across the rod.

When she'd first gotten her dog, Lucky, whenever she had to leave the house for work, he would cry and howl for her to return. The vet explained that it was separation anxiety … he was afraid she wouldn't ever come back. When he became comfortable enough to trust her, he relaxed.

In the shower, Kit suddenly knew with greater clarity than ever before how Lucky felt. Separated from her gun, she experienced a rush of claustrophobia. Her chest grew tight, and once again, she couldn't breathe. She whipped the curtain aside and stepped back into the bathroom.

Teddy shot to his feet.

She raised a calming hand toward him. "I'm all right. I just felt closed in and trapped in there."

Teddy's brows knitted in concern. "Leave the curtain open a little. Maybe that'll help."

She nodded and tried again. Though his idea made the situation tolerable, she still wasn't entirely comfortable, so when she stepped into the stream of water, she kept her eyes open. What followed was the fastest shower she'd ever taken. Moving cleverly yet with warp speed, she managed to wash her face and hair without closing her eyes longer than to blink. She gave the rest of her body a quick pass and got out of there.

A few minutes later, in fresh clothes, her gun back on her calf, Kit sat at the counter between the kitchen and the living room. While Teddy worked on breakfast, she plugged her hair dryer into a nearby receptacle and flicked the thing on. As usual, the noise filled her ears, cutting her off from any other sound. Unable to bear even that kind of isolation, she switched it off. Leaving the dryer on the counter, she got up and walked to the window onto the courtyard.

Where was the cop who was supposed to be there? An adrenaline surge washed over her.

Then he strolled out into the courtyard from the lattice-ceilinged walkway. Even though she now saw there had been no cause for her sudden spike in anxiety, it wasn't easily ignored. As she walked back to the counter, she wondered if one cop was enough.

She took her seat and watched Teddy add some chopped mushrooms and onions to a pan already containing melted butter.

Sitting there, Kit wondered what was wrong with her. Why was she acting so damned paralyzed? God knows this wasn't the first time her life had been threatened since she'd come to work for Broussard. It wasn't even the second ... or the third. And she'd handled all those better than this. What was different about this one?

In reviewing the previous times she'd been in danger, she saw that with one exception, the threat had been acute and was permanently resolved within a very short interval. There hadn't been hours and hours to dwell on a danger that still existed. Even when she and Teddy had been kidnapped, she knew who to fear. This time, she had no idea who had attacked her. Or when he would try again. That was it ... the uncertainty of this situation ... how could she not be unnerved?

But there was another reason, one she now harbored in a small dark place where little light reached. In each of those other situations, she had responded as any sentient organism would when its existence was threatened. She had fought with every resource at her hand to keep living. But that was before she knew she had a destiny yet unfulfilled. She had not yet loved as the Hendrins had loved their daughter or the Munsons their son. She could not die without having had that experience. Now, even though she wasn't fully aware of it, she had much more to lose. That's why she couldn't handle the thought that her latest attacker might try again and this time succeed.

Because Teddy made the meal, Kit volunteered to do all the clean-up while Teddy watched. When she was finished, he suggested they get some air.

"What do you mean?" Kit asked.

"Take a walk in the Quarter, go for a drive ..."

Kit's eyes caught fire. "I can't. He could be out there, waiting. What are you thinking?"

"That he wouldn't dare try anything in daylight."

"We don't *know* that. I have to give Andy and Phillip time to find him. I have to stay here until it's safe." This wasn't what she wanted to do. She wanted to be out there helping resolve the problem. But what could she do ... she didn't have any idea how to do that, and, God help her, she was afraid. And her fear disgusted her.

"Okay," Teddy said. "I want to do whatever makes you feel comfortable."

They spent the rest of the day in edgy companionship in Kit's apartment. For lunch, Kit called down to Bunny's and had a couple of burgers sent up along with two orders of her famous Cajun-spiced french fries and a gallon of sweet iced tea. She also placed an order for the day-shift cop watching over her. He picked up the food at the gate and brought it up to the apartment. Believing it would compromise the security he was providing for him to remain in the apartment and eat, he took his back to the courtyard.

Kit and Teddy spent the evening watching movies from Kit's classic DVD collection, which ran largely to epic films with Richard Burton in them.

For dinner, they had a couple of steaks from Kit's freezer. After dinner, they watched *Cleopatra*. Around ten o'clock, Kit want into the bathroom to wash her face. Looking into the mirror she was horrified to see how the stress of the last twenty-four hours had caused her eyes to look dark and sunken.

Dark and sunken …

Her mind flashed back to the day before, when she was looking at the morgue admission photos of Jennifer Hendrin. Dark and sunken …

A vague presence that had been trying to swim up out of her subconscious got close enough to the surface so it shimmered just below perception.

She went back into the living room, where Teddy was looking out the window. "I have to go to the office."

Teddy turned toward her, his surprise at this announcement obvious. "What for?"

"Something he hasn't been able to define has been bothering Andy about one of those frozen bodies. I may know what it is."

CHAPTER 20

TEDDY BROUGHT HIS TRUCK down Toulouse and stopped at Kit's gate, which opened the moment he arrived.

Kit emerged and hurried the few steps to the truck. She pulled the door open and climbed in. Behind her, the cop on guard watched through the open gate until they pulled away. He had offered to get his squad car and follow them to the ME's office. At first Kit agreed, then, more worried about returning home after it had been left unguarded, she changed her mind and asked that he stay behind and keep the place secure.

The NOPD had established a curfew in the city. In the Quarter and the business district, no one could be on the streets after midnight. In other areas, the curfew was less generous. Since it was now only ten o'clock and Kit and Teddy's route to the bridge out of New Orleans would stay entirely within the midnight curfew zone, they didn't have to worry about being stopped by the cops and questioned.

Of course, that wasn't the foremost issue on Kit's mind. In the truck, she nervously kept her eyes roving: rear-view mirror, intersection ahead, the lone man strolling down the sidewalk on the right, the deep, dark doorway on the left.

Behind them, about a block away, she noticed a vehicle at the curb flick on its lights. It pulled onto Toulouse and slowly began moving.

Teddy hung a left at Chartres Street.

As they reached the intersection with St. Peter a few seconds later, Kit saw headlights behind them turn onto Chartres from Toulouse and head their way.

Teddy turned left on St. Peter.

Telling herself it was just a coincidence the car behind them had also gone east on Chartres, Kit kept her eyes on the rearview mirror, hoping the mystery car would sail through the St. Peter intersection and disappear.

Instead, it turned onto St. Peter just as they had.

Okay, Kit thought. *Don't overreact. This is just the quickest route out of the Quarter. It's not surprising we're both going the same way.*

The vehicle remained a block behind them all the way to North Rampart, where Teddy took another left. Her eyes riveted to the rearview mirror, Kit silently urged the vehicle behind them to turn right.

It didn't.

"I'm not certain," Kit said, "but someone may be following us."

"I've been watching him too," Teddy said. "Still too soon to know for sure."

Just to be prepared, Kit reached for her Ladysmith and held it in her lap.

There was very little traffic on Rampart and many of the streetlamps and stoplights were not working, so outside the Quarter, the city was a more desolate place than within. That made the presence of the trailing vehicle seem like much more than a random event.

At Canal Street, Teddy made a right.

A few seconds later, the suspect vehicle did the same.

Kit's grip on the Ladysmith tightened.

This went on for seven blocks. At Claiborne, Teddy turned left.

Twenty seconds later, Kit said, "Here he comes."

"Let's see if he follows us onto the expressway."

He did.

"Now are you convinced he's following us?" Kit asked.

"I'm getting there." Teddy leaned back in his seat, unfastened a lower button on his shirt, and did a dry reach for the .22 pistol holstered inside his pants.

"He doesn't seem to be getting any closer," Kit said, watching the mirror.

"Maybe he's going to make his move after we stop."

"There's a police substation on the way to the office. Gretna wasn't flooded, so it's bound to be staffed. We'll stop there and tell them we're being followed."

"Suppose we aren't?"

"We'll apologize for bothering them."

When Teddy left the expressway in Gretna, the vehicle followed. On this side of the river Katrina had caused much less havoc, so while the street wasn't heavily traveled, there were now other cars in each lane.

"If he was going to try something, seems like he should have done it back in New Orleans, where there are fewer people around," Teddy said.

Behind them, Kit saw a car pull out of a side street so it was now between them and the suspect vehicle. "That does seem odd."

A block from the police substation, Kit saw the trailing vehicle make a left and disappear.

"He's gone," Kit said, the tension draining out of her. "He *wasn't* following us." She put the Ladysmith back in its holster.

"Maybe the attack on you was just a spontaneous one-time thing," Teddy suggested, "and he has no intention of trying again."

"I can't afford to think like that."

"You're right. We have to stay alert."

They passed the police substation, which had lots of lights visible through the windows. A couple of squad cars were parked out front.

"You never said what it is you think might be on the autopsy photo," Teddy said a couple of blocks later. "... Damn, what's wrong with that guy ..." He flicked his high beams on and off to tell the oncoming vehicle in the opposite lane that his were on full blast.

The other driver ignored the message.

"What a jerk," Teddy said. "Somebody should ..."

The windshield suddenly exploded into a huge cobweb as something tore through it and buried itself in the seat beside Teddy's left shoulder. Another hit the windshield to the right of the first, spreading the web and zipping past Kit's left ear before it smashed into the rear window, which shattered and fell onto the back seat. As the vehicle in the opposite lane roared by, the driver's window of Teddy's truck shattered. A projectile ripped through the cab and ticked the tip of Teddy's nose. It traced a fiery trail across Kit's forehead and then smashed out the passenger window.

Flinching in surprise at the shocking onslaught, Teddy jerked the wheel to the left. Unable to see anything through the windshield, but knowing the truck was out of control, he hit the brakes. The rear end of the truck fishtailed to the right, then it tipped up so both right wheels were a foot off the pavement. It crossed the opposite lane on two wheels, then settled back to earth before crashing into a lamp pole. The impact sheared off the pole, and it fell onto the truck, collapsing the roof.

Fifty yards away, the vehicle from which the attack had come turned onto a side street and sped into the night.

CHAPTER 21

KIT HAD NO IDEA if she was hurt. She seemed able to breathe without pain and thought she could feel all her extremities. The caved-in truck roof formed a partition between her and Teddy. All she could see of him was his lower half. He wasn't moving.

Despair possessed her. He couldn't be dead … he just couldn't be. "Teddy … are you hurt?"

His left foot moved. *He moved.*

She heard his voice: "I'm okay. Are you?"

"I think so." She turned and tried to open the door, but it wouldn't budge. "My door is jammed."

There was a reverberating bang as Teddy threw his warped door open. "Be right there."

Three seconds later, he appeared on her side. He grabbed the door handle, braced one foot against the truck body, and heaved. With a screech of metal, the door opened. He reached in and unhooked Kit's seatbelt. She grabbed his offered hand, and he hauled her from the wreck.

For a moment, they stood looking at each other as though they'd been apart for years. They fell into each other's arms.

"I saw you weren't moving, and I was *so* afraid," Kit breathed into his ear.

"Just before you called out to me," Teddy said. "I was trying to get up the courage to check on you."

They released each other, and Kit's hand went gently to Teddy's left temple. "You've got a cut there … you're still bleeding. And also one on your nose."

"You've got one, too, a long one, running horizontally across your forehead. It doesn't look deep. The blood is already clotting."

"A bullet did it. That must have been the guy who was following us. He turned off so he could get in front and come at us head on."

"Not much doubt there."

They were suddenly caught in the glare of oncoming headlights from the near lane. Fearing their attacker had returned, they bolted for the opposite side of the truck and reached for their weapons as they dropped into a crouch.

"Hello there," a female voice called out. "Do you need help?"

Kit rose and carefully looked out between the hood of the truck and the fallen lamppost suspended above it. From the streetlights on the opposite side of the road, she saw that the question had come from a woman dressed in a waitress uniform standing on the far side of her car.

Feeling it was safe, Kit stood and came into view, making sure she kept her gun hand behind her. Teddy did the same from the rear of the truck.

"We're not hurt," Kit said, "but would you stop at the police station just down the road and tell them we've had an incident here?"

"I will." The waitress got in her car and drove off.

"We should get out of sight until the cops arrive," Teddy suggested.

They moved behind some shrubs, and Kit got out her cell phone.

"Who are you calling?" Teddy asked.

"Andy."

BROUSSARD CROSSED HIS LEGS in the big leather chair next to the wall of books in his study and shifted his weight onto his left buttock. In his hand was a well-worn paperback edition of *Crossfire Trail* by Louis L'Amour, one of his favorites by that author. Apart from enjoying the western setting in L'Amour novels, he loved the moral clarity in them, good always prevailing over evil. Tonight, facing frustration and anger over his own inability to find the monster who'd killed Jennifer Hendrin and attacked Kit, he sought refuge in a fictional world where he could succeed.

He read another half page before his stomach growled again. In the refrigerator was a lovely spinach quiche he had made four hours ago. He sometimes had his most insightful thoughts while cooking. But even that hadn't helped him find the answers he needed.

In the refrigerator, too, was a nice lively bottle of Beaujolais, which would perfectly compliment the quiche.

Those were to have been his dinner. But like a little boy who has been bad, he had decided he should not be rewarded for his work that day, but go to bed hungry. It was the only penance he could think of for failing Kit when she needed him.

He read another half page.

His stomach growled again, much louder this time. He looked toward the study doorway, imagining a large piece of quiche on his fork, heading for his mouth.

No, he wouldn't give in.

At the bottom of the next page, just as Rafe Caradec shot the skulking Gee Bonaro, Broussard's stomach threatened him. He looked toward the door. That quiche wouldn't stay fresh forever. Be a shame to let it spoil ... criminal, actually.

Not wanting to be a criminal, he got up and put the book on the end table by his chair. He would do his penance tomorrow, when he wouldn't be wasting food.

Ten minutes later, as he sat back at the kitchen table, savoring the last splash of wine in his glass, the phone on the wall rang.

He got up and answered it. "Broussard."

"It's Kit. Teddy and I have had a problem."

"What do you mean?"

"We were on our way to the office and were shot at in Teddy's truck, most likely by the same guy who attacked me."

Alarmed and upset that his poor investigative skills had apparently put Kit in danger again, he said, "Either of you hurt?"

"We're fine, but the truck is in bad shape. We hit a light pole."

"Where are you?"

"On LaFayette, a few blocks from the office."

"I'll be right there."

"I'm going to see if the cops will take us to the office. If we're not at the scene, that's where we'll be."

A POLICE PATROL CAR arrived a few minutes later, and Kit and Teddy told them their story.

"What kind of car was it?" the older of the two officers asked, looking up from the little note pad where he was entering the facts as Kit related them.

"We never got a good look at it. When it was following us, it was too far away, then when it was coming toward us, the brights were on, blinding us."

"You're not giving us much to go on."

"It's not by intention."

The cop glanced at Teddy's truck. "You can't drive that anymore. Is there someone you can call to come and get you?"

Kit said, "We've already done that. He's going to meet us at the ME's temporary offices down the street in the Gretna Green shopping center. Could you drop us there?"

"Sure. We'll have to wait for the wrecker first. And we need to have someone take a look at those wounds before we let you go. There's an ambulance on the way."

"Where will they take my truck?" Teddy asked.

"I'll give you the address." The cop flipped to a fresh page in his note pad. He jotted down an address and phone number, tore out the page, and gave it to Teddy, who looked at it briefly and tucked it into his wallet.

An ambulance appeared from the same direction the cops had come. For the next few minutes, Kit and Teddy received more medical attention than either felt was necessary. While their wounds were being cleaned and bandaged, the tow truck arrived.

Eight minutes later, after Kit and Teddy had repeatedly refused the suggestion by the paramedic tending them that they go to the hospital for a better medical evaluation than could be conducted in the field, Teddy's truck was towed off to the Gretna version of pick-up heaven. Broussard had not yet arrived.

"We can give you that ride now," the cop said.

The cop's partner, a square-jawed young man wearing frameless eyeglasses with wire temples, said, "Sure you want to go to the office? Suppose the guy who shot at you shows up over there?"

"I hope he does," Kit said.

The older cop gave her a hard look. "That sounds like your carrying."

"We both are," she replied. "It's okay; we're legal."

"Just don't shoot him in the back."

"I'll have to think about that."

Kᴵᴛ ᴋᴇʏᴇᴅ ᴛʜᴇ ꜰʀᴏɴᴛ door of the ME's offices and went inside, Teddy following. Seeing they were safely off the street, the cop behind the wheel of the cruiser that brought them pulled away.

Before moving in, Broussard had the glass-paneled front door and the big glass windows facing onto the mall painted black, so when Kit flicked on the lights, it wasn't obvious from the outside that anyone was there.

She locked the front door and looked at Teddy. "I'm sorry about your truck. It's all my fault."

"How do you figure?"

"The guy who shot at us was after me."

"It wasn't you who shot up the truck; it was him."

"You know what I mean."

"I do, and I reject the suggestion you're responsible in any way. Besides, it's just a truck. I know where I can buy another one. See, I go to this place, knock on the door, and when somebody comes to the little sliding peep hole in it, I show them my credit card."

"I appreciate you saying that."

"It's what I really think."

"Let's do what we came here for."

With Teddy trailing behind her, Kit headed for Broussard's office.

"What exactly *is* the purpose of our trip?" Teddy asked a few moments later as they waited for Broussard's computer to boot up.

"To take another look at something I saw yesterday."

"Because …"

"I'm not sure."

When the computer was ready, she navigated to the folder containing Jennifer Hendrin's autopsy photos and opened it. She clicked on the close-up of the face she had looked at earlier.

A sound came from the front door, and they both turned their heads in that direction, even though all they could see was the hallway.

"Anyone here?" a voice called out.

It was Broussard.

"We're in your office," Kit shouted, turning her attention back to the disgusting image filling the computer screen.

Seconds later, Broussard appeared in the doorway. Behind him was Phil Gatlin.

"What the devil are you …" Broussard began.

"Come look at this picture of Jennifer Hendrin."

Broussard walked over to Kit's chair. Teddy moved out of the way so Broussard could see the image. He studied it and said, "What am I lookin' for?"

"Her body floated in flood waters for over a week, right?"

"Yes."

"And she was found face down in the water …"

"Also correct."

"Why then is she still wearing eye make-up?"

CHAPTER 22

E*YE MAKE-UP*, B*ROUSSARD THOUGHT* as he pushed the speed limit on the now nearly deserted expressway, heading to the morgue in St. Gabriel. *That's* what had been bothering him about Jennifer Hendrin's body. What was wrong with him? How could he have missed that? It was so apparent on the photo Kit had shown him. Not seeing it on Hendrin was bad enough, but the pictures he'd just looked at of the other two bodies found with Hendrin ... They had it, too. It was embarrassing and demoralizing. This kind of thing was just not acceptable. Maybe after this was over, he ought to think about retiring. But right now, he had a killer to catch, and he wanted to see the eye make-up in person, because there was no way it should have survived that kind of exposure to water. He nudged the gas and increased his speed, so absorbed in thought he forgot that Gatlin, Kit, and Teddy were following in Gatlin's Pontiac.

"W*HAT'S THE MATTER WITH* that old geezer?" Gatlin groused, as Broussard's T-Bird suddenly shot forward into the night, leaving him behind. "If I had a ticket book with me, I'd write him up."

"He's angry with himself," Kit explained from the passenger seat beside him, surprised Gatlin didn't get that. "… for not seeing the make-up on those bodies."

"That's the trouble with him," Gatlin said. "He thinks he's perfect. When he finds out he isn't, he can't handle it. Now I gotta break the law, too." He stepped on the gas, and the Pontiac responded with a shudder and a hesitation. It found its stride, and Kit was thrown back in her seat as they went after Broussard, whose taillights were now barely visible.

The way both cars were speeding, Kit didn't have to worry about anyone overtaking them from behind. But whenever they passed someone in the oncoming lane, she flinched, expecting another attack. By the time they reached the turnoff at St. Gabriel, she was exhausted from the tension.

They drove for nearly a mile more and didn't see another car, but Kit was still frazzled when, through the windshield of the old Pontiac, she saw Broussard turn into a driveway and stop at a small security kiosk. The guard looked back at the Pontiac and waved an acknowledgement that they'd be allowed in.

Broussard led them up the long drive to the mortuary, where he parked his T-Bird in an unmarked spot at the foot of a tall light pole. Gatlin maneuvered the Pontiac around and backed into a spot beside the T-Bird. By the time he came to a stop, Broussard was outside motioning for him to roll down his window.

"We're not workin' two shifts any more, so I'm gonna need a hand," Broussard said through the open window. "Preferably somebody tall, with a sour disposition … I guess that'd be you, Phillip."

"I didn't see anyone following us," Kit said from the passenger seat. "But I'm not comfortable sitting exposed out here."

"You and Teddy can wait inside in clerical while Phillip helps me."

They all got out of the Pontiac and headed for the mortuary's side door. The light pole where Broussard had parked cast eerie shadows on the warehouse dock serving the line of refrigerated trucks that housed the dead not yet identified or released. Kit had heard about those trucks, but this being her first visit to the site, she had never seen them. The thought of so many lost souls languishing inside them made her momentarily forget her own problems.

Broussard keyed the lock in the side door, and everyone followed him inside.

With all the bodies locked away, the air conditioning had managed to evacuate all but the tiniest trace of an odor.

Tonight, the security desk was being manned by Romeil Bettis, owner of Bettis First Response Security, who, like so many others, was volunteering his services.

When the place was empty as it was tonight, Bettis did a walk around every half hour. In the few minutes between circuits, he'd read. Tonight, it was *The Art of War* by Sun Tzu, a book Broussard had loaned him.

"Dr. B.," Bettis said, putting down his book and standing up. "Didn't expect you tonight." Bettis had a wide face with a long chin. His short beard was totally gray, but the thick hair on his head was the color of the roan gelding Broussard had once lost money on when Phillip said he was a sure thing.

"Spur of the moment visit," Broussard said. He did a quick introduction of everyone with him and said, "We probably won't be here long. I want to take a look at a couple of our clients. We're gonna stop in clerical to see where they are, then we'll need a gurney out on the dock and whichever truck they're in unlocked."

"After you all sign in, I'll get right on it," Bettis said.

He watched them to make sure everyone put their name on his sheet, then he flicked on a few more light switches and accompanied them down the blue tarp-lined corridor to clerical.

As they walked, Kit felt the heavy weight of death all around her. She glanced at Teddy and saw that he looked apprehensive and uncomfortable. She couldn't tell how Gatlin was reacting because he was in front of her.

Reaching the clerical area, Bettis said, "I'll go ahead and get a gurney lined up."

Broussard asked, "You got rubber gloves?"

Bettis patted his pocket. "Always carry a few."

"Thanks. We'll be out in a minute."

Everyone else followed Broussard into clerical, where he went to the rolling file cabinet containing the records for bodies with numbers between 400 and 500. He thumbed through them until he found 427. Noting that the tab on the file now included Jennifer Hendrin's name, he checked her location. It was likely 428 and 429 were in the same truck, but he checked those locations as well just to be sure.

From somewhere close by, they heard the squeal of an overhead door opening: Bettis preparing to take a gurney out on the dock.

Broussard looked at Kit. "We'll be back soon as we can. Phillip, come on, we should suit up."

Broussard led Phillip to the dressing area, where he helped the old detective into a disposable jump suit.

"I'm not gonna have wet stuff sloshing on me, am I?" Gatlin said, zipping up his suit.

"We're not washing a car," Broussard said, stepping into the legs of a suit.

"Then why we doing all this?"

"Protection against the unexpected."

"The unexpected ... Yeah ... That's always what gets you."

They finished dressing, put on masks and gloves, and headed for the loading dock, Broussard carrying the flashlight he'd brought from his car.

Their route led them through body reception. When they emerged onto the dock, Bettis was waiting.

"Number six, if you please," Broussard said.

"Say, what happened to those two people with you ... those bandages on their faces?" Bettis said.

"They were in an accident earlier tonight."

"Glad to see they both walked away from it." He headed over to a truck with a big red number six taped to the side near the rear. He keyed the lock in its overhead door and rolled it up with a clatter that, to Gatlin, seemed blasphemous, like shouting in church. The cold air inside rolled out and curled around Phillip's legs.

"You don't need me in there, I hope," Bettis said.

"We can handle it," Broussard replied.

"Then I'll just get out of your way and have a smoke."

Broussard flicked on the overhead lights in the truck, illuminating the metal racks lining each side of the interior. On those racks, stacked three high, were black body bags, each looking, Gatlin thought, like some huge cocoon. Except nothing was going to emerge from those cocoons, at least not on their own power.

"Get that gurney will you?" Broussard said.

Gatlin pushed the gurney to the truck, where Broussard helped it navigate the little height difference between the truck and the dock. Broussard then started down the aisle, reading the numbers on the racks. He found Jennifer Hendrin halfway back on the lowest rack.

"Here she is."

Gatlin pushed the gurney to where Broussard waited. He lined it up so it was opposite the rack containing Jennifer Hendrin's remains.

"On three," Broussard said, reaching down for his end of the bag. When Gatlin had a good grip on his end, Broussard started the count. At three, they lifted her gently onto the gurney. Broussard unzipped the bag partway and pulled it down so the cadaver's head was accessible.

Gatlin stepped back and turned away.

Broussard pulled his flashlight from where he'd stowed it in a pocket of his jumpsuit, then flicked it on and bent over. He played the light onto Hendrin's bulging dead eyes and looked at her more closely than he ever had.

Oh for the love of … How had he missed that? "I'm ready to put her back."

Gatlin turned. Picking up on the anger in Broussard's voice, he said, "What's wrong?"

"That's what I'd like to know."

"So you're mad … but you don't know why?"

Broussard zipped up the body bag and put his flashlight back in his pocket. "On three …"

They lowered her onto her shelf.

Broussard backed up, pulling the gurney with him. He pointed at the body on the upper shelf of the next rack. "Now that one."

Because it was higher, the reach to get this one was awkward, and Broussard felt a twinge in his back as the bag slid off the shelf. He almost lost his grip, but managed to hold on long enough to get her down onto the gurney without dropping her. As Broussard unzipped the bag, Gatlin once again moved away and averted his eyes.

Ten seconds later, staring down into the flashlight-illuminated mouth of this bag, Broussard experienced a rush of pleasure at the pattern he saw emerging. But it was wrapped around a stab of pain because of his incompetence at missing it earlier, not once but twice. And it was almost a certainty that after he looked at 428, it would be even worse.

He zipped up the bag. "Hands needed."

Gatlin stepped back to the gurney and waited a moment to see if Broussard was ready to tell him what the hell he'd seen. With no explanation forthcoming, Gatlin grabbed hold of the bag, and they returned 428 to its temporary home.

They repeated their ritual with 429. When it was replaced on its shelf, Gatlin forced the issue. "Okay, I'm officially tired of waiting. Talk."

"I have no idea why I didn't notice it earlier, but whoever killed these women tattooed eyeliner on them."

CHAPTER 23

"MAYBE I SHOULD RETIRE," Broussard said, looking at Gatlin over the empty gurney where, a moment ago, he'd seen the same tattooing on body 429 as on the other two murdered surrogates.

"What are you talking about?" Gatlin asked.

"I looked at all those bodies earlier twice, and I never noticed those tattoos. I'm not fit to do this anymore."

"You made a mistake. Big deal. Something got past you."

"Ten years ago that wouldn't have happened."

"Ten years ago I didn't have to get up five times a night to take a leak. Neither of us is what we once were. Get over it."

"Don't think I can."

"Look, up till a few days ago, you were working ridiculous hours. It was probably just fatigue catching up with you."

"I can't accept that."

Gatlin leveled his index finger at his old friend. "There's your *real* problem. It's not that you're getting old, or you occasionally lose focus when your glutes are dragging in the mud. You're just so accustomed to being this perfect intellect who's smarter than anyone else, you're not willing to come off your pedestal and mix with the commoners."

"Is that really who I am?"

D.J. DONALDSON

"It hasn't been … until now. But that's because you never had to face it. Now you do. How you handle it will determine if you're really that person. If you're not, you admit to a mistake and move on. You don't take your ball and go home."

Broussard looked at his old friend without responding. He'd never thought of himself as Phillip had described him. It was true he loved always being a step ahead of everyone else in analyzing a crime scene, but was he a snob about it? Because that's what Phillip was saying. The shock of this new perspective took his mind off the mistake he'd made.

"Could we get out of here now?" Phillip said. "I'm starting to hear the people in these bags whisper things."

"Let's go then."

They wheeled the gurney back onto the dock and turned it over to Bettis.

"We're gonna spend a few minutes in clerical before we leave," Broussard said.

"Okay," Bettis said. "If I hear any noises in there, I won't start shooting. Did you find what you were looking for in the truck?"

"I did."

In CLERICAL, KIT AND Teddy got out of their chairs as Broussard and Gatlin entered.

"We know something now that we didn't before," Broussard said. "He tattooed eyeliner on all three victims. And it was crudely done, so he's not a pro at it."

Okay, Kit thought. *Now we're getting somewhere.* She'd seen Broussard do so much with far less in the past, she was sure he could use this new information to huge advantage.

"Any idea why he'd do that?" Teddy asked.

"We think he liked to play dress-up with his frozen victims," Broussard said. "My guess is when he took 'em out of the freezer for his fun, they'd thaw a little and their eyeliner would run. He must like eyes to look just right."

Exactly, Kit thought. Her hopes they would soon be hot on the trail of the man who attacked her escalated.

"Where do these nuts come from?" Gatlin said.

"If I knew, I'd put a stop to it," Broussard said.

"What do we do now?" Kit asked.

"Add this to the details we've already sent VICAP … see if this helps them in any way," Broussard replied.

That's it? Kit thought. *Where were the brilliant insights she was expecting?* "What are the chances that will help?"

"Let's just do it and not speculate on the outcome."

Kit nodded. His reluctance to express any optimism at all over this meant he didn't feel any. And why should he if that's all he could think of? The best VICAP could probably do would be to tie the Ninth Ward victims into other cases in their files. It wouldn't help catch the guy. If he'd been a professional tattoo artist, maybe it would have clarified a suspect for them. But Broussard said he was an amateur. VICAP wouldn't help at all.

"Fire up one of those computers, would you?" Broussard asked Kit. "We'll relay this new information from here."

Though she felt it was likely a waste of time, Kit simply said, "Sure."

"I believe the phrase is 'boot up,'" Gatlin said.

Realizing Gatlin was testing him to see if they were still friends, Broussard said, "Aren't you the guy who once did an oil change on a car with the drain plug in his pocket?"

"I might be."

"Then you won't be offended if we wait for technical advice from someone a little more credible."

"Your choice."

They looked at each other for just an instant. Kit was focused on the computer they were going to use, and Teddy was watching her. So neither of them saw the slight nod of understanding Gatlin and Broussard exchanged.

When the computer was ready, Kit drafted an e-mail to Broussard's friend at VICAP and they sent it on its way.

"That's all we can do tonight," Broussard said. "Unless Teddy wants to follow up on his damaged truck."

"There's nothing I can accomplish this late."

"Guess then we'll just go back to my place," Kit said. She looked at Gatlin. "Will you give us a ride?"

"Of course."

ON THE WAY BACK to New Orleans, Broussard thought about what Gatlin had said regarding him being an intellectual snob. He didn't want to be that. But he also couldn't accept the way things had been going. Take that look of disappointment on Kit's face when she'd asked what their next step would be, and all he could come up with was to send the information on to VICAP. It hurt that he couldn't do better. How could Phillip expect him to just shrug something like that off? Was it snobbery to be upset with your inability to help your friends when they desperately needed you?

KIT WAS JUST AS fidgety on the ride back as she had been coming to St. Gabriel, still flinching every time an oncoming car passed, worried about every vehicle behind them. Despite her concerns that they'd be attacked again, they made it back to New Orleans without any problems.

"WHAT HAPPENED TO YOU two?" the cop in Kit's courtyard inquired when he saw Kit and Teddy.

Reminded of its existence, Kit touched her bandage. "Somebody shot at our truck, and we hit a lamp pole."

"Sounds like you're lucky to look as good as you do. He get away?"

"So far."

"I'm sorry I wasn't there to help."

"Don't be. It was my call to have you stay behind."

Reaching her apartment, Kit locked the door and sagged back against it. "Lord, I am *so* tired."

Teddy came close and tenderly stroked a stray lock of hair away from her forehead. "You should get some sleep."

She shook her head. "I can't. He might try to get us even here. We can't let him find us asleep."

"We'll sleep in two-hour shifts. I'll watch while you sleep, then we'll switch."

"Guess that'd be all right. But we should stay in the same room … not separate. And we shouldn't watch TV. We want to be able to hear any unusual sounds."

"I'll read," Teddy said. He walked over, pulled a book from the shelves flanking the fireplace, and checked out the jacket blurb. "This one looks good."

"What is it?"

"Old Man's War."

"Good choice. Now I have to make a pit stop."

"Would you like me to …"

"Watching me shower is one thing … I'll do this by myself, thanks."

She returned a few minutes later and stretched out on the sofa.

"Two hours ... then it's your turn."

Teddy nodded and opened his book.

BROUSSARD WASN'T *AFRAID* TO sleep. He was still so upset with himself sleep was impossible. He wandered into his study and once again picked up *Cross Fire Trail*.

He read for nearly two hours, pausing at intervals when thoughts of his impotence to move the investigation forward pulled his vision inward. Finally, he read the last sentence and fondly closed the book. Sated and satisfied with his vicarious achievements *a la* L'Amour, his head slowly fell forward and he, too, slept.

But even in slumber, Broussard was troubled, his mind a loose storm door rattling with each stentorian breath he took. Eventually, a great exhalation blew that door wide open with such force the sound of it ripping from its hinges woke him, a possible way to advance the investigation standing on his doorstep.

CHAPTER 24

BROUSSARD HAD NEVER BEEN known to distrust knives because sometimes they were used as murder weapons. He had never blamed a hammer for killing anyone. But he had a strong dislike for computers because they could provide an avenue into your life by which your privacy could be compromised. When Gatlin had once pointed out the inconsistency in Broussard's view of hammers versus computers, Broussard had said, "No hammer ever stole anyone's identity." Unable to argue with someone who thinks like that, Gatlin had given up all further discussion on the point. All of which explains why Broussard didn't have a computer in his home and had to go back to the office to check out his idea.

Sitting in front of his office computer, Broussard entered *KILLER WHO TATTOOS HIS VICTIMS* into the Internet search box. He was well aware that the likelihood of this endeavor yielding anything of immediate significance was about as remote as the possibilities associated with his report to VICAP. That he was turning to a computer for help showed how desperate he was.

A second later, the first 10 of 419 hits appeared on his monitor.

The very first entry caught his attention: *Guardian Angels Join Search For West Atlantic City Killer*. The few sentences accompanying the title line mentioned four victims and some tattoos found on a third victim. He clicked on the link. But all that produced was a thumbnail story with no further mention of tattoos.

It was now nearly eight o'clock. Broussard had left the house without even having a cup of coffee. It was, therefore, no surprise his stomach felt like it had been bored out by one of those giant machines that tunnel through mountains. Ignoring the discomfort, he went back to the list of hits his search had produced. Most of them concerned serial killers with tattoos on their own body.

He clicked on the next set of results.

This page was cluttered with references to fictional events on TV shows.

He tried the next set. And the next.

After he'd combed through a hundred entries, most of which hadn't the slightest pertinence to what he was looking for, his enthusiasm was noticeably waning. But at least he was doing *something*.

He moved on to the next ten results.

At the top of the page, the first entry was titled, *Night Demon*. He read further: *Stalk your victims and elude capture. Find a safe place for the freezer to store your victims.*

What the devil *was* this?

He followed the link.

This took him to what was obviously a thumbnail sketch of some video game.

His first impulse was to move on, but *freezer to store your victims ...* that seemed too much on point to ignore.

He picked up the phone and punched in a number. It rang twice and was then answered by a familiar voice.

"Dis is Gramma O. Why you callin' me so early?"

"Mornin'."

"City Boy. You comin' in for breakfast?"

"I'm not sure. I've got somethin' I have to do first, and I need Bubba's help. Is he there?"

"He's in da kitchen, peelin' potatoes. I don't mind if he stays with me 'till he gets his insurance money to rebuild his place, but he's gotta earn his way. Which means he can't be runnin' off to fool around with you ... unless a course it's important."

"I think it might be."

'You jus' think ... you don't know?"

"Not yet."

"I'll get him."

After a short interval, Bubba picked up. "Dr. B ... what's wrong? One of da birds actin' up?"

In addition to his mechanical skills, Bubba was a noted video game addict. If anybody had knowledge of Night Demon, it would be him.

"The cars are fine. Do you know anything about a video game called Night Demon?"

"Dat's a sick one. I never played it, but I heard about it. Whoever plays it takes da role of a serial killer who hunts down women. Dat's all I know. Why you askin' about ... Oooh, you thinkin' dere's a tie-in with da case you're workin'?"

"At this point, I have no idea. But I'd like to explore the possibility. Any place locally I could get a copy right now?"

"Dere's a guy over in Westwego ... Billy Daughtry, he owns all kinda games ... He especially likes nasty ones. He might have it."

"Can you call him and find out?"

"He doesn't have a phone."

"Do you know him well enough that if he does have a copy, he'd let you borrow it?"

"He might."

Westwego, where Daughtry lived, was west of Broussard's temporary offices and on the same side of the river. "I'm at the Gretna office. Could we go over to this guy's house together now?"

"I don't know … I'm kinda workin' here in da kitchen."

"I already got you a reprieve on that."

"On my way …"

B ROUSSARD OPENED THE DOOR to let Bubba in and saw he was carrying a paper bag.

"Thanks for gettin' me out a dere," Bubba said. "I peeled so many potatoes dis mornin' I was startin' to *feel* like one."

"Exactly what goes through a potato's mind?" Broussard asked.

"He wishes somebody would call and get him a reprieve."

"What's in the bag?"

"Somethin' from Gramma O."

Bubba handed Broussard the bag.

The old pathologist looked inside, inhaled over the bag deeply, and smiled for the first time in days. "Fresh croissants."

"Along with some blackberry jam," Bubba said. "And a course, some coffee and cream. I'm supposed to be sure you eat somethin' before we go get dat game."

"I'm not about to disobey Grandma O. Come on back to my office."

Reaching his office, Broussard went behind his desk and offered Bubba the other chair.

"There's only one cup in here," Broussard said as he emptied the bag.

"I already ate. So you jus' go ahead."

Grandma O had even thought to include a real case knife and some napkins. For the next few minutes, the hard edges of life since Katrina seemed a bit more bearable as Broussard ate the flaky, buttery croissants generously spread with Grandma O's homemade blackberry preserves and drank the rich, earthy coffee she made from her own blend of five different coffee beans whose names she had never divulged. But when he washed down the last bite with the final mouthful from his cup, it all came back sharp as ever.

BILLY DAUGHTRY LIVED IN a small white clapboard house with a dirt driveway and a hard scrabble yard where even weeds had a hard time growing. Near the house, as close to the porch steps as it could be parked, sat a battered old green Volkswagen.

"Dat's his car, so looks like he's home," Bubba said.

"What's he do for a livin'?" Broussard asked as he pulled into the driveway.

"Manages Game World in Kenner."

The windows of the little house were covered on the inside with pull-down shades. As they walked up to the cement block porch, Broussard observed someone push a shade aside and look out.

Bubba saw it too, and waved.

As Bubba reached the foot of the steps, the front door swung open. A barefoot man wearing khakis and a collared, blue, pullover shirt bearing a Game World logo on the pocket stepped onto the porch. Even though Bubba had said Daughtry managed that business, Broussard was expecting a kid. But this guy, who badly needed a shave, was in his mid-thirties.

"Smurfette," Daughtry called out to Bubba. "Good to see you. Thought maybe you'd drowned."

"Nahh. All us Oustellettes float. See you still got a roof."

"I would have thought, seeing my vast estate here, it would have been obvious I've always been blessed by good fortune. Who's your friend?"

"I'm Andy."

"Andy what?"

"Broussard."

"That your car?"

"Yes."

"Sweet ride. Had it long?"

"Quite awhile."

"Have you noticed it's starting to get a little snug on you?"

Broussard thought of a cutting comeback, but in the interest of getting his hands on Daughtry's copy of Night Demon, instead chose a benign response. "Now that you mention it, I have."

"So what's up?" Daughtry said.

"You got a copy a Night Demon?" Bubba asked.

"Yeah, I do. Why?"

"Could we borrow it for a few hours?"

"Hey man, you know what your askin'? That's a rare game. One of my favorites. I can't take a chance of losin' it."

It was unusual to be able to see the color of someone's eyes from as far away as Broussard was standing, but Daughtry had gray irises that seemed to shine with a glacial light.

"You've borrowed games from me," Bubba said.

"Yeah, but that was different."

"How?"

"You were the one takin' the risk. Order yourself one. You could go online and find it."

"We want to play it dis mornin'," Bubba said. "I thought we were friends."

Daughtry looked at Bubba for a few seconds and said, "I'll make you a deal. I gotta get to work, but my car won't start. You get it runnin', you can have the game, but just for twenty-four hours."

Broussard's hopes rose. If anybody could get that Volkswagen started, it was Bubba.

Without even a glance at the Volkswagen, Bubba said, "Will it crank?"

"Yeah."

"Get da game."

CHAPTER 25

Bubba finished connecting the wires from his gaming console to Broussard's computer monitor, which Broussard had turned on his desk so it faced the larger part of the room.

"Okay, we're ready," Bubba announced.

Just then the phone rang.

Broussard walked over and answered it. "ME's office."

"I know it's only been a few hours since we last spoke," Kit said on the other end of the line, "but have there been any developments?"

"I'm not sure how it'll help, or if it will at all, but I've located a video game that seems to have elements in it similar to our case. Bubba is sittin' right here beside me, ready to start the game. So I should know more in a half hour or so."

"I want to see, too. Can you wait until I get there?"

"You could be wastin' your time."

"I don't care. I want to be there. Will you wait?"

Broussard was so eager to see the game the thought of *any* delay was hard to accept. But since Kit had such a personal stake in finding the killer, he reluctantly said, "Okay, but I'm only gonna give you twenty-five minutes to get here. After that, we're gonna proceed."

"We're leaving now."

"Be careful."

The line went dead.

Broussard looked at Bubba. "Show's gonna be delayed."

"Who's comin'?"

"Kit and probably Teddy."

"And you only gave 'em twenty-five minutes?"

"At my age, a minute is worth more to me than to them."

KIT HUNG UP AND turned to Teddy. "Will you get my car and bring it to the gate?"

"Has Broussard learned something?"

"Maybe. We'll know better after we get to the office and see what he's got."

"What if we're followed again?"

"I'm going to take care of that."

"How?"

"You just get the car. I'll do the rest. If I don't come out as soon as you pull up to the gate, don't worry. I'll be there shortly."

Before the door shut behind Teddy, Kit again had the phone in her hand.

SIX MINUTES AFTER TEDDY stepped onto Toulouse Street, He Daisy came out of Bunny's side door, carrying a large purse. He was wearing a white blouse and black slacks, his favorite red wig, the same intense red lipstick from the night before, and sunglasses. He walked down to Kit's gate and knocked. The gate opened and he went inside.

Two minutes later, Teddy arrived at the gate in Kit's car and tapped the horn.

The gate swung open. A cheap-looking redhead wearing sunglasses and carrying a large purse came to the car and got in.

Teddy protested. "I'm sorry, Miss, but ..."

The redhead looked at Teddy and slid her glasses down her nose.

Shocked, he gasped, "Kit?"

"Let's go."

This time, no car followed.

"How'd you manage that disguise so fast?" Teddy asked.

"After you left, I called a friend of mine who lives down the street and asked if he could come over and help. If anyone was watching, I was counting on them thinking I was him."

"He was dressed like you are, wearing the wig and lipstick?"

"It was He Daisy. I'm sure I've mentioned him."

"No, this is the first I've heard of ... He Daisy?"

Kit shrugged. "That's what he wants to be called."

"How'd you know he could help on such short notice?"

"He's a painter, likes to work from about eight p.m. till midnight and six till noon. So I knew he'd be home. And he once told me he can get dressed up in five minutes."

"He Daisy ..."

"Right."

"You've got some odd friends."

"And you're normal, being an alligator farmer and all."

Teddy nodded. "Good point."

W HEN THEY REACHED THE ME's office, Kit took off the wig and wiped away as much of the red lipstick as she could. They walked into Broussard's office a minute before his deadline expired.

"Any trouble?" Broussard asked.

"The car doesn't have any bullet holes in it, so I'd say we did okay." She looked at Bubba, who was sitting with the game console in his hand. "Hi Bubba, are you going to be our guide?"

Bubba turned in his seat. "Guess so. Andy told me about you bein' attacked ... twice. I'm sure sorry about dat. Teddy, I wish your truck hadn't hit a pole."

"Which reminds me, I should contact my insurance guy about that some time today," Teddy said.

"How'd you discover this game?" Kit asked Broussard.

"I ran an Internet search for killers who tattoo their victims." In response to her surprised look, he added, "I was desperate. Let's all sit down and let Bubba get started."

While waiting for Kit and Teddy, Broussard and Bubba had brought in the two chairs from Kit's office and placed them in front of the monitor so everyone would have a seat.

They all settled in and Bubba started the game.

"I got a cheat sheet from da Internet while we were waitin', but I haven't looked at it," Bubba said. "I thought we'd just start playin' and see how it goes. From da little book dat came with da game, we're supposed to be a guy stalkin' women. Our goal is to overpower our victims and not get killed or caught."

"Oh, this is a healthy thing to have in stores," Kit said.

"Lotta dese games are on da weird side," Bubba said. "Our main character's name is Nathan."

The game opened in a scene where Nathan was sitting in a car, watching a row of brownstone apartment buildings on a city street similar to what you might see in Boston or New York. The front door on one of the buildings opened, and a stream of young women came out. When they reached the sidewalk, they split up. One went down the sidewalk to the right. Two more went to the left. Two crossed the street to the side where Nathan was parked. One of those who crossed started walking toward Nathan's car. The other went the opposite way.

When the women had dispersed a bit, the scene changed to an aerial view showing all the players. The little movie that had been playing shifted to Nathan's point of view inside the car. The movie stopped.

"Now we have to choose which girl to follow," Bubba said. "Let's take da one dat passed our car."

Bubba worked the console controls, and Nathan left his car and began following the girl Bubba picked. The point of view remained Nathan's.

For the next block, Nathan and the girl passed a number of businesses that were open. Bubba had Nathan stay well behind the girl. Then they hit a block where everything was closed, and there was no traffic.

"I think dis is supposed to be his chance," Bubba said. He manipulated the game controls, and Nathan began walking faster. For a while, the girl didn't appear to know Nathan was closing in.

Nathan began walking faster. He reached in his pocket and pulled out …

"Oh my God," Kit said. "It's a plastic bag. That's what he used on me."

"I don't like dis game," Bubba said. Nathan stopped walking, but the girl didn't.

"We have to see more," Broussard said. "I know it's difficult, but we need you to continue."

Bubba took a deep breath and resumed pressing controls on the console. Nathan began moving again. He quickly shifted into a speed walk that closed the distance between him and the girl.

Now he was only about fifteen feet back. Then ten … five …
As close as he was, the girl didn't appear to know he was there. It
seemed so real, Kit wanted to call out and warn her.

Nathan was now right behind her. He raised the bag. *What
was wrong with that girl? Why didn't she hear him coming? Jesus,
was she deaf?*

Suddenly, the girl turned and opened fire with a snub
nose .38. Nathan collapsed on the sidewalk, and the game screen
mushroomed into a red and black cloud. Green letters blazed
across the screen.

GAME OVER. THANKS FOR PLAYING.

Kit felt like cheering at Nathan's death.

"Well, dat was da wrong girl," Bubba said. "Guess you all
want a try again?"

There was a subdued murmur of assent.

Bubba started a new game. This time, before Nathan got
out of the car, Bubba had him look at the passenger seat. On
it sat a knife and a gun. Nathan picked up the gun. Bubba also
tried to pick up the knife, but he was allowed only one weapon
or the other. Sticking with the gun, Nathan left the car and went
after the girl heading to Nathan's right on the other side of the
street.

The girl turned left at the first intersection. This took her
onto a deserted cityscape that seemed like the opportunity
Nathan was looking for. He began walking faster. This time,
instead of having his plastic bag already out, he had the gun in
his hand. He caught up to the girl, grabbed her, and put the gun
to her head. She screamed.

Up ahead, a cop car suddenly pulled out of a side street.
It screeched to a stop. A cop piled out and aimed his pistol at
Nathan. At the same instant, another cop car squealed to a stop
behind Nathan. The girl squirmed away and ducked into a dark

alley. Nathan raised his gun and fired at the cop ahead of him. Both cops then began blasting away. Nathan fell to the sidewalk riddled with gunshots.

The now-familiar red and black cloud washed over the screen, followed by the green letters: *GAME OVER. THANKS FOR PLAYING.*

Bubba looked at Broussard. "Maybe it's time we used da cheat sheet."

Broussard nodded. "Do that."

Bubba pulled a sheaf of stapled papers off the desk beside the monitor. He read through the first page. "So *dat's* da secret." He looked at Broussard. "*None* a dose first girls we saw are safe to follow."

Bubba started a new game. This time, he had Nathan stay in the car until the girls who had come out of the brownstone were out of sight. The scene shifted back to the brownstone's front door, where another girl emerged.

"Dere's da one we want," Bubba said.

The girl came down the steps and turned to her right, taking her away from Nathan's car.

Nathan got out and followed.

Like the previous two girls, this one quickly reached a dark section of the city. Nathan began to move faster. Soon, he was barely six feet behind her, plastic bag in hand.

Though it was just a game, Kit felt sick to her stomach knowing there was nothing this girl could do to save herself. In the game avatar, she saw Jennifer Hendrin. And she saw herself.

Nathan rushed the girl and slipped the bag over her head. She struggled, and just as Kit had done, slid to the ground.

"It ain't me," Bubba said, putting the console in his lap and lifting his hands up so all could see he wasn't working the controls.

The girl struggled to live, but Nathan twisted the neck of the bag hard against the back of the girl's head. She bucked and kicked, emitting muffled screams.

Kit looked away.

Then it was over. The girl lay still. Nathan waited for Bubba's instructions.

"Do I *have* to keep goin'?" Bubba pleaded to Broussard.

Broussard put a chubby hand on Bubba's shoulder. "We understand it's not you doin' this. You're just demonstratin' the game to us."

Bubba nodded.

Using the cheat sheet for guidance, Bubba had Nathan drag his victim's body into a nearby alley. Nathan returned to his car, drove it to the alley, and loaded the victim into his trunk. He then set out for his lair.

Faced with four different routes he could take, Bubba avoided the one that would have killed Nathan in a collision with a runaway propane truck, another in which he would have drowned when an old bridge collapsed, and a third where he would have been killed by two carjackers.

When Nathan safely reached his hideaway, an abandoned one-room schoolhouse in the country, the game took away Bubba's control.

Nathan carried the body in the back door and put it on a large table with a work light clamped to it. He adjusted the light so it illuminated the victim's face. He wiped off the victim's eye make-up, then reached down to a shelf under the table and brought out a bottle labeled "India Ink". Using a large hat pin, he repeatedly drove the ink into the victim's skin, mimicking eyeliner.

Astounded by the similarity of the game to their real case, Kit muttered, "Jesus."

"I know," Broussard agreed, unable to take his eyes off the monitor.

When Nathan was finished tattooing the victim, he undressed her, carried her to a chest freezer, and dumped her in. He returned to his car. A fade-out occurred, followed by a fade-in that now showed Nathan in his car, cruising a campus parking lot at night. Scattered through the lot, isolated young women were getting out of their cars and heading for the crosswalk that led to the main part of the campus.

"Can we take a break for a minute?" Bubba asked.

"It's pretty gruesome, I agree," Broussard said. "How does this kind of thing get on store shelves? Is there no sense of decency out there?"

"Not really," Bubba replied. "If somebody will buy it, someone will sell it."

"There's no question in my mind that the guy we're after knew about this game and modeled his actions on what he saw here," Kit said. "But that's all it tells us. It doesn't bring us any closer to finding him. They could have sold thousands of copies of the game. And who knows how many original owners have given or traded away their copies."

"All true," Broussard said. "But we're not dealin' with someone who simply copied what he saw in the game. He added a twist of his own."

"All his victims, before he went after me, were surrogates," Kit said.

"Exactly. Whatever caused him to choose that class of victim makes him unique."

"I still don't see how knowing about this game helps us find him."

"Let's watch the rest of it before we think about that. Bubba, can you continue?"

"I think so."

Over the next thirty minutes, Nathan collected and tattooed two more women. Like his first victim, he undressed each of them and put them in his freezer.

After a fade-out and fade-in, everyone watching got to see Nathan do what Broussard had deduced the real killer had done with his victims.

He took each cadaver out of the freezer and fit it with a contraption that circled the torso in two places with metal rings connected by a rod along the victims' spine. Using a loop welded to the rod, he attached each body to a pulley system screwed to the ceiling. He hoisted the bodies until they were suspended with feet barely off the ground. From an adjacent storeroom, he pulled a rack of clothes over to the hanging bodies. While Kit and the others watched with horror, Nathan dressed each of them from the rack. He then sat down in a chair and admired what he'd done.

The scene abruptly shifted to an exterior shot. Five police cruisers pulled into the schoolyard and fanned out in a line. A pair of cops from the first car in the line and another pair from the last one jumped out of their cruisers. Weapons drawn, they circled around to the rear of the schoolhouse. The six cops in the other three cars crouched behind their open doors, weapons ready. One of them called out to Nathan over a megaphone.

"You inside. This is the state police. Come out unarmed with your hands on your head. Do not resist. We are here in numbers. There's no way out of there but through us. You have one minute to make your decision."

Inside, with Bubba controlling the ensuing events, Nathan went to a cache of weapons on a nearby table. Avoiding a grenade launcher that would have exploded in his hands, a machine gun that would have jammed, and a flamethrower whose tank would have been punctured by a police bullet, engulfing him in flames, he chose a pair of semi-automatic shotguns with drum-shaped magazines. He shouldered one of the guns using its carrying strap and cradled the other in his left arm. He emptied a box of cartridges into a pocket in his cargo pants.

The game once again began to play on its own. Grinning smugly, Nathan went to a trapdoor, opened it, and dropped into a prepared tunnel so large he could move through it standing up. He ran down the tunnel to its end and climbed a small ladder.

The scene shifted to a wide-angle exterior shot of the cops hiding behind their cars. In the woods behind them, a camouflaged trap door on the ground opened. Nathan climbed out. He turned and began blasting at the cops with one of the shotguns.

Taken by surprise, the cops by their cars were massacred as Nathan emptied the first gun at them, firing so rapidly the scatter shot couldn't miss.

Hearing the gunfire, the cops behind the schoolhouse came running. But in the time it took them to reach the action, Nathan had switched to his other gun. In seconds, the last four cops lay dead on the ground.

Through the trees, Nathan saw two more cop cars turn onto the school drive from the main road. He popped open the magazine of the shotgun in his hand and reloaded. He then ran to the cruiser nearest the drive and hid in front of it. When the two fresh cruisers arrived, Nathan easily killed the four cops in them.

The game cut to a scene of Nathan listening to the radio in his car, riding happily away from the school. The camera cut to a long shot of Nathan's car disappearing in the distance. Over the image a message appeared. *CONGRATULATIONS. YOU ARE A WINNER. WATCH FOR NIGHT DEMON 2, COMING SOON.*

"I need to wash my hands," Bubba said, getting out of his chair.

"Down the hall to your left," Broussard said. He watched Bubba leave, then said, "That was disappointin'. Watchin' the rest didn't help at all."

"I'm not so sure of that," Kit said, suddenly standing and pointing to the screen.

Broussard turned just in time to see what she meant.

CHAPTER 26

"GAME DESIGNED AND DEVELOPED by Marion Marshall," Broussard read from the credits. "Are you thinkin' ...?"

"Go with me a minute," Kit said excitedly. "Suppose Marion Marshall created this game because he's always wanted to do what Nathan did. Then, he finally followed those impulses and became Nathan, killing and tattooing the three women from the LeDoux Street freezer. Suppose further, he's a relative of Jude Marshall, maybe Jude's brother. Jude knew his brother was unhinged and capable of murder, yet he did nothing about it. Then, Jude learned about the three bodies in the freezer. Feeling responsible and guilty for having let his brother do that, Jude committed suicide."

"Quite a string of assumptions."

"Where is it weak?"

"Do Jude and Quentin even have a brother?"

Kit shook her head. "I've no idea."

"Why were surrogates chosen?"

"Work in progress. Doesn't mean my theory is wrong."

Broussard continued probing. "We don't even know that Marion Marshall is related to Jude."

"Let's get busy and find out, unless you've got a better idea."

"How do you propose to do that?"

"Give me a minute ..."

While Kit mulled that over, Teddy said, "Guess it wouldn't be a good idea to just ask Quentin Marshall if he has a brother named Marion."

"If I'm right, Quentin might also have known what Marion did," Kit replied. "Asking him anything like that could warn Marion we're closing in."

"Jude's wife might know if there's a third brother," Broussard said. "She likely wouldn't know anything about him being a killer, and, therefore, would think the question was innocuous."

"It's still risky," Kit said. "And we didn't part on the best of terms. I don't think she'd even speak to me again."

"What are we talkin' about?" Bubba asked, returning from the bathroom.

"Strategy for future action," Broussard said.

"We finished with da game?"

Broussard looked at Kit, who said, "We might need it down the line for evidence, but for now we're through."

"Can I return it?"

"I'd like to hold on to it for awhile."

"I promised I'd have it back by tomorrow mornin'."

"Okay, go ahead and return it. If we need it again, we'll re-borrow it or find another copy."

While Bubba set about disconnecting the game from the monitor, the others thought about the problem at hand.

A few seconds later, Broussard said, "Why don't we ..."

At the same instant, Kit said, "It's extremely ..."

Broussard deferred. "Go ahead ..."

"It's extremely likely the killer lived in Louisiana before the hurricane. Let's call the Baton Rouge PD and see if Marion Marshall has a Louisiana driver's license."

"I was about to suggest the same thing."

"Have you got the direct number for dispatch?"

"I think so." Broussard reached for his Rolodex.

"You need me anymore?" Bubba asked.

"Not at the moment," Broussard replied. "But you've been a big help."

"Guess I better get back to dose potatoes den."

As Bubba left, Teddy said, "There's not going to be anybody in my insurance agent's office on a Sunday morning, but I should call him and leave a message about what happened. Be right back." He stepped out in the hall.

"Here's that number," Broussard said.

He called it out and Kit punched it into his phone. After she'd made her request to Baton Rouge and hung up, Broussard said, "How'd you like to call the Hendrins and tell 'em how and where they can claim Jennifer's body?"

"You ready to release it now?"

"It's time."

"I'm sure that'll give them a measure of closure. But finding her killer will do more. As for *me* calling them ..." She stepped away from the phone and gestured toward it with both hands. "Your turn."

While Broussard called Jennifer's parents, Kit monitored his e-mail for a reply from Baton Rouge. Considering how slow their response had been to her earlier request on a weekday, she was worried they'd be even slower on the weekend. But barely three minutes after Broussard finished speaking to Mrs. Hendrin, the awaited e-mail arrived.

"What have we got?" Broussard asked.

"Marion Marshall does have a Louisiana license."

"Where's he live?"

"In Paradis. Look at his picture."

Broussard stepped around to the front of the monitor and leaned down.

"What's that on his face?" Kit asked, referring to the dark purple coloration on the left half of Marshall's face below his eye.

"Looks like a port wine birth mark."

"Can't they be treated?"

"Some improve with laser exposure; some don't."

"Be pretty hard to grow up normal having that burden to deal with. Might even cause a latent sociopath to express those tendencies. I'm liking this guy better and better as our killer. Think we got enough to issue a search warrant for his house?"

"Lookin' for …"

Kit shrugged. "Hat pins that have been dipped in India ink … the ink itself … souvenirs he might have taken from his victims."

"Let me call Phillip and ask what he thinks."

Broussard picked up the phone and punched in the number of Gatlin's cell. "Phillip … Andy. I need your advice on somethin'." Broussard paused, then said, "I might take it, or I might not. Depends on how sound it is." He explained the situation at length. He listened to Gatlin's reply, then said, "Okay, thanks. We'll get back to you." He hung up and looked at Kit. "He said forget it. No judge would issue a warrant on what we have."

"Then let's get more."

"How?"

"We can start by driving over and taking a look at where he lives."

"It can't be far now," Kit said thirty minutes later from behind the wheel of her car. She pointed to a tiled roof in the distance. "Bet it's that next house."

They were in a remote area where scattered mansions and manicured estates were separated by huge tracts of swampy wilderness. Broussard was in the passenger seat next to her. Teddy was in the back.

As they drew near the upcoming home, they could see the estate was surrounded by a tall wrought-iron fence that ran between red brick pillars each topped with a granite cap and ball. The house itself, a sprawling structure with a domed portico reminiscent of Monticello, was at least two hundred yards back from the road.

"Designing computer games must pay pretty well," Teddy said.

"Someone is leaving," Broussard said, remarking on the red car coming down the drive.

Kit eased up on the gas. "What do we do? I don't want anybody from the house seeing us."

"Maybe they'll go the other way."

The red car came through the gates and turned left so it was coming right at them.

"If you do anything now, you'll just draw attention to us," Broussard said.

Kit replied, "Pretend like you're sleeping ... turn your head to the side. Teddy, you do the same."

While both men did as she asked, Kit flipped down her visor and straightened in her seat so the visor would hide more of her face. This meant she could only see the small section of road just in front of her car.

In no time at all, she saw the hood of the red car as the vehicle was about to pass. Though she shouldn't have done it because it exposed more of her face than she wished, she slid her head to the left and, with one eye, took a quick peek at the driver.

What she saw was a shock.

The car whizzed past.

"I saw the driver," Kit said. "It was Quentin Marshall."

"Did he recognize you?" Teddy asked.

"No. He was talking on his cell phone and looking straight ahead. A morning visit to his brother … Makes me wonder just how close they are."

"You don't happen to know Quentin's address, do you?" Broussard asked.

"I can find out pretty fast."

Kit drove past the estate's grounds until she found a wide part of the shoulder where she could pull off the road. She got out her cell and navigated to a set of Internet-linked area white pages. A few more pushed buttons and she turned to Broussard with a surprised look. "Quentin wasn't visiting his brother. He lives there."

CHAPTER 27

"THEY LIVE IN THE same house," Kit said. "What are the chances Marion could have killed those three woman without Quentin knowing?"

"It's possible, I suppose," Broussard replied.

"But if Jude killed himself because he knew what was going on, doesn't it seem likely he'd have told Quentin what Marion was doing?"

"Not necessarily. From what you said, Jude and Quentin weren't close."

"Could you get a search warrant now?" Teddy asked.

Broussard looked over his shoulder. "What we've just learned is interestin', but from a legal perspective, doesn't advance our case."

"I'd like to get a better look at his home and grounds," Kit said.

"To what end?" Broussard replied.

"I don't know … just to get a better handle on them."

"You can't go wanderin' around their property."

"No … that wouldn't be smart."

"Or legal."

"What about a helicopter?"

"Isn't that a bit …"

"A bit what?" Kit said, anger suddenly flaring. "Marion knows where I live. He attacked me almost in my apartment. I want to know as much about him as he does me. And I will know that, with or without your help."

Broussard had been around Kit long enough to appreciate how stubborn she could be. So he took her at her word. He also knew that sometimes her zeal overcame her better judgment. To make sure her fervor didn't compromise the investigation, he decided to help her get what she wanted. "Let me see what I can arrange. But it won't happen today."

TRYING TO GET OUT of her apartment that morning unseen by anyone who might be keeping her under surveillance had been so much trouble, Kit decided to risk a different approach. She and Teddy spent the next few hours renting a motel room and buying enough toiletries and fresh clothes for the next few days, thinking that, at least now, Marion wouldn't have any idea where she was. When she called and told Gatlin about the motel, he thought she was making a bad decision. But he couldn't change her mind. Even though she wouldn't be there, Gatlin told her he would keep a cop in her courtyard.

"THAT'S IT COMING UP," Kit said into the boom mike attached to her helmet and pointing through the windshield of the Kiowa reconnaissance helicopter, where she was sitting in the co-pilot's seat. Next to her at the controls, Jeff Lyons, the cadaver escort and navy reserve pilot Broussard had met at the FEMA mortuary, nodded. Even with the noise-suppressing helmet on, the sound of the helicopter blades throbbed inside her skull.

"Better take her up a little," Broussard said into his mike from the back seat next to Teddy. "If there's anyone outside, we don't want 'em to know they're the purpose of the flyover."

Lyons changed the pitch of the main rotor and twisted the throttle for more power, sending the chopper higher in the sky.

In seconds, they were over the Marshall estate, which sat like a green gem among wilderness chaff. Their course took them across the rear of the property. As they passed the mansion, Kit caught a glimpse of what looked like three people sitting at a table on the back patio. She tried to see them better through the binoculars she'd brought, but by the time she got the lenses to her eyes, the angle was wrong and she couldn't even find the patio.

Over the receiver in her helmet, Kit heard Lyons say, "If you'd like a better look at those people, I'll get you a close-up digital photo of them and the grounds on the return."

Kit gave him an okay sign.

"We should go downrange at least ten minutes before we come back," Lyons said. "That should be far enough to keep them from becoming suspicious."

THIRTY MINUTES LATER, LYONS and his three passengers were standing by the now silent Kiowa at Alvin Callender Field, the naval air station airport in Belle Chasse, where they'd departed.

"Thanks so much for your help," Kit said, shaking Lyons's hand. In her head, the helicopter blades were still whipping the air.

"The photos should be on your computer by the time you get back to the office," Lyons said.

Broussard and Teddy added their thanks and followed Kit to her car.

"Anybody want to lay bets whether they're here?" Kit said, twenty minutes later, as she booted up her computer.

"He seems like a competent guy," Teddy said. "I wouldn't bet against him."

The little on-screen hourglass icon disappeared, and Kit opened her e-mail program. Just below some spam with a gibberish topic line, she saw a message: *FLYOVER PICS*. She opened the message and selected the first attached image. Broussard and Teddy moved in for a better look.

The screen quickly filled with a wide-angle shot of the Marshall estate and its surrounding environs that included the complex system of bayous that criss-crossed the wilderness at the rear of the property.

The next shot, at a much higher magnification, was restricted to the back of the house. In this one, the three figures seated at the table were clearly visible, but their features were not discernible.

The third picture was the money shot: a close-up in which each of the three faces, which were all turned up to look at the helicopter, was captured in such clarity it was easy to see that one of those present was Quentin Marshall. There was also an older woman there and …

"It's him," Kit said, pointing at the second man. Even Broussard and Teddy, who didn't have the best view, could see the port wine stain on Marion Marshall's face.

"I'm obviously all for doing anything necessary to catch the guy who attacked you," Teddy said, "but I don't understand why it's legal to fly over someone's backyard and take their picture. Shouldn't we have had a court order to do that?"

"I don't know all the fine points of the legal issues surroundin' surveillance," Broussard said, "but the primary issue in any of these things is whether the subject has a reasonable expectation of privacy. What we just did was okay because no one could reasonably expect they'd never be seen sittin' in their backyard."

"But we didn't just see them. We photographed them with a zoom lens."

"That's less clear. I know it's legal to use the zoom function on a camera to enhance what can be seen, but when we took the pictures, we may have been over the line. I don't really care."

"I'd love to know what they were talking about," Kit said. "And you know ..." She clicked back to the wide angle shot. "They're only about thirty yards from the water in this bayou. I'll bet if someone was in a boat back there, they might be able to hear them."

"But then they'd stop talking," Teddy said.

"Not if the boat was hidden in these grasses and cattails."

"You're not thinkin' you should do that, are you?" Broussard asked.

Kit shook her head. "No."

Remembering all the other times Kit had put herself at risk with ill-advised behavior, Broussard said, "Promise me you're not gonna do this."

"Somebody should."

"I disagree. If he's the killer, he's too dangerous to be around, especially when he's in his comfort zone. Besides, what do you think would be heard that'd be useful?"

"Who knows? But at least we'd be doing something that might help prove he's our guy. What's our plan now?"

"Right this minute, I don't have one."

"There you are."

"I'm workin' on it. Meanwhile, I'm still waitin' for your promise."

"I promise."

"Say it in a sentence."

"I promise I won't try to overhear any conversation in the Marshall's backyard. Satisfied?"

Broussard shook a finger in her face. "Don't disappoint me."

"I'll be good."

In truth, there was no chance Kit would go back on her word. She was simply too frightened of Marshall to get that close.

"I've got to drive over to St. Gabriel ... see how things are goin'," Broussard said. "Be back in a few hours. Maybe I'll get some ideas on how to proceed durin' the drive."

"Then we'll see you later."

It wasn't far into his trip that Broussard began to wonder if maybe a sting could be set up to trap Marshall into attacking Kit in front of witnesses. They could get a policewoman, disguise her as Kit, and put her in a boat behind the Marshall estate. Have a lot of other cops positioned in the weeds where they could see what was happening ... fake Kit pretends to be doing surveillance behind the property, but purposely gives herself away somehow.

No ... That's no good. Even if he fell for it, all he could be charged with was assault.

After Broussard left the office, Kit returned to her computer and sent her fingers flying over the keyboard.

"What are you doing?" Teddy asked.

She initiated the Internet search she'd set up and gave him a satisfied look. "I've got an idea,"

CHAPTER 28

Kɪᴛ sᴄᴀɴɴᴇᴅ ᴛʜᴇ sɪɢɴs along the street. "There it is." She pulled into the parking lot that served a small brown-painted brick building and shut off the engine.

"My Little Eye, Private Investigations?" Teddy said, reading the sign.

"Yeah, I would have preferred a more aggressive-sounding operation myself, but this is the only detective agency anywhere close."

"What are we doing?"

"I promised Andy I wouldn't go back to the Marshall house. I didn't say I'd forget the idea. I'm going to hire a professional to do it. Bring those pictures." She got out of the car and headed for the agency's front door.

Inside, they found a young blonde in a crisp yellow-and-white-checked linen suit standing on a chair. She was arranging the tendrils of a plant that had grown almost completely around the room from a surprisingly small clay pot. Kit found the extensive growth reassuring, as it indicated the agency had been there awhile and was, therefore, likely a good one.

Hearing them enter, the girl stepped off the chair. "May I help you?" She had great receptionist eyes: bright and shiny that made you feel you'd made her day simply by coming in.

"I'd like to speak to Mr. Hennepin," Kit said, referring to the M. Hennepin addendum under the agency's name on its sign.

"Of course. Just one minute."

The girl went to a door in the rear of the room, knocked, and stuck her head in. "Someone's here to see you ..."

The girl opened the door fully and turned to Kit and Teddy.

"You can go in."

Kit was expecting that Hennepin would be a heavy-set, tough looking guy in his fifties. She was right about the heavy-set part and the age, but she missed the sex, for M. Hennepin was a woman, dressed in bib overalls.

"Marge Hennepin," she said, rising from her chair behind her big desk, where she had apparently been looking through several stacks of photos that now lay face-down.

Kit crossed the room and shook Hennepin's rough hand. "I'm Kit Franklyn. This is my friend Teddy LaBiche."

Hennepin and Teddy shook hands, and Hennepin said, "Have a seat and tell me what's troubling you."

It was probably the first time Kit had ever seen rocking chairs provided for clients in an office. As she sat, she said, "Ms. Hennepin, I have to say ..."

"Call me Marge."

"Marge, you're not what I expected."

"I wouldn't be a very good detective if I was, would I?"

"What I meant was ... This job I have could be very danger-ous."

"So it needs a man?"

"That *is* what I was thinking."

"Would you like a list of all the males whose ass I've kicked in the last twenty years?"

"Well ... I ..."

"If it makes you feel any better, after I got out of the army, where I was trained in every infantry weapon system they had, I became a professional female wrestler. I am not someone to be underestimated, not by you, not by anyone."

"How's your hearing?"

"*Your* watch is working." She pointed at Teddy. "His isn't."

Teddy looked at his wrist. He raised his arm and held his watch to his ear. "She's right. The battery must be dead."

"Okay," Kit said. "Here's the situation. I'm a death investigator for the Orleans Parish medical examiner ..."

For the next several minutes, Kit laid things out for Hennepin and showed her the photos taken from the Kiowa. "Since I'm employed by the ME's office, I'm bound by the same legalities as the police. As my agent, you will be as well. That's why I asked about your hearing. Anything you overhear with the unaided ear will be admissible in court. If you use any sound-amplifying device, it all could be suppressed."

"Got it."

"We did our flyover this morning a little after eight. I have no idea if they're out there every morning, but we're going to assume they are. So I'd like you to be in position tomorrow morning by seven o'clock. Will that be a problem?"

"We haven't discussed my fees."

"What will this cost?"

"Let's establish some ground rules first. Say they don't appear by eight, or eight-thirty. How long should I wait for them?"

"I guess the longer you wait the more it'll cost ..."

"Time is money."

"Ten o'clock. If they're not out by then, call it off until the next morning."

"Was it a covered patio?"

"No."

"Then weather could be a factor."

"If it's rainy, don't go."

"It's not that simple. If I've made plans to do something, that means another job doesn't get done."

"So it's going to cost me either way."

"Half if it rains."

"What's the total tab going to be for good weather?"

"Five hundred."

"Can we do it day to day?"

"Decision each day by noon; payment daily in advance. Any morning the weather doesn't cooperate, next day's advance will only be two fifty."

Kit reached in her bag and took out her checkbook. "Make it out to My Little Eye?"

"If you would."

Kit scribbled out a check for five hundred and handed it across the desk. "Don't think I'm underestimating you when I say this, but there's a decent chance the guy with the birthmark on his face has access to a semi-automatic shotgun."

"That'll make two of us."

CHAPTER 29

MARGE HENNEPIN SHIFTED ONTO her left cheek to restore circulation in the opposite half of her rump. She'd been sitting in her camouflage-painted flat-bottom boat surrounded by cattails and rushes since sunrise, waiting for the sound of a human voice. But apart from the occasional splash of a bream snatching something off the bayou's surface, the intermittent call of a red-winged blackbird, and the frequent drone of a mosquito trying to fly into her ear, she'd heard nothing.

She checked her watch: eight-forty ... another hour and twenty minutes before she could pack it in for the day.

At her side was a rod and reel, its line hanging limply in the water, the hook unbaited. If discovered, she hoped to appear as nothing more than an old woman out fishing. If her disguise failed and her hand was forced, she would fill it with the Street-sweeper shotgun lying in the bottom of the boat under an old shirt. But that was not her only protection.

She reached into one of the big pockets on the cammies she was wearing and got out her cell phone. She navigated to the text message function and sent a template she'd made yesterday after Kit had left the office: *How are you doing?*

Across the bayou, also well-hidden by cattails and grasses, Mark Dabaldo, her former wrestling manager and current operations back-up, felt his phone vibrate. He checked the message and returned one of his own: *Bored to shit. You?*

Marge sent back: *Enjoying not hearing you talk.*

Mark typed his reply: *Sure. Piss off your protection.*

But before he sent the message, he saw someone come onto the patio from the back door. Hastily, he changed the message: *Subject now in view.*

Seeing the message, Marge began to listen harder.

Her phone vibrated again: *Subject coming … object in hand.*

Oh shit, Marge thought. *They know we're here.*

She bent down and threw the shirt off the shotgun. She snatched up the weapon and looked toward the Marshall's boat dock. A few rapid heartbeats later, a man walked into view. She was close enough to verify that it was the guy with the facial birthmark in Kit Franklyn's aerial photos.

He did a quick look around. Muscles all over Marge's body contracted as though they could make her smaller. But by the time his head turned in her direction, she was still as bulky as ever.

In the next instant, he seemed to be looking right at her. She wanted to raise the shotgun in his direction, but couldn't afford to move.

Then he turned away.

As the tension in the situation dropped just below Marge's red zone, the guy did something she didn't understand. He knelt and picked up a baseball bat that had been lying on the dock. He began to hit the bat rhythmically against a dock piling on her side.

Clunk. Clunk. Clunk.

What the hell was he doing?

The water in front of Marge's boat suddenly surged and rolled. Something beneath the surface slid by. Whatever it was headed out into the bayou, then turned toward the dock. The top of a huge scaly snout and a pair of evil eyes rose to the surface.

In the boat, Marge almost peed her pants. *Jesus. That thing had been sitting next to her for God knows how long. Jesus.*

The guy put the bat down and picked up the object he'd been carrying. He unwrapped it from what appeared to be a towel, and for the first time, Marge could see what it was.

Oh my God. He was going to …

She thought about screaming at him to stop, but from the object's appearance and the rough way he was handling it, it seemed a scream wouldn't accomplish anything but give her presence away. So instead, she snatched her camera phone from her shirt pocket.

The man swung his arm backward.

Marge got off two shots with the camera as the object flew through the air, both unobstructed, she thought. She was less sure about the one she took as the huge alligator caught the thrown object in his open mouth and sank out of sight.

CHAPTER 30

MARGE HENNEPIN CLICKED THE sharpen command on Adobe Photoshop. She bent closer to her computer monitor and looked at the effect on the blurred photo she'd taken behind the Marshall estate. "It's still not great, but you can tell what it is." She vacated her chair.

Kit took her place and looked hard at the picture. "It's definitely an infant," she said. She lifted her hand to the screen and pointed. "You can see the arms here, and these are the legs."

From behind Kit, Marge spoke again. "Like I said. I'm sure the baby was dead when it was thrown into the water. God help me if it wasn't, because I didn't do anything to stop what happened. I just snapped a few pictures. It looked limp and lifeless. I hope it wasn't just unconscious. Lord, I pray that wasn't the case."

"Where the devil do you suppose that baby came from?" Teddy asked.

"I have no idea," Kit responded. "But I want to see it."

"You can't," Marge said. "I told you the alligator ate it."

Kit turned to Teddy. "Digestion is relatively slow in an alligator right?"

"Yes …" Teddy's brow furrowed. "You're not thinking …"

"I want to get hold of that animal and open it. If the Marshalls killed a baby, we can get them for that."

"Alligators are protected. You can't just kill one whenever you feel like it." Seeing Kit becoming angry at his uncooperative comment, Teddy quickly added, "But I'm sure if we explained the situation to Fish and Wildlife, they'd grant us a permit."

"How long would *that* take? We can't get involved in a lot of red tape on this and let that baby get dissolved."

"I know some people there. I'll get things expedited."

"And you could catch it?"

"If we can find the right one." He looked at Marge. "Did this animal have any identifying features?"

"It was huge."

"That and the fact they're territorial will certainly help us find it. But Fish and Wildlife will want more proof that we know exactly which individual we're after."

"I didn't actually see much of it," Marge said. "But now that you're forcing me to think harder … It had an irregular white line running diagonally from the top of its head to down under its left eye. Don't know if it had one under the other eye."

"I've never seen any natural marking like that on a gator," Teddy said. "Sounds like an injury of some sort, either fresh or one healed without normal pigmentation. That's what we're looking for."

"From where I stand," Dewey Lazare, sheriff of St. Charles Parish, said, pouring himself a cup of coffee, "you folks are messin' in my business."

Lazare had a remarkable gut that spilled in a fleshy avalanche over his belt, making him look like a walrus in a brown uniform.

"This is not about turf," Kit said. "We're trying to bring a killer to justice."

Lazare shot Kit a hard look. "Missy, I don't appreciate bein' lectured to by anybody, least of all a woman."

Kit was about to rip him a new southern egress, but Broussard reined her in with a touch on her hand and a little warning nod. He turned to Lazare. "Sheriff, I understand how you might feel that way. But that's not our intent. We're here because we need some direction and figured since the Marshall estate is in your parish and you've been at this kind of work a long time, you'd know what to do. Am I on the right track do you think, wantin' to get a look inside this gator? Dr. Franklyn here thinks it'd be better to go out there and just question the people who live there … see what might come from that."

Lazare took a sip of his coffee and looked hard at Broussard.

Kit was sure Lazare would never fall for such a transparent attempt to play to his ego. She was likewise convinced he'd see though Broussard's ploy of getting him to cooperate by using his obvious dislike of women against him.

Lazare's body language softened, and he lost the defensive glint in his puffy eyes. He looked at Kit. "Questionin' them would just be stupid. Then they'd know they were bein' watched." He shook his head, waggling his jowels. "No … you gotta check out that gator. How you gonna get hold of it?"

"That'll be my job," Teddy said.

"You know what you're doin'?"

"I'm a professional alligator farmer."

"You got a permit?"

"We do."

"I can't have you crashin' around in my parish unsupervised. So I'm gonna send my deputy, Theo Lancon, with you."

"That's good," Teddy said. "An extra hand will be useful."

"When you plannin' on doin' this?"

"That's kind of a problem," Broussard said. "There's not enough time left today to get everything together, and we can't do it at night and risk the lights we'd need bein' seen from the Marshall house, so we're gonna start at sunup tomorrow mornin'."

"Didn't you say the Marshalls eat breakfast out on the back patio?"

"It is risky. But we hope to make the capture down bayou a little and be quick and quiet and gone from the area before they come out."

"Why not wait until later in the day?"

"Can't say that'd be any better. For all we know, they may have a yard crew out there workin' later. Or somebody may come out to sit on the dock and birdwatch. And the longer we wait, the less of that child there's gonna be to examine. We'll post a watch to keep an eye on the house. If anybody comes out while we're still in a vulnerable position, we'll call it off."

"Where should Theo meet you?"

Broussard laid a map out on Lazare's desk and showed him the spot they'd chosen for the operation's staging area.

CHAPTER 31

Theo Lancon was a walrus in training. In a few years, if he didn't change his habits, his gut would surely equal Lazare's in size. But he was a congenial fellow and willing to help where needed. Teddy posted him in the woods adjacent to the Marshall estate property line, where he could keep an eye on the back of the house.

Teddy was situated in a second set of woods, across the bayou and down about fifty yards to Lancon's right. He was located far enough from the Marshall's house that the trees where Lancon was hiding would block the view from anyone looking out a window when the time came for Teddy to take his shot with the sound-suppressed Ruger automatic rifle he'd borrowed from Fish and Wildlife.

Bubba was facing Teddy directly on the opposite side of the bayou, ready to call the gator into their trap. Back aways, behind a tree, stood Phil Gatlin with another Ruger.

Forty yards farther down to Teddy's left, Kit and Broussard waited at the boat-launching area where the operation had gotten underway. To keep any local fishermen from stumbling onto what they were doing, they'd blocked the access road with

Lancon's cruiser along with a sign saying the road was temporarily closed for repairs.

So everyone present could follow the progress of the operation, they were each wearing an earpiece and a tiny boom mike connected to a short range, voice-activated Walkie-Talkie, courtesy of the NOPD via Gatlin.

"Are we clear, number two?" Teddy said into his mike.

"Clear," Lancon responded.

"Number three, get started."

Across the bayou, Bubba put the fat end of one of his two baseball bats into the water. Pressing that bat into the bayou mud, he began striking it on the side with the other one.

Teddy cringed at how loud it was. "Easy does it, three."

Bubba's next blow was much softer, but still probably hard enough for the gator they were after to sense the vibrations being sent into the water … *if* the animal was anywhere in the area.

But even if the creature was nearby, other factors could cause their plan to fail. Among these was the possibility that Bubba wasn't generating vibrations similar enough to those the Marshalls used to summon the animal. Another flaw was that this unfamiliar location for the call might make the gator too skittery to show itself.

Concerned that the sound they were making might carry to the Marshall house, Teddy checked with Lancon. "How we doing, number two?"

"Still good," Lancon replied.

The gator did not make an immediate appearance. Nor did another five minutes of calling it change the situation.

"How you holding up, number three?" Teddy asked.

"I'd rather be peelin' potatoes."

Bubba carried on for another five minutes while Teddy scanned the bayou for any sign of a wake that indicated the gator was coming.

Bubba was crouching near a fan-shaped shallow that extended about five feet out into the bayou. They'd chosen the spot so it wouldn't be possible for the gator to sneak up on him totally submerged. But, because gators can cover a lot of distance fast when they lunge for prey at the water's edge, it was necessary for Bubba to keep a sharp eye on the point where the water deepened.

Teddy believed the gator would be wary enough to surface and take a look in Bubba's direction before making any attack decision. It was also extremely likely that after the gator surfaced, it would find the situation too dangerous to proceed and would submerge, never to be seen by them again. For that reason, Teddy had decided he should take the first shot available. If the gator came from Teddy's left and surfaced, it would be up to Gatlin to determine, using the scope on his rifle, if the gator had the identifying mark. He would then communicate that to Teddy, who would make the shot. If the animal came from the right and surfaced, Teddy could judge for himself if it was the one they wanted. In either case, Teddy would get one shot to hit the thumbnail-sized lethal spot an inch behind the alligator's eyes. If he missed, or hit it anywhere else, the gator would submerge and swim away.

But Teddy wasn't going to miss. He would send his slug directly into the animal's brainstem. Then, in the few seconds, before the animal sank, he would use the grappling hook at his feet to haul the creature to shore.

That was the plan.

And that was exactly how it was going to play out.

Or so Teddy thought.

CHAPTER 32

Bᴜʙʙᴀ ᴄᴏɴᴛɪɴᴜᴇᴅ ᴛᴏ ᴄᴀʟʟ the gator. Eyes continually scanning the surface of the green water, Teddy watched closely for signs the creature was approaching. Suddenly, Teddy heard a sound behind him. Lowering the Ruger, he turned and couldn't believe what he saw. The gator had come out of the adjacent bayou and was charging at high speed, its legs under it like a mammal, jaws open so wide Teddy could see the manhole-size opening into its gullet at the back of its throat.

Teddy snap-fired the Ruger and sent a slug down the animal's throat just as the creature lunged for him. Teddy leapt to the side and the big jaws snapped shut on nothing but his heat signature. But as Teddy jumped, the rifle barrel hit a tree and the gun spun out of his hand. Mouth gaping, the gator swept its big head in Teddy's direction.

As he dove out of the way, Teddy screamed into the mike. "I'm in trouble here!" The gator's jaws snapped again, just clipping the heel of Teddy's left boot.

Across the bayou, Bubba sprang into action. Spinning like an Olympic hammer thrower, he lofted the bat in his hand over the water onto the opposite shore. He then ran into the bayou and dove headfirst into the green water.

It was a good thing Gatlin had not shown up in a suit, but had arrived in clothing appropriate for an alligator hunt, because he, too, ran for the water. Being much heavier than Bubba, when his feet hit the mud near the shore, he sank two inches into it and sprawled face down in the water. His Ruger flew out of his hand into the bayou.

Teddy's shout rang in Theo Lancon's earpiece. As Lancon turned toward the bayou, the rays of the morning sun filtering through the trees reflected off his badge. They hit the metal again a few steps later. In less than a minute, Lancon was at the water's edge, and he could distinctly see what was happening to Teddy. Nothing in him wanted to get any closer.

Hearing Teddy's distress call, Broussard started running toward the point where Bubba and Gatlin had gone into the bayou, Kit matching him stride for stride. They reached the fan-shaped shallows as Bubba and Gatlin climbed out onto the opposite shore. Beyond the two men, Kit and Broussard could see the thrashing gator.

Broussard's eyes went to Gatlin's deep shoeprints in the mud. Realizing it would be an even greater trap for him, Broussard ran back a few steps to his right and launched himself, his white shirt, bow tie, and dress slacks horizontally into a deeper part of the bayou, producing slightly less splash than when the USS *Ronald Reagan* was launched.

Kit stopped at the water's edge and watched Broussard swim across the bayou. She was astonished at what he had done. But now, there was no need for her over there. What could she do that four men couldn't? So she stayed where she was.

The bad thing about Teddy's leap to evade the gator's jaws was that he ended up lying on his side in the weeds, where he saw a heavily armored case of the worst breath he'd ever encountered coming fast, the pearly white oral avenue to the animal's stomach about to engulf him.

He rolled onto his back just as the gator snapped at him. Teddy was acutely aware that it would take the animal no time at all to react to the miss, so he kept rolling, knowing this was a race he couldn't win. Then the small of his back collided with a tree, ending the contest.

The great reptile came at him so fast Teddy had no time to get his little .22 pistol. He twisted and brought his feet around so he could kick at the animal, knowing he was less than a second away from having the bones in both his legs crushed.

Seeing Teddy in dire trouble, Bubba rushed the gator and smacked it on the back with the baseball bat he'd thrown across the bayou. The animal jerked its head in Bubba's direction and grabbed the bat, splintering it with the force of its bite. It shook off the wooden shards and went after Bubba. Trying to lure the creature farther from Teddy, Bubba didn't turn and run, but backpedaled. With the gator lurching after him, Bubba's left heel caught in a grass hummock and he toppled over backwards.

Gatlin pulled his 9mm automatic from his belt holster and charged the animal.

Scrambling to his feet, Teddy yelled, "An inch behind the eyes. It's the only lethal spot!"

Gatlin put the gun against the gator's scaly hide and pulled the trigger.

Nothing happened.

He tried again with the same result. The gun was jammed from being immersed in mud when Gatlin fell. From Gatlin's right, Broussard came flying through the air. He landed on the gator's back with a loud thump and a groan as the gator's dorsal scutes rammed into his chest.

Somehow, Broussard got the gator in a headlock that compressed the creature's jaws until they were fully closed. Gators can generate an unbelievable amount of force when they close their jaws, but the muscles that open the mouth are weak. So Broussard was able to keep those fearsome teeth out of play. But the animal was racking its head violently from side to side, trying to shake Broussard off him. Its other weapon, its great tail, was slashing back and forth between Broussard's legs, looking for a way to do some damage.

Broussard's unexpected act saved Bubba's life, and the little Cajun scrambled to his feet. Needing to do something, fast, Teddy spotted the rifle he'd lost during the first stage of the attack. He snatched it up and ran to the gator, intending to finish what he'd started, but Broussard's headlock was covering the kill spot.

"You're in the way," Teddy shouted. "I can't get a clean shot!"

Unable to dislodge Broussard, the animal began clawing at the earth, propelling itself toward the bayou. If it got into the water, it would not only be able to drown Broussard, but would get away.

There were now *two* reasons Broussard needed to let go of the animal, but the question was, how to do that? If Broussard released his hold, there was a good chance the gator would turn on him, and there was no doubt about which of them was quicker.

The gator was now about eight feet from the water and making steady progress.

Suddenly, Bubba got down on his knees, crawled close to the gator's head, and smacked it on the side of the snout with his fist. Its cold reptilian eyes glaring, the gator yanked its head around. It dug into the turf and lunged at Bubba, dragging Broussard along. The gator's snout hit Bubba in the side. With a quick jerk of its head, it threw him into the weeds.

The great reptile then tried to go after Bubba, but Broussard shifted his weight to the right, using his bulk as leverage to slow the animal down. Bubba scrambled to his feet and came back to the creature, staying just out of range of another snout swing, but standing where the animal could see him.

"Okay, he wants *me* now," Bubba said. "Dr. B, you let him go an' roll hard to your right. Teddy, when he comes after me, let him have it."

"What if goes for me instead?" Broussard said breathlessly.

"Den I'll owe you an apology."

CHAPTER 33

BROUSSARD RELEASED HIS HOLD on the gator and rolled away from it. On cue, the animal swung its head toward Bubba and came after him in an explosion of claws and teeth. But Teddy was waiting.

He squeezed the trigger on the Ruger.

There was a sickening sound of the projectile striking the animal. The huge body gave a great shudder, and all the energy that suffused it a moment earlier was gone. Though he had no doubt it was dead, Teddy approached the animal carefully and pushed on it with the barrel of the rifle.

There was no response.

Though they had prevailed, not one of the four men standing over the great animal felt good about it.

"What a magnificent creature," Teddy said.

"He certainly gave us all we could handle," Gatlin added reverently.

"I got a lotta gator stories I like to tell people," Bubba said. "But right now, I don't think dis is gonna be one of 'em."

"We had to do it," Broussard said. "But we don't have to like it."

WHEN THEO LANCON SAW that the gator was dead, he returned to his post, glad no one had been hurt. If they had, questions might have been raised about why he hadn't come to help. As he looked out between the trees at the still-empty backyard of the Marshall house, he realized that even though everyone across the bayou was safe, they still might wonder why he hadn't been there too. *Well, it was because I've been trained never to leave my post when I'm doing surveillance. And …*

A blur suddenly passed in front of Lancon's eyes. Before he could process what that might have been, he felt a sharp pain encircling his neck. His hands went to the spot, and his fingers felt a hard ring sinking into his skin. At the same time he realized he couldn't breathe.

The ligature tightened, cutting through his skin and dividing his thyroid. His hands clawed at the constricting band, but there was no way he could get his fingers under it. With the incessant pressure, the band cut deeper, slicing and parting tissue until it went entirely through the wall of his trachea. Blood and air rushed into his respiratory passage and down into his lungs through the opening in his neck. For an instant, Lancon's oxygen-starved brain received what it needed, delaying his slide into unconsciousness. He exhaled, sending bloody froth bubbling from around the ligature where it had cut into his trachea. The ever-increasing pressure then compressed the large vessels in Lancon's neck, so that blood could neither enter nor leave his brain. The deputy's sun, already dim, disappeared behind a permanent cloud. He went limp, and Marion Marshall let him fall.

Marion pulled off Lancon's ear bud and mike and put it over his own left ear. He relieved Lancon of his Walkie Talkie and ran off into the woods to end the threat facing his family.

DURING THE GATOR ATTACK, Kit had heard a few electronically unaided shouts and grunts from the combatants, but had no real ear onto the events. The communication gear they'd been wearing was variously damaged by water and/ or lost during the action. Though Theo Lancon's equipment had been fully functional during the attack, Marion had put him down so efficiently Lancon had not been able to utter a single word. Thus, Kit didn't realize Lancon was no longer in play.

THE WEIGHT OF THE big gator was a staggering burden, but Teddy and the others managed to load it into the boat Teddy had used to get on that side of the bayou. With Teddy poling the craft forward from the back and the others sitting where they could find room beside and on the gator, Teddy maneuvered the boat around the turn and headed back up the bayou.

"I'm not bein' critical," Broussard said to Teddy from his seat on the gator's chest, "but how'd this thing get the drop on you?"

"I was checking behind me every once in awhile … often enough to have spotted an ordinary gator leaving the water. Then I turn and there's this one high-running right for me full blast. I've seen them do that lots of times trying to get *away* from danger. But I never saw one high-run toward it."

"Guess he thought he could take you."

"I won't make that mistake again."

"Any day we learn somethin' new is a success."

"Or any day we don't get eaten and digested," Bubba added.

"That'd be right up there too," Broussard said.

"The way you been flying through the air today, we need to get you a cape," Gatlin said to Broussard.

"I already have three on order. I'd get *you* one, but you were disqualified when you fell in the mud."

"Careful, or I may charge you for all the communication equipment we ruined."

"By the way," Broussard said, "where's your Ruger?"

Gatlin looked toward shore and pretended he hadn't heard the question.

Kit was waiting for them when the nose of the boat touched shore.

"Things didn't go quite as planned," Teddy said to Kit. "But we got it."

"Everyone okay?"

"We'll all probably be sore tomorrow, but we've still got our finger and toes," Teddy replied.

"And no tooth marks on us," Bubba added.

Seeing how disheveled and dirty they all were, Kit became acutely aware of how clean her clothes were … clear testimony to her cowardice. How could she have done that? Teddy's life had been at risk, and she'd done nothing. She had put her own welfare above his.

"Our communication gear is all messed up," Broussard said to Kit. "Anything from Lancon?"

"No."

"Check with him, will you?"

"Number two, please respond. Everything okay?"

Through her earpiece, Kit heard, "No problem." Until now, she hadn't heard Lancon say more than a few words over the system, so she didn't notice the voice she'd just heard was different than before. She gave Broussard a thumbs up.

"Did you bring the gloves and a knife?" Teddy asked Bubba.

"In my truck."

"I'll get them," Kit said, wanting to do *something* to help.

Bubba said, "Under the passenger seat."

The four men wrestled the gator out of the boat and laid it on the shore with its belly facing the water. By the time that was done, Kit was back with the gloves and a big serrated hunting knife. "Who gets these?"

Bubba pointed at Teddy.

Teddy took the gloves first and pulled them on. Kit then handed him the knife. Following old habits that wouldn't let him damage a perfectly good skin, Teddy didn't open the belly along the midline, but rather cut along the junction with the useless back armor, carrying the cut up along the jaw and down the other side, stopping where the ground prevented him from going further. He returned to the vent end of the animal and made a cross cut. This allowed him to lay the abdomen open.

"That's what we're after," he said, using the tip of the knife to point out a large, elongated white object streaked with red.

Everyone jockeyed for the best view.

"Here goes." He sliced the stomach open and a putrid, pearly green fluid spilled out. The stench was indescribable. It was all Kit could do to keep from gagging.

Teddy plunged his fingers into the cut and began exploring. He came out with something hard and shiny. He cleaned it off and examined it, then looked up at the group. "Somebody around here is missing a cat or a dog." He tossed the tag onto the ground and plunged his hand back into the stomach. This time, he scooped out a baseball. Returning for a third time, he came out grasping a pulpy white mass with tentacles. "Catfish head," he said, tossing it onto the sand.

He went in again and groped around for a few seconds. "Uh-oh. This may be what we're looking for." He pulled a small, white leg with a perfect, little foot out of the gator's stomach. Afraid to exert any more tension on the tiny appendage, he reached back inside for a more substantial grip. Using his other hand to widen the opening, he delivered the mucousy, partially-digested remains of an infant.

Unable to hold it in any longer, Kit turned to the side and dry heaved. She turned back to see Teddy lay the baby's body on its back. He cleaned it with his hand, and everyone was shocked to see a line of sutures running down the middle of its abdomen.

"What the hell *is* this?" Gatlin muttered.

Broussard said, "Cut the sutures."

Scissors would have been more useful now, and it took Teddy an interminable amount of time to sever all the sutures with the knife. But, finally, the job was done. He spread the edges of the incision apart as much as he could. Even though Gatlin and Bubba didn't know their way around the inside of a human body, they leaned in to look with as much interest as Kit and Broussard.

It took Kit a moment to get oriented, then ... *Oh my God ...* Everything that had been happening fell into place. She looked toward the Marshall's mansion. *Oh my God.*

"We have to get to the house," she said. "... The Marshalls' house, now."

A blast of gunfire suddenly erupted from the tree line. Broussard groaned in pain and grabbed at his left bicep, blood welling through his fingers. Gatlin was hit too, his left arm bloodied at the elbow. Swearing, Gatlin seized Broussard by the belt with his right hand and pulled him away from the gator. Together, they ran and stumbled toward a big cypress stump a few yards away. There was another blast, and dirt kicked up all around them. A third shot shredded the stump as they dove behind it. While this was happening, Bubba ran for the boat and threw himself headlong into it. Teddy dropped to the ground behind the gator carcass, pulling Kit down with him.

The sound of gunfire was now nonstop. Bubba had brought a wooden boat to minimize any sound they might make by things striking against the hull. One shot chewed a hole in its gunnel. The next hit the raised front leg of the gator, nearly severing it.

Through the mayhem, Kit realized that the amount of havoc each round was creating could only have been made by a shotgun. She flashed on the shootout in Night Demon and realized it was surely Marion Marshall firing on them with the gun he'd depicted in that game.

There was another blast, but this time the sound was different. It was Bubba returning fire with the Ruger left in the boat. The next three shotgun blasts from the woods worked their way down the boat's gunnel, gouging out great chunks of wood.

Teddy got his little chrome .22 pistol from his belt holster. He raised his arm and blindly got off two rounds in the general direction of the threat before the shotgun found him, hitting him in the wrist. His hand flew open and backward, flipping the gun into the air. The pistol fell onto the gator's side and slid down its back out where there was no chance to retrieve it.

Teddy looked at his wrist.

"Are you hurt?" Kit asked.

"Not bad. He's using buckshot. Only one of the balls hit me. But I lost my gun. Even if I had it, I don't think I could hold it."

A round from the shotgun splattered at Kit's feet, and she pulled them closer to her body.

"We need help, fast," Kit said. "You got your phone? I left mine in the car."

"So did I."

A piece of the cypress stump where Gatlin and Broussard were hiding flew into the air. Behind the stump, Gatlin was staring at the screen on *his* phone. Apparently angry that it wasn't working, he threw it into the bayou.

The fusillade continued, alternately chopping holes in the boat, tearing chunks out of the stump, and slamming into the gator, raining reptilian blood and tissue onto Kit and Teddy.

Kit could see little hope in their dire circumstances. Gatlin had lost his Ruger into the bayou when he'd fallen in the mud. He wasn't even trying to return fire with the pistol he carried, so the mud must have fouled it. Bubba had abandoned the other Ruger when he'd been driven out of the boat and into the water behind it.

A round of shot peppered the ground in front of the gator's snout.

Kit reached down and got her .38 from under her pant leg. Another round of buckshot smashed into the carcass, splattering blood into Kit's hair and onto her face.

She was the only one with a weapon. But what the hell could she do with it? Firing blind as Teddy had done wouldn't accomplish anything. And if she showed any part of herself, she'd be shot. There was no way around the truth. They were all going to die.

CHAPTER 34

THE SHOTGUN KNOCKED ANOTHER chunk out of the boat. The gator carcass jumped as it absorbed another round. A piece of the cypress stump exploded.

Kit felt that any minute Marion would move in for the kill. He would be exposed then, but with his rapid firing speed, she wouldn't even be able to get off a shot.

A form of premature death settled over her. She grew calm and began to accept what was to come. At least she hadn't yet bought the new dog she'd spoken to Bunny about. She didn't have to worry about leaving a pet behind with no one to care for it. In truth, there was no animal or person that was dependent on her. She could leave this earth, and it just wouldn't matter.

A round of buckshot blasted off the gator's hind leg.

But then, the old Kit began to surface, the one that existed before this case began. She grew angry at what Marion Marshall had done to her. He had made her someone she despised: a coward who wouldn't even help when her boyfriend's life had been threatened by this alligator.

She saw, too, that she was wrong about no one depending on her. There *was* someone ... in the Marshalls' house. She was sure of it a moment ago when they had opened that child's abdomen, but she'd let the thought get away from her when they'd come under fire … another self-serving, cowardly act. Someone *did* need her. And time could be running out.

The gator carcass bucked as another round punched into it.

Kit flashed again on the shotgun scene in Night Demon. Nathan's onslaught had been relentless, cutting those cops down with sheer overwhelming firepower. But there had been a moment in the game when the firing stopped … when Nathan had to reload.

Her eyes took on a steely glint. The muscles in her jaw flexed as she clamped down on her teeth.

It grew quiet.

Praying she was right about why that happened, Kit jumped to her feet, vaulted the gator, and ran toward the shotgun.

CHAPTER 35

Kit sprinted for the tree line, expecting at any moment to be blasted in the face with multiple rounds of buckshot. But if that happened, at least she wouldn't have died shaking in fear.

She was now halfway there ... and still alive.

The weeds that started just in front of the tree line were coming up fast. Ten feet away ... The anticipation of being shredded by dozens of steel balls made her light-headed. What she was doing was nuts, but she had no choice. Now she saw the problem she hadn't considered before she'd jumped the gator. From the moment the gunfire began, she'd been hiding, had never seen the exact location of the shooter. He could be behind a tree to her right or her left. If she chose wrong, she might not have time to correct her mistake.

The weeds were now five feet away. Still no gunfire.

She hit the weeds two seconds later and vaulted into the air, her face and gun hand turned to the left, because that was a more natural direction for her. But even before she hit the ground, she saw there was no one there.

Hairs on her neck prickling, she let her legs crumple under her when she landed. She rolled to the right, onto her back, and there he was, trying to reload one of the two shotguns he'd brought. His hand went for a holster strapped to his leg, where Kit could see the handle of an automatic pistol.

Kit began firing. She was a great marksman on the practice range, but now discovered she wasn't nearly as good under duress. Her first three rounds left no visible evidence of their existence as they embarked on a field trip of the woods. This gave Marshall time to pull his sidearm.

But Kit's fourth round hit him in the right shoulder. He jerked backward at the impact and dropped his gun. A bloodstain blossomed into his khaki T-shirt. Swearing, he grabbed at the wound.

As Kit scrambled to her feet, he dropped to his knees and reached for his pistol. Before he could grab it, Kit rushed him and kicked him in the side, knocking him over. With her free hand, she picked up his gun and shoved it in her back pocket.

She was safe.

She wasn't going to die.

Most importantly, she had saved *herself*. She wanted to howl like an animal. Instead, she shouted at the others. "I've got him. But I could use a hand." Then to the man at her feet, "I know what your despicable brother is doing. Where is he?"

"In the operating room he installed in our house," Marion whined. "I'm hurt. I need help."

"He's still going ahead with the operation, despite what just happened here?"

"He probably doesn't even know about this. The room is soundproof, and I didn't tell him anything before I left. I'm bleeding to death. Do something."

"Where in the house *is* this room?"

"Ground floor, right wing as you face the place from the backyard. You'll tell the DA I cooperated with you, right? They'll cut me a break then, won't they?"

Bubba appeared at her side with the Ruger. "Keep an eye on him," Kit said. "I've got more to do." She only had a single round left in her .38, so she returned that gun to her calf holster, pulled the automatic from her back pocket, and showed it to Teddy, who had come up behind Bubba. "How do I use this thing?"

He was puzzled. "Why do you …?"

"No time to explain. Talk …"

Teddy reached out and turned her hand so he could examine the gun better. "It's ready to go, but you should drop the magazine out of the butt so we can see how many rounds it has. This is the release lever. Don't let it fall in the dirt."

Kit let the magazine slide into her hand and saw that it was full.

"Now just slip it back in until it clicks."

She slammed the magazine home as though she'd been doing it her entire life. "I'm heading to the Marshall house. Phone for help. Send someone to the house to back me up, and get an ambulance in here for Andy and Phillip."

"And me … don't forget me …" Marion whined.

Ignoring him, Kit said, "And have the medics look for Lancon. This guy has his radio gear, so Lancon is likely in serious trouble, or maybe beyond it."

"Why are you …?"

Without answering, she turned and sprinted off into the woods.

Four minutes later, she reached the iron fence surrounding the rear of the Marshall estate. Rather than try to climb over it, she turned and followed it to the edge of the bayou, where she squeezed between the last fence post and the water and stepped onto Marshall real estate.

Before Teddy left Bubba alone with Marion Marshall, he
relieved Marion of Lancon's ear bud and mike and the Walkie
Talkie clipped to his belt. Frisking Marshall, Teddy found a gray
metal box in the man's back pocket.

"What's this?" Teddy asked, holding the box in front of
Marshall.

"It blocks cell phones. You'll have to turn if off, or you won't
be able to GET ME SOME HELP."

Teddy flicked off the device and headed for Kit's car to call
911.

Kit didn't understand all of what had been happening,
but when she saw that the body in the alligator had no liver,
she'd instantly realized Organogenesis Inc. wasn't making livers
at all. It was somehow making kids, cloning the sick ones who
needed a liver. And last week, when Quentin was complaining
about Jude taking his own life, Quentin said he had two transplants coming up … one yesterday and another today. The child
they'd found in the alligator had provided the liver for the first,
and Quentin was going to need another one today. From what
Marion had told her, there was no doubt in her mind that he
was, this very minute, about to kill another infant.

Unless she was already too late.

Marion said their operating room was in the right wing of
the house. As Kit sprinted for the bank of French doors opening
onto the patio, she saw there were no windows over there, a fact
that seemed to show Marion was telling the truth.

She crossed the patio and darted up the steps. She grabbed
the nearest doorknob and yanked.

Locked.

Unwilling to waste time checking any other doors, she smashed out the glass with the butt of the automatic and cleaned the remaining shards from the opening. Though Marion said the OR was soundproof, Kit hoped she'd set off a security alarm that might be wired into it. That would have surely stopped the operation. But no such alarm sounded.

She reached inside and twisted the doorknob. She flew through the open door and across a sitting room whose expensive furnishings made no impression on her and entered a vast kitchen, not even noticing the black onyx floor and countertops as she searched for a doorway to the right wing.

There …

Skirting a work island, she crossed the room and darted into the hallway on the other side. Thirty feet down, she saw a large doorway on the right.

A few seconds later, she stood in front of a pair of metal pocket doors that opened by sliding left and right into the wall. She slipped her fingers into the handhold on the left one and threw it open.

Across the room, two gowned and masked figures stood over an operating table. The shorter one on the opposite side looked up. The taller, whom she believed to be Quentin Marshall, turned to face her. There was a scalpel in his hand.

Pointing the automatic at them, Kit said, "Both of you, get over there against the wall."

The smaller of the two began moving. Quentin did nothing. Then he spoke. "How much do you know?"

"More than you'd like, I assure you."

"You didn't see anyone else in the house?"

"If you mean your brother, Marion, he's not in any position to help you."

"You don't know what you're doing. There's a very sick child who needs me today. His parents have gone through hell with him. And today, I'm going to cure him. Do you understand that? Can it possibly penetrate your tiny brain?"

"I swear, if you don't move now, I'm going to shoot you in the kneecaps. Bad a shot as I am, I might shoot your dick off by mistake."

Quentin moved slowly over to the wall. "You're acting irrationally, do you know that?"

"All the more reason not to screw with me."

Keeping the gun on both of them, Kit went to the operating table, her heart thumping at what she might be about to see. She leaned over and looked at the tiny figure on the table.

There was an endotracheal tube taped to his mouth and an IV line fixed to the back of his little hand. A blue surgical drape with a big window in it covered the rest of him. Kit checked to make sure the two against the wall were staying there. Then she turned back to the child. Her mouth dry with worry, she leaned in so she could see the operating field.

All she saw was a big, smooth, orange patch—uncut skin swabbed with Betadine.

UNCUT.

She'd arrived in time. The child would live.

But now she had to get him awake.

She turned to the two against the wall. She motioned to the smaller one with her gun. "You, take off your mask."

That person responded, revealing the face of a woman in her sixties. The same woman Kit had seen in the flyover photos.

"Who are you?" Kit asked.

"Nita Marshall," the woman said. "… Quentin's mother."

"Good God, how can you be a party to this?"

"You obviously don't understand."

"I get it completely. Can you bring this child out of the anesthesia?"

"Yes."

"I want you to do that. And if you hurt him …"

Quentin pulled his mask down around his neck. "That proves you're confused. We're not evil. If we can't perform the transplant scheduled for today with the organ we had planned to use, we have no other agenda."

"Then wake him up."

"Of course," Nita Marshall said. She went to the side of the table where the anesthesia machine was breathing for the child and made some adjustments in the setting. "It'll take a few minutes."

Kit backed up so she could keep an eye on both of them.

"You realize the subject on that table isn't really a person, don't you?" Quentin asked.

"What the hell are you talking about?"

"He was conceived in a dish to be a provider for a child who had real parents and a real home, where he would be loved and guided as he matured. That's a *thing* on the table; it has no name, no future, no reason to exist other than to provide …"

"The more you talk, the more I want to hurt you," Kit said. "So you'd better just shut up. Sit on the floor."

Quentin slid to the floor and sat skewering Kit with a hostile stare.

He was still there fifteen minutes later, when his mother said to Kit, "He should be coming awake any minute." She proceeded to remove the tube before the child was conscious enough to fight it. She then detached the IV from the back of his hand.

"Get that surgical drape off him too," Kit demanded.

There was a commotion in the hall. Sheriff Lazare and three deputies, all with automatics in hand, poured into the room.

The child on the table began to cry softly.

"Sheriff, take those two into custody," Kit said. "The charge will be multiple murder."

While Lazare's men led Quentin and his mother away, Kit put her gun on a nearby stand holding a tray of surgical instruments, went to the operating table, and picked up the crying child. "Hello, little man," she crooned. "You don't have to worry. You're safe now. I won't let anyone hurt you." The child stopped crying. He looked up at her with impossibly bright blue eyes and with all he had been through, smiled at her.

"Is he okay?" Lazare said, walking over to them.

"He seems to be fine."

"There's an ambulance outside. We should let them take him to the hospital for a check-up."

"He's not going without me."

"Then you'll both go."

"What about the others? Have you seen them? How are they doing"?

"The only one in any real trouble is Theo. He might not make it."

Kit was relieved to hear her friends were going to be okay, but her pleasure at hearing that was mitigated by Lancon's situation. "I'm so sorry."

"You didn't do it."

"Still …"

Lazare solemnly nodded. "Yeah …"

KIT HELD THE INFANT in her arms all the way to the hospital, never taking her eyes from his delicate little face. Though it was a short ride, it was long enough for her to weave a tapestry for the child's future. He was alone in the world, had no home, and didn't even have a name. He needed someone to love him, someone to tuck him in at night and read to him and comfort him when he scraped his knee, someone to put money under his pillow when he lost a tooth, someone to help him become a man. In short, what he needed was *her*.

And she needed him.

CHAPTER 36

"So, can I assume dose at da table with full use a all dere arms are da smarter ones?" Grandma O asked.

She was referring to the sling on Gatlin's left arm and the cast and sling on Broussard's left arm.

"I'm afraid that was more a matter of good and bad luck," Kit said.

"I don't know," Bubba said. "I had a feelin' somethin' bad might happen. Dat's why I was crouchin' down when da shootin' started."

"You might have mentioned that to the rest of us at the time," Gatlin said.

"Didn't think you'd pay any attention."

"Damn brave thing you did, charging Marshall like that," Gatlin said to Kit.

"At the time, it didn't feel like I had much choice."

"You actually did," Gatlin said. "So stop being modest. I hate it when people won't accept a compliment."

"You all play nice now," Grandma O said as she left them and went to the kitchen.

Wanting to get the topic off her supposed bravery, Kit said, "I checked on Theo Lancon this morning. They think he'll recover."

A murmur of support for the injured deputy ran around the table.

"I still got some questions about what happened," Bubba said. "I know Marion liked to kill women an' dress 'em up after dey was dead." He shivered. "Gives me da creeps jus' sayin' it. Why'd he choose women who had been ... what was dat word?"

"Surrogates," Kit said.

"Dat's it. Why'd he choose dem?"

"Until late yesterday afternoon, I was a little fuzzy on that myself," Gatlin said.

"What happened yesterday?" Kit asked.

"Because the bodies were found in New Orleans, and we'll need to iron out who has jurisdiction in the case, Lazare agreed to send me copies of statements any of the three Marshalls made. I got two yesterday, one from Marion and one from his mother. Quentin is still not talking. Guess you've all figured out Surrogacy Central was operated by the Marshalls to find women who would carry the embryos they made."

Broussard had been sitting there not saying much. At this point, he spoke. "Though the three surrogates had signed contracts givin' up all rights to the child they carried, Jennifer Hendrin and the other two women couldn't live by those terms. They threatened legal action if Surrogacy Central wouldn't let 'em see their babies. Of course, that wasn't possible because the children were dead. The women had to be silenced."

"I wasn't aware Lazare sent *you* copies of those statements," Gatlin said.

Broussard shook his head. "Didn't have to. Hendrin's best friend said Hendrin had changed her mind about givin' up those rights and that the clinic had refused to listen to her pleas. Then she turns up dead ... All pretty obvious now."

"Okay, how'd Marion get involved?" Gatlin asked.

"I'm guessin' that as a child he did somethin' sociopathic, and his family covered up for him. When they needed someone to get rid of those women, they turned to him."

"Not bad," Gatlin said. "When he was fourteen, Marion crushed a classmate's skull with a rock. Before the authorities found the body, Quentin went to the scene, picked up the murder weapon, and buried it in the woods, miles away. Marion was never implicated in the crime."

"I think I see the rest now," Kit said. "The family didn't know about Marion's little dress-up fantasy. He was supposed to dispose of those bodies, but instead, he decided that was his chance to act out the events he put in Night Demon. He collected the bodies and stored them in the LeDoux Street building until the flood washed the freezer into the street. Knowing they'd be discovered, Marion must have then confessed to his brothers what he'd done." She looked at Gatlin for comment.

"Exactly," he said.

"That has to be what drove Jude to take his own life," Kit said. "... fear those bodies would cause everything to unravel."

"Guess that makes him the sensitive one," Teddy said. "I don't understand why they'd trust someone as unstable as Marion with killing those women."

Gatlin responded. "The interviewer asked Nita Marshall that. She said they felt they had no choice. They didn't want an outsider having that to hold over them. And like Kit said, they didn't know about Marion's cadaver dress-up fetish."

Teddy shook his head. "*There's* a gene pool that needs to be drained and filled in."

"Did either of the statements say where they got the eggs to make the embryos for their scheme?" Kit asked.

Gatlin shrugged. "Apparently didn't need any."

"Why not?"

"They figured out a way to make embryos directly from the marrow cells they took from each client."

"I didn't think that was possible."

"I only know what they said."

"So all the embryos they made were clones of their clients," Teddy said. "Is that what I'm hearing?"

"It's how they were able to provide livers that didn't require their clients to take any drugs to prevent rejection," Kit said.

"Didn't you tell me the kid whose father you spoke to needed a new liver because the drainage system in his son didn't develop right?"

"Yes."

"If the liver the Marshalls were going to give him came from a clone, wouldn't that one develop wrong as well?"

Kit shook her head. "No. The father said there's no genetic basis for the disorder. It just happens. Nobody knows why. You could make a hundred clones from a child where it went wrong, and they'd all be normal." Kit looked at Gatlin. "Did either Marion or his mother say why Marion came after me?"

"Quentin told Marion about you investigating Jude's death, and he ragged Marion again for keeping the three bodies. Quentin used your visit as an example of the kind of trouble Marion's stupidity could create. Marion decided, in his disturbed way of thinking, he'd make up for his earlier mistake by taking you out of the picture. I don't know if Quentin has figured that out yet."

At this point, Grandma O appeared and began to distribute their lunch orders. Over the next half hour as they ate, the conversation ran heavily to the great alligator hunt and the subsequent shotgun attack. Kit noticed that Broussard did not join in the discussion. Nor did he seem to be enjoying his food with his usual obvious fervor.

When they had all finished and the gathering was breaking up, Broussard remained at the table, nursing an iced tea. "I'm going to see Teddy to his car, then I want to talk to you about something," Kit said to him. "Can you wait?"

"Sure."

Teddy and Kit walked out to the parking lot, where Teddy's rental car waited. A few steps before they reached it, Kit's cell phone rang. She removed it from her bag and took the call.

"Kit Franklyn."

Teddy watched as her expression, initially expectant, became one of disappointment.

"I understand," she said. "That's perfectly reasonable. Don't know why it didn't occur to me. Thanks for letting me know."

"Who was that?" Teddy asked as she put her phone away.

"Social services. I'm not getting the baby. The parents of the child who provided the marrow cells the Marshalls used to make him are taking him. It was stupid of me not to see that's what would probably happen."

Teddy stepped close and took her in his arms. "It wasn't stupid. You were just blinded by your affection for the little guy."

"I just feel so *depleted* now."

"You know, kids are still being made the old way."

She leaned back and looked at him. "The old way?"

"I understand it's not difficult. I'll bet even you and I could figure out how to do it."

"Are you saying …?"

"Clear your schedule and come over for a visit in the next few days. We'll talk about it." He gave her a lingering kiss on the lips, and they walked to his car. He got in and rolled down the window. "I'll be waiting to hear from you."

Kit watched his car until it was out of sight. Feeling so light it seemed as though she was floating over the pavement, she returned to Grandma O's and walked back to where Broussard was sitting limply in his chair like a bag of dirty laundry, fiddling with some sugar packets. She sat down beside him. "What's going on with you?"

"What do you mean?"

"You hardly said anything during lunch, and you just generally seemed disengaged."

"Guess I am. The hunt for the killer of those women was all that was keepin' me goin'. Now that it's over, all I see is my own wanin' abilities and a destroyed city with an uncertain future."

"As for your waning abilities, you were the one who found the freezer, located the building where it was stored, and discovered Night Demon. On the physical side, there's the way you handled those thugs and jumped on that gator."

He tossed a sugar packet across the table. "Okay, I had a few good moments. Now, can you fix the city?"

Kit stood. "Let's take a ride."

"Where?"

"You'll see."

They went to the parking lot and got into Kit's car.

"How far is this place?" Broussard asked.

"Don't be so impatient."

Broussard managed to hold his tongue for most of the trip. But when they got to Caffin Street, he said, "What's goin' on?"

"I brought Teddy down here yesterday to show him where Marion kept the bodies, and I noticed something you should see."

They turned onto LeDoux. She drove another half block and stopped the car. Pointing at one of the dead trees Broussard had lamented over after visiting the Hendrins, she said, "Look at that first big branch."

Broussard's eyes followed the direction she indicated. He craned his head around, looking at the branch from various angles while Kit waited for his reaction. Finally, he looked at her and grinned. "It's growin' new leaves."

"A lot of them are."

"You know the sayin': it ain't over 'till the fat man sings …"

"Isn't it fat lady?"

"I'm makin' a point here."

"Which is …"

"I may have to cancel my vocal debut."

ACROSS THE RIVER AT the Three Pines nursing home, there was a knock on Jimmy Bolden's door.

"Yeah … come in."

The door was opened by one of the male attendants. He was carrying a small white sack. "This just came for you."

"What is it?"

The attendant crossed the room and put the sack on Jimmy's dresser. He unrolled the fold in the sack and looked inside. He took out a deli container and opened it. "Looks like rice pudding."

Jimmy managed the best smile he could, his first attempt to do so in weeks. "Who brought it?"

"A little Cajun guy with a beard. Said he was delivering for a friend of yours. Also said you'd be getting one of these from now on every Thursday."

Epilogue

W HEN BROUSSARD GOT HOME after Kit had taken him down to the Ninth and shown him the budding tree, he went to his study and pulled his Webster's dictionary from his bookshelf. He took the book to his reading chair and sat down. Phillip had called him an intellectual snob. He opened the dictionary and turned the pages until he found the entry for "snob": *One who has an offensive air of superiority in matters of knowledge or taste.*

He thought about all that had happened and the mistake he had made in not seeing the tattooed eyeliner. Maybe it *was* time to admit he was getting old and accept that for most of his life he *had* been a snob. Perhaps he should simply admit he was fallible and sometimes might no longer be the most observant person in the room ... stop trying to be so perfect. He had great colleagues and friends ... all very intelligent and capable. There was certainly no shame in being their equal. No one could call him a snob then. Wouldn't that be a comfortable way to live out his remaining professional years?

He ruminated over these things for a while, then got to thinking ... the definition of "snob" implied that a snob didn't have the goods, he merely *acted* as though he did. So, if a person was *really* always the most observant or smartest or most cultured person in any group, then being a snob was in the eye of the beholder.

It was clear what he needed to do.

He'd just have to tighten up and quit making mistakes.

Author's notes

At the time this book was written, three-dimensional tubes of living tissue had actually been created using a desktop printer equipped with cell suspensions rather than ink. Will this ultimately lead to production someday of entire organs on demand as some believe? I, for one, hope so.

With regard to the title, I've use BAD KARMA in the sense of the general feeling of a place. As in: I'm getting really creepy vibes from this town.

About the Author

D.J. Donaldson

I grew up Sylvania, Ohio, a little suburb of Toledo, where the nearby stone quarries produce some of the best fossil trilobites in the country. I know that doesn't sound like much to be proud of, but we're simple people in Ohio. After obtaining a bachelor's degree at the U. of Toledo, I became a teacher of ninth grade general science in Sylvania, occupying the same desk my high school chemistry and physics teacher used when

Photo/Credit: Jennifer Brommer

he tried unsuccessfully to teach me how to use a slide rule. I lasted six months as a public school teacher, lured away into pursuit of a Ph.D. by Dr. Katoh, a developmental biologist I met in a program to broaden the biological knowledge of science teachers. Katoh's lectures were unlike anything I'd ever heard in college. He related his discipline as a series of detective stories that had me on the edge of my chair. Stimulated to seek the master who trained Katoh, I moved to New Orleans and spent five years at Tulane working on a doctorate in human anatomy. Stressed by graduate work, I hated New Orleans. When Mardi Gras would roll around, my wife and I would leave town.

It wasn't until many years later, after the painful memories of graduate school had faded and I'd taught microscopic anatomy to thousands of students at the U. of Tennessee Medical School in Memphis (not all at the same time) and published dozens of papers on wound healing that I suddenly felt the urge to write novels. And there was only one place I wanted to write about ... mysterious, sleazy, beautiful New Orleans. Okay, so I'm kind of slow to appreciate things.

Practically from the moment I decided to try my hand at fiction, I wanted to write about a medical examiner. There's just something appealing about being able to put a killer in the slammer using things like the stomach contents of the victim or teeth impressions left in a bite mark. Contrary to what the publisher's blurb said on a couple of my books, I'm not a forensic pathologist. To gear up for the first book in the series, I spent a couple of weeks hanging around the county forensic center where Dr. Jim Bell taught me the ropes. Unfortunately, Jim died unexpectedly after falling into a diabetic coma a few months before the first book was published. Though he was an avid reader, he never got to see a word of the book he helped me with. In many ways, Jim lives on as Broussard. Broussard's brilliant mind, his weight problem, his appreciation of fine food and antiques, his love for Louis L'Amour novels ... that was Jim Bell. When a new book comes out, Jim's wife always buys an armful and sends them to Jim's relatives.

My research occasionally puts me in interesting situations. Some time ago, I accompanied a Memphis homicide detective to a rooming house where we found a man stuck to the floor by a pool of his own blood, his throat cut, and a big knife lying next to the body. Within a few minutes, I found myself straddling the blood, holding a paper bag for the detective to collect the victim's personal effects. A short time later, after I'd listened to the cops on the scene discuss the conflicting stories they were getting from the occupants, the captain of the general investigation bureau turned to me and said, "What do *you* think happened?" The house is full of detectives and he's asking *my* opinion. I pointed out a discrepancy I'd noticed in the story told by the occupant who found the body and next thing I know, he's calling all the other detectives over so I can tell them. Later, we took this woman in for questioning. I wish I could say I solved the crime, but it didn't turn out that glamorous. They eventually ruled it a suicide.

Other Books by D.J. Donaldson

* Published by Astor + Blue Edition- www.astorandblue.com

*Louisiana Fever
*New Orleans Requiem
*Sleeping With The Crawfish

Cajun Nights
Blood on the Bayou
No Mardi Gras for the Dead
Do No Harm (Recently reissued as The Killing Harvest)
The Judas Virus
In the Blood (Recently reissued as The Lethal Helix)
Amnesia (Recently reissued as The Memory Thief)
The Blood Betrayal